CONTEMPORARY AMERICAN FICTION

THE WIDOW'S MITE

Dr. Ferrol Sams is a practicing physician in
Fayetteville, Georgia. His new novel is
When All the World Was Young. Penguin
also publishes *Run with the Horsemen* and
The Whisper of the River.

THE WIDOW'S MITE

& *Other Stories*

FERROL SAMS

PENGUIN BOOKS

PENGUIN BOOKS
Published by the Penguin Group
Viking Penguin, a division of Penguin Books USA Inc.,
375 Hudson Street, New York, New York 10014, U.S.A.
Penguin Books Ltd, 27 Wrights Lane, London W8 5TZ, England
Penguin Books Australia Ltd, Ringwood, Victoria, Australia
Penguin Books Canada Ltd, 10 Alcorn Avenue, Suite 300,
Toronto, Ontario, Canada M4V 382
Penguin Books (N.Z.) Ltd, 182–190 Wairau Road,
Auckland 10, New Zealand

Penguin Books Ltd, Registered Offices:
Harmondsworth, Middlesex, England

First published in the United States of America by
Peachtree Publishers, Ltd. 1987
Published in Penguin Books 1989

3 5 7 9 10 8 6 4

With the exception of the story entitled "Saba (An Affirmation)," all places
and persons represented in this book are fictional, and any resemblance to
actual places or persons, living or dead, is purely coincidental.

"Thursday" by Edna St. Vincent Millay. From *Collected Poems*,
Harper & Row. Copyright © 1922, 1950, by Edna St. Vincent Millay.
Reprinted by permission.

LIBRARY OF CONGRESS CATALOG IN PUBLICATION DATA
Sams, Ferrol, 1922–
The widow's mite and other stories/Ferrol Sams.
p.   cm.–(Contemporary American fiction)
ISBN 0 14 01.1250 2
I. Title. II. Series.
PS3569.A46656W54   1989   813'.54–dc19   88-21859

Printed in the United States of America
Set in Goudy O.S.

CONTENTS

To
Helen

The Widow's Mite

I WOULD BE THE first to admit that I wasn't born a Branscombe or yet a Vollenweider, don't you know? But still and all, I feel down in my heart that I'm as much of a lady as any of them. And down in your heart is where Jesus looks, and I hope it's only Jesus what looks down in there, for I've personally got no desire to. My stars alive, what may be going on even in my very own heart is enough to scare me to death. Which is what that psychiatrist was trying to tell me about that time. That it's what's down inside that you don't ever let out that's important, and we need to bring it up and face it and even talk to somebody about it. What he meant was me bring it up and talk to him about it and me pay him to listen. I'll tell you right now, I never went to him but once. It makes me mad as all get-out to go to a doctor anytime what's too busy to talk to me or worse yet acts like he's not interested in what I've got to say. I don't feel like he's proper earning his money. But there's something plumb indecent about going to a doctor that's not going to do a blessed thing but listen to you and charge you by the hour for it, and not even throw in no iron and vitamins or even a eensy-weensy B12 shot and has the nerve to tell you ahead of time that's the way it's going to be.

Well, they can keep their listening and I'll keep my money. I guess I wasn't born yesterday. And I guess I know a good doctor when I see one. A really good doctor has got a knife in one hand and hormones in the other and I mean he's coming at you. He's not sitting there in no leather chair with his legs crossed and sucking on no pipe and acting like if you got the money, he'll take the time.

Which is where I differ from the Branscombes and the Vollenweiders, for they throw their money around on you wouldn't believe what all, and I'd bet you five hundred dollars — if I was a betting woman, which I am not — that I've had more operations my ownself than the whole kit and caboodle of them together, and that includes their in-laws, too. Course they was all raised in big white houses or pillowed mansions or whatever you want to call them, and my daddy sharecropped and sawmilled from here to yonder and pieced that out by making a little whiskey now and then, but he never got caught at it, and at least I can truthfully say that not a drop of it has ever crossed my lips. Not even back when I had the cramps so bad ever time I minnerstrated that I'd holler and moan for two days hand-running, and my aunt what stayed with us after Mama died would beg me to take a dram and hush. But even when I was a teenager I was a handmaiden of the Lord, so to speak. I knew in my heart that ladies don't ever let down and drink alcohol, and Jesus can look down in there all He wants and He won't find even the first little old temptation to sin against my body with liquor.

Which is something that Waldene Branscombe has for sure and certain not learned yet. She buys all her clothes in Atlanta and has not ever took the down elevator when she walks into Rich's. Prances into the Regency shop there, she does, in the size sixes at that, and buys fancy clothes to wear to cocktail parties in Atlanta. She drinks liquor when she's at them, too, and she goes regular to one of them psychiatrists but has never yet had the first operation. Which we all have a pretty good idea of what's down in her heart, but if she shows the psychiatrist or yet Jesus more than she does the rest of us when she's flouncing around town in those lowcut, high-faluting clothes from the Regency shop, then somebody ought to be embarrassed, but it's sure not Waldene. I personally think she'd do better for herself just to go ahead and have something cut plumb out of her and be done with it.

People who was born with money don't have peacock brains about the real value of it and how to get the best return on your dollar. They spend it like it was always just gonna keep rolling in. She could get her gall bladder out for three hundred and fifty dollars, and I know that's a lot to shell out in one piece, but the psychiatrist will nickel and dime the same amount out of her over the long haul. And at least with the gall bladder out she wouldn't be bothered with gas for awhile, which is a great comfort and money well spent, and psychiatrists won't even discuss gas with you as I discovered that one and only time I went to one. Not that I for one minute want to be understood as saying I think Waldene's gall bladder is what ought to be cut out. I never yet caught Waldene in the unladylike conduct that gas causes and if I was going to recommend an operation for her I don't for the life of me know whether it would be to cut something out or put something in, but rich folks don't like to lay money out on something what's not a sure thing.

Take tithing for instance. Waldene wouldn't even consider that. She might spend a sight more than a tenth at Rich's, but a dollar in the collection plate is plenty on Sunday. I am a good Christian and always have been. I was born one, I guess, because I read my horoscope every day in the *Atlanta Constitution* and my Bible every night. And of course I have always tithed and been regular in the Eastern Star. I have flat set aside that tenth for the Lord even when I worked at the button counter at Kress's. Nobody could call me a religious fanatic or nothing like that, unless you was a Methodist, and of course they think that anybody what runs their lives by rules is a fanatic, which is the same as saying all of we Baptists are. Well, everybody knows about sticks and stones may break my bones but words will never harm me. That's not Holy Writ, as they say; it's just a saying. But it's so old and so true that it ought to be in the Bible. It would fit in real good in Proverbs like it was right at home. In fact, I may just write it in the margin of mine. In red ink. Like Jesus did all his talking in. The which I have already underlined the last chapter of Ecclesiastes in red, in fact I painted the whole white page of it with a red color crayon. I know as well as the next one that Jesus never said it, but all that about a virtuous woman, if he'd a thought of it he would of. And if I'd ever had a little girl, I was always aiming to name her Ruby and raise her up so that's what her price would have been greater than. That is one more holy piece of Scripture, I am here to tell you.

But I set out to tell you about tithing and how I became to look on it in an adult way and all. It's easy enough to give that tenth when you're making ten or twenty dollars a month, and if some emergency comes up and you're too sick to go to church on Sunday, you can always skip the tithe with a clear conscience — that is, if you're really sick and have been under a doctor and not just laying out because you didn't get your hair set or something like that. Even Jesus don't expect you to pay for something you don't get.

When you have a heap of money though, it makes you sing a different tune and do some real serious soul searching. You can almost understand how come the Branscombes and Vollenweiders are Methodists, although that is an extreme step and risking your immortal soul to eternal hell-fire and I wasn't never really tempted to change over. I am certainly not one to trade my soul's salvation for a mess of pottage. I have never knowed exactly what that was anyhow, but it sure doesn't sound very good. Bout like turnip greens or some such, and that's certainly not worth the risk of hell-fire.

Well, there I sat. All of a sudden I had an unborn baby in my womb and $125,000, cash, tax-free, in my lap. I had just that month turned twenty-one, which kept Pa from running my business although I did have to holler Law at him a couple of times to impress him that I was legal of age and also a widow woman to boot. If Pa had ever got his hands on my money or his nose in my business, it would have been Katy bar the door and shirt sleeves to shirt sleeves in about thirty minutes. I had only been married a year, and John George had in fact just took out the insurance policy as my anniversary present. It was our paper anniversary, like they say, and he was being appropriate, but it sure turned out to be a heap of paper. We made it double indemnity because it didn't cost but ten dollars more, not ever dreaming we was going to cash in on it so good and so quick. And, of course, we wasn't dreaming about Leon Jr. Talbott, either, whose mother was a Vollenweider.

Leon Jr. wasn't but fourteen and didn't have no business atall driving his daddy's Buick automobile across the playground at recess which it was also the ball diamond, but he done it. He done it on a dare, his friend L. M. Bottoms claimed, to prove that he could drive, and he was aiming to cut a doughnut out in center field and scatter them children like chickens, he said. Everybody in town knows Leon Jr. has got problems. He just never has been what you could call right. The very idea of him setting there hutten, hutten, hutten in a black Buick while them children finished their sack lunches, except for Little Bobby Brookshire whose Mama still packed his in a lard bucket even though he was in the eighth grade and fat as a killing-size hog.

The Board of Education had decided to put in outside lights for the ball diamond and had hired John George to do the wiring. He come down off his ladder when Leon Jr. scratched off and he seen that he was aiming for them children. John George hollered for them all to run and was trying to wave Leon Jr. off at the same time. L. M. Bottoms claims that they was all out the way except Little Bobby Brookshire who had to waddle in place of running, and that Leon Jr. would have hit him as sure as gun's iron if John George hadn't dived in front of that black Buick and give him a shove.

Even then everything would have been all right if Leon Talbott Sr. hadn't left that metal fence post sticking out the back window, but then he wasn't to fault for how could he have known that Leon Jr. was going to snitch his car to show out? Anyhow, when John George straightened out from pushing Little Bobby Brookshire to safety, that post caught him across the back of the neck going about forty miles an hour and cut his head clean off. They say it rolled almost to the pitcher's mound from out in center field, and even if somebody had of been at shortstop it wouldn't have of made no difference, because everybody was just too stunned to even move until it quit rolling. It scraped a good deal of the skin off one side of his face and messed up his ear real bad. Luther and Son embalmed the head and body separate and then stuck them together, and although you could tell the shirt collar was riding a little high, we was able to open the casket at the service, which was a comfort to me. And I will say the insurance company never even raised a murmur about it and was real nice about paying off prompt. They never even done no whining about double indemnity. Course there was no way they could have said all that wasn't to be classified accidental death, and John George had even died like a hero and that was a comfort also. So was the insurance company in their own way.

Leon Talbott Sr. come to see me before the funeral with some papers to sign, saying I didn't lay no blame nor hold no claim on Leon Jr. Talbott. Everybody knows that every dollar in that family was Vollenweider, and they give me twenty-five thousand of them to sign the paper and said they hoped I'd build a nice house and be comfortable. I never let on to them about the insurance policy. What folks don't know won't hurt them and sometimes what they don't know helps you out a heap.

The only thing that really worried me about the funeral was that John George wasn't saved. I don't mean he didn't believe. I am sure that he did, but he hadn't never professed Jesus Christ as his personal Saviour out in public at the front of the church and all that and been baptized with the water and the Spirit. And every time that we was by ourself, so's we'd have a chance to talk about such, it seemed like John George always had something else on his mind and when he did he could sure distract you. I was aiming to work on him real hard for the second anniversary, which they say is tin and I'd rather of had John George saved than anything I ever seen that was made out of tin. But all things considered, I guess things turned out for the best. If we hadn't got the insurance, all our child and I would of had when it was over and done with would of been the twenty-five thousand dollars from Leon Talbott Sr.'s in-laws, and we could of made do real nice with that but we wouldn't have been so prominent in the church and the community.

I am still coming to tithing. It was about a month after the funeral. I know it was a month cause I had slacked up from going to the cemetery every day and had cut it down to three times a week, and after two months I was going to cut the trips back to once a month and then, of course, later I could just go on Christmas and Easter and John George's birthday. I know that only God sees our insides, but it don't hurt a thing to remember how hard folks look at the outside, and Faceville is strict about grieving widow women and the cemetery. The news leaked out about the insurance money and here come Brother Whatever.

That was my private name for him, of course, and I never let him hear me use it. His real name was Leland L. Laurens and he was the pastor of the First Baptist Church of Faceville, Georgia, and why we called it First Baptist I have never understood, unless it just had a grander sound to it, because it was the only Baptist church in Faceville. And still is, for that matter, unless you count the colored one and nobody ever does. I had found a home in the First Baptist and the congregation was, I wouldn't say more Christian than any I'd ever belonged to before, but certainly more what you would call genteel.

And I'd always liked the preacher well enough, too, although nothing like Mildred Mitchell, which her husband always said that when Mildred died she wanted to go to Leland, and she very nearly did when he got the call to Alabama and left Faceville for good. Die, I mean, not go to him. First place, he wouldn't of had her and second place, it would have flat tore Faceville up. She didn't have no use atall for the next two preachers we had at First Baptist and it wasn't for no reason in the world except she was still moaning for Leland L. Laurens, and them preachers was both just as involved and consecrated as they could be, and to this day Mildred don't do all she should in the WMU. I will say, though, that Leland L. Laurens was the cause of Mildred finally joining the Eastern Star, because when he left and Mildred dropped out of prayer meeting, WMU, and the Eve-to-Judith Bible Study Group, she had to have somewhere to get out of the house that was respectable and Eastern Star was it.

She went right on up, too. Within a year she was in the East and it wasn't but three years before she became Worthy Grand Matron. She would of done better to put it off awhile because Rotell Robinson was Grand Master that year and he can't keep from belching, even when he's in the East, which is not a suitable place at all for gas what with the ladies of the Court dressed up in evening gowns and all. Mildred had blue chiffon, the which it didn't do much for her, her skin being what I've always called sallow, but doctors nowdays don't know what you're talking about when you say "sallow." In fact, they don't even recognize "bilious" anymore.

And I know sure as I'm standing here that Rotell has got a hiatal hernia. I call mine "my hyena" and Dr. Mason always knows right off what I'm talking about. I told Rotell oncet that he ought to get hisself x-rayed and lose fifty pounds and he'd feel better, but he won't go to no doctor. All the Robinsons are tight with their money where doctors are concerned. Of course, the way I handle my hyena is when I know ahead of time I'm going out like to church or the Eastern Star, I get up early and take two enemas and you don't ever catch me belching in public. Or nothing else. A proper enema, if you give it right, is not only a tool of good health but makes you mindful of good manners. Rotell acted so disinterested I didn't bother to tell him about the enemas, and for that matter I've never told Dr. Mason. You can't ever be sure what them doctors have decided from one visit to the next that folks ought to give up. They can sure hem you in.

The reason I always called Leland L. Laurens "Brother Whatever" was that it looked like every time I got around him he'd wind up saying that. "Whatever," he'd say. The preachers in the little country churches I growed up in didn't have all that much education. They'd felt the call and got theyselves ordained and they preached on Sunday and worked at the Ford plant or some such during the week. But they was all full of the fire of the Lord and would talk to you and argue with you about the Scriptures all night long. Any church that is called First Baptist is bound and determined to have a preacher what's been off to college and to the Seminary, and of course they don't work. They just preach and visit.

Every time I would stop Leland L. Laurens on the street or even go by his office, which he called it his study (that comes from going to the Seminary, too, in my opinion) to discuss the way I personally was interpreting something I'd read in the Bible, he'd wind up rolling his eyes extra patient like and saying, "Whatever," and just keep walking on. Take, for instance, the first miracle, the one at Cana, where the Philistines or some such run out of wine when they was carousing at that wedding. I run into him on the curb one day just as the mail run and told Leland L. Laurens that my faith wouldn't let me believe that the Lord Jesus Christ condoned alcohol in any shape, form, or fashion or had anything at all to do with it. I told him that I had become to interpret that Bible passage as Jesus turned that water into plain grape juice, just like we have at Communion in First Baptist with the Nabisco saltines all crumbled up. It hadn't never sowvered or fermented, and that bunch of Vollenweiders and Branscombes whooping it up at Cana hadn't drunk anything like that in so many years they'd plumb forgot how good fresh grape juice tastes and that's how come they said it was the best of the evening. And that didn't take nothing away at all from the Lord Jesus Christ, for it's as plain as the nose on your face that it takes every bit as big a miracle to turn a barrel of water into grape juice as it does into wine. Leland L. Laurens shut his eyes for a extra long moment and then he says, "Whatever," and then he tipped his hat to Miss Lorraine Graham and walked on in the post office. And ever since that day I've been calling him Brother Whatever behind his back and down in my heart, where only Jesus can see and that psychiatrist wanted to go prying and plundering around except I wasn't about to let him.

If I'd told Brother Robert K. Price that interpretation, he'd of preached a whole sermon on it at the Holly Grove Tabernacle and have received at least two or three new souls into fellowship when he opened the doors of the church. Not that I'd trade back. Brother Price does murder the King's English — comes from not finishing nothing but the seventh grade and working all his life at Dundee No. 2 in Griffin. You can tell he is happy in the Lord, though, and he will always take time to talk to you. He told me oncet that when he was young he thought he'd be an evangelist. He was called to a little church in Dawson County way up in north Georgia for a whole week's revival. They guaranteed him twenty dollars plus all the love offerings he could get, which wasn't bad atall for that day and time. But Brother Robert K. Price had done bit off more'n he could chew as he very quickly come to find out. He come on back home on Tuesday and has been happy as a dead pig in the sunshine ever since, just preaching at Holly Grove and working at Dundee No. 2. He told me about Dawson County. Said he didn't mind the drums and cymbals but he wasn't going to do snakes for nobody.

Brother Whatever reads the Scripture as smooth and grand as Billy Graham and never stumbles over big words or hard names, and I do respect him for it as a man and as a servant of God and all that. I do wish, though, that every now and then he'd holler just a little bit. I never saw him raise a sweat over a sermon, and I never saw Brother Price wind one up lessen he was sopping wet. Now that's what I call the Fire of the Lord.

The day Brother Whatever come to call on me about my insurance money, I knew I had to have my wits about me, and I breathed a little personal prayer when I seen him coming up the walk.

I knew the news was out because Cousin Sara had went by Montine's to pick up a loaf of bread. The Bamby truck runs on Wednesday and Kate Greer always shows up to get a loaf while it's fresh and before everybody in town has had a chance to squeeze it or paw over it, she says. I do believe she is more conscientious than I am about germs. On top of which her doctor has told her that she has capillaries, so she is extra careful about a lot of things. Kate gets Rachel to set her aside a loaf under the counter in case the bread truck runs while Kate is taking her nap. Rachel is Montine's sister-in-law, and everybody in Faceville does love a family business. Cousin Sara heard Rachel and Kate talking about me, and Kate was saying that Leon Talbott, Sr. had bought off Leon Talbott, Jr. by paying me twenty-five thousand dollars.

Rachel said that wasn't the end of it by a long sight, that John Addison had come by and told Montine that a fellow had told him the insurance policy was for fifty thousand dollars, double indemnity. Course John Addison hadn't told who a fellow was, but anybody who's lived in Faceville long knows that it's a fellow always tells John Addison everything and they're usually dead center on the truth and John Addison has never yet the first time let down and told anybody who a fellow is.

When Rachel told Kate that, she said, "Well, now, hasn't she popped her butt in a tub of butter! I've got to run by Catherine's and tell her. Thanks for saving out the bread." Kate didn't mean no harm nor yet even no disrespect when she said that about my butt and the tub of butter. All it meant was that I'd done a heap

better than anybody ever expected me to and they was surprised.
It's just another one of those old sayings, although not one that I
have ever even thought about writing down in red anywhere and
most certainly not in Proverbs. I learned a long time ago that
some old sayings are better than others, and to tell the truth,
some of them don't hardly bear repeating. Kate, of course, will
repeat anything. Almost anywhere. But, come to think of it,
not to just anybody.

It was the day after that when Brother Whatever come a-call-
ing, and I knew when I saw him what he had on his mind. He's
always about a day and a half picking something up, but then
Brother Whatever don't have a fellow and has to rely on the
WMU. After five or ten minutes and a really sweet prayer,
which Brother Whatever could do better'n anybody else — I
mean he could flat bring the Heavenly Father right in the room
with you when you were grief-stricken and all — he set down in
John George's rocker and says, "Well, I hear you've come into a
little money."

I was setting there thinking the whole time he had been
praying. I knowed that he knew but he didn't know that I knowed
that he knew, and that always gives a lady a little edge. So I come
out with it straight. I said, "Yessir. John George had took out an
insurance policy for fifty thousand on hisself for our anniversary
present. It was our paper anniversary and I give him a Bible, one
of them with Jesus talking to Hisself in red, that he could mark
up whenever he got around to studying on it, and he give me the
insurance policy. Next year I was going to get him baptized for
our second anniversary, but I'm sure you understand, Preacher,
that you have to go one step at the time and you have to walk
before you can run, and that insurance policy was sure the first
step to salvation on account of my intentions and all being so
good, and I am not really scared about John George's soul. I
figure if he's not with Jesus yet that sooner or later they'll find
each other. After all, they got all eternity to do it in. The Bible
says, 'Seek and ye shall find,' and I figure that applies to Jesus

same as John George, and John George was sure a patient man, the which if anybody ought to know I do."

I explained about the policy being double indemnity and then I told it all. Like I said, I knowed he already knew it anyhow, so I told him about Leon Jr. Talbott and I asked Brother Whatever to pray for him because we all know that, regardless of how the law gets tangled up and confused about involuntary manslaughter and such, Leon Jr. Talbott had took another human's life and was in danger of hell fire on account of it, double indemnity notwithstanding. Although it's a sweet thought I'd never had before that maybe the good Lord gives all of us double indemnity if our sins are accidental and we can prove it. Then so help me, he come out with it. "Whatever," he said.

That was a good sign I was winning. I lined it right on out: twenty-five from Leon Talbott Sr. and the Vollenweiders, fifty from the policy and fifty from the double indemnity.

"That makes $125,000, Preacher," I said. "And there's no sense atall in either one of us wasting our breath on the widow's mite. The which I'm a widow my own self now and I realize if that one in the Bible had amounted to anything or had anything besides just a mite, she wouldn't have had to throw it all in the collection plate at one time, she could have just give a tenth. You can't divide a mite, Preacher, there's not ten parts to it, I suspect, but I am certainly going to tithe my fortune which I have come up with so unexpectedly. I am grateful to God for His bountiful goodness and this fallen sparrow is going to repay Him and keep the hairs in my head numbered."

When I stopped for breath, Brother Whatever said, "Amen," and had a sharp gleam in his eye and I could tell he felt like I was losing ground. I never let on. I just kept talking. I could tell he had done his arithmetic in his head and he was dead certain that ten percent of $125,000 was $12,500. Well, I had news for him, and Brother Robert K. Price would of thought on the Lord giving double indemnity for a whole week at Dundee No. 2 and then come up on Sunday morning with a sermon that shook the rafters and brought new men in from the field of sin, as they say. But then some folks is so educated you couldn't inspire 'em for nothing, short of a lightning bolt and a thunderstorm.

Then I told Brother Whatever that I had been praying on my knees about this matter. I learned a long time ago that if you are going to have a argument that the first one what says he has been praying about it, just up front and open and all, has got a considerable advantage, like a school teacher or your grandparents or even a judge. It takes more than a average person to ignore you praying about something and go on with the sense behind what you was talking about in the first place. And if you say it was on your knees, then if somebody disagrees it sounds like they coming between you and the good Lord and they feel like they are more than likely to displease the Lord a little. The which I had been praying, and if it wasn't really on my knees, at least I'd thought about being on them, and Jesus Hisself says that thinking about something is the same as doing it, so I wasn't really lying.

I could tell that Brother Whatever believed it anyhow, for he looked down at them real quick-like. My knees. But they was crossed. Mama had learned us that soon as we was old enough to wear lipstick and silk stockings. You can't ever tell who's trying to get a peek, and it's better to be prepared and help your fellow man avoid even the appearance of evil. Some of them Branscombes and Vollenweiders can flop down on a sofa or yet a glider and take your picture from clear across the room, but I am a Baptist lady. That is no way to attract a man, besides the which you can't never tell what might come up that you've got no desire to handle. The only time I ever went to the Methodist church, Waldene Branscombe got to giggling with her cousin over the responsive reading, which it was about a rod that come forth out of the stem of Jesse. They kept it up plumb through Epworth League, and if you are going to get nasty-minded about the Holy Bible, no wonder you need a psychiatrist and all such. It is better to avoid the appearance of evil.

"Preacher," I said, "let me tell you about this tithe and ten percent business. You think we talking about $12,500 for the Faceville First Baptist, and I have no doubt in my heart that you are sincere in the light of what all you have learned at that Seminary in Louisville, but I myself know all about two plus two and ten percent and all, and I never had to leave Little Flock school house to learn it. You think ten percent is $12,500 and that's what you looking at, but it ain't." I never say *ain't* because Mama preached at us about it and said it was common to say it, but didn't seem like nothing else would fit right then. Another thing Mama used to do was make us girls wear bonnets and gloves and long sleeves in the field so as folks couldn't tell we'd been out in no sun or ever touched a hoe handle, and I would pray that Waldene or none the other girls at school would come by and recognize me. Sister rubbed buttermilk on her face, too, up under the sun bonnet and all, because she was bad to freckle, but all I wanted was just not to be recognized.

"First off, Preacher," I went on, "you can drop the double indemnity. I feel like that's something the Lord granted because of good stewardship, like in the parable of the ten talents and all, and it didn't cost me and John George but ten dollars to start off with, so that's forty-nine thousand nine hundred and ninety dollars right there ought not to be tithed on again. That leaves fifty thousand, and from that we need to subtract at least ten percent because you know that the insurance company had done paid out that much on income tax and corporate tax and it is un-American to have double taxation or taxation without representation, which is what caused this country in the first place at the Boston Tea Party, the which Myrtle Crouch and me like to never of learned from Mrs. Cole in American History, but once we got ahold of it I bet you neither one of us will ever forget it. So that leaves forty-five thousand."

I could tell that he was weakening. The first sign is his eyes get sort of a glazed look they call it, and he quits looking at you plumb straight all the time.

"Now, Preacher, out of that forty-five thousand we ought to take the funeral expenses, to my way of thinking. After all, that was a very religious ceremony the way you preached it, and now we talking just a little about separation of church and state, but I won't do nothing more that just touch on that."

He took a deep breath and swallowed, but he didn't say nothing.

"Luther and Son's bill come to $2,445.50, which included the embalming, the solid copper coffin, the hearse, the funeral home, and twenty-four dollars for digging the grave. He's got the whole thing itemized, which is just good business and I do appreciate it, and he was real sweet and supportive and just wonderful through it all, but I disremember exactly where the fifty cents comes in at. So now we talking about $42,554.50.

"But from that we need to deduct the florist's bill. I don't want you to think I'm being cheap, Preacher, but all this was spent on John George, you know, and I have not been able to find the first thing in the Bible about tithing dead men. It stands to reason that if there's to be no giving or taking in marriage in heaven, then for sure and certain the tithe ought to be shut down, too. I paid out a flat one hundred dollars for that blanket of red roses and baby breath what was on the coffin with the one orchid right in the middle of it. Laverne wanted to make the orchid white to match the baby breath, but I liked the purple better, and it is still fresh in that little test tube what Laverne put it in and I've yet got it in the refrigerator. I have pressed six of the roses, and when the orchid starts to fade I aim to press it too, and then I can have them framed and hang them on the wall under our marriage license.

"Also, while I was at Laverne's picking out the orchid, I come across this offering that I just couldn't resist, which you may have noticed at the head of the coffin. It was the carnations around the pink ceramic telephone that was laying off the hook and had golden letters under it that said, 'Jesus called.' Laverne charged me twenty dollars for the phone and five dollars for the carnations, but to me it was worth it. It's just so sweet and sentimental and tells it all, and I still choke up when I think about it. I have got the offering with the telephone on it in my closet, but I didn't press none of the carnations. They are so fat they'll stain the Bible or dictionary every time and they get flaky and crumbly when you finally do get them dried. Laverne wanted I should choose white carnations, but I stood firm on pink. That Laverne is really hung up on white, you have to watch her. And that's another $125 right there."

I took a quick look at Brother Whatever and knew I was doing all right. You could hear the air blowing way in the back of his nose when he breathed. But if he thought I was even close to being done, he had another think coming.

"Preacher, I hadn't told you yet about the house I'm getting built. John Milsapps is going to build it except for the brick, which James Callaway is going to put up. John George's baby and widow are going to have a brand-new house by the time the baby is born, and John George's baby is going to be raised in a solid brick house. James said everybody puts up brick veneer, but I argued him down and my house is going to be solid brick all the way to the roof. I told James that nothing else would do, since it was going to be built with John George's insurance money and I wanted solid brick for sentimental reasons if nothing else, because John George used to say that was what I was built like. James said solid brick tends to sweat, but I told him John George did, too, at least ever time he made that remark, and James said it was fine with him and we didn't need to talk about it no more.

"James is the best brick mason around, Preacher, even before he give up drinking, and John George told me one time that you wouldn't find no hogs in one of James Callaway's walls and I laughed fit to kill, but it turned out that's just brick mason talk, and a hog to them is a slanting line of bricks that is a monument to sloppy work when somebody stands off and looks at it. It's there forever and you can't hide it for nothing. I told James about what John George said and he come down on his price, too. He has got real respect for a widow woman.

"John Milsapps is a different cat. I had to talk cash at four o'clock every Friday to get his prices off any. He's the one what built K. W. McElwaney's house, and he'd make a dog laugh telling about how come they kept calling him back every year or so to put on a new addition. John's got a sharp tongue, but he's got a true eye and I've always heard that his corners are square. He give me a little trouble about me wanting two bathrooms, and I won't repeat his remarks about what a girl raised like me wanted with more'n one on the inside the house. It wasn't that I hadn't already heard the words he used at one place or another, it was just that his thoughts was what you would call coarse and a lady wouldn't repeat them. I know he'll make a funny story about it before he tells it down at John M. Jackson's store and it'll get all over town, but it helped me get another two hundred dollars off his bill. Course I had to let a tear come up and my chin tremble, but it takes that to make John feel guilty. I've knowed him since I was a little girl and Pa sold him whiskey now and then, which means ever Tuesday and Saturday, just between me and you, Preacher. John talks rough and blusters around like he's disrespectful, but he's got a heart like summer butter, if you know how to get to it. It's tedious, but it's all part of being a good steward, Preacher, of the earthly goods that the Lord has placed in our hands."

Brother Whatever had commenced to rocking, but he never said a word.

"I know you wonder why I'm telling you all this, Preacher, but it still has to do with tithing. John George use to say I ramble more'n anybody he ever saw to finally get to where I was headed for in the first place. The upshot of all that with James and John … and I hadn't even thought of it before but that sounds like I'd been dealing with the disciples, don't it? James and John. I declare. Course James Callaway's daddy wasn't Zebedee and John Milsapps has never been what you'd call all that close to Jesus, but still and all isn't that interesting? Anyway, for one afternoon and half a morning's dickering I got a solid brick, three-bedroom, two-bathroom house with a glassed-in sun porch for $8,400 instead of $10,000. The sun porch is nowhere near as big as Mrs. Vollenweider's, which is where I got the idea, but it'll hold a little sofa and also some ferns and African violets in the winter time. If you've been following along, that leaves $34,305.50. Right?"

He never said it then. He just said, "I guess so."

Then I told him, "The lot was four hundred dollars, which may sound a little high for no more'n one acre of land in this town, but it sets on a corner just one block from the court house and I hear tell that someday they're going to pave the street in front of it. Also it belonged to Mr. Hulon Gosset, and I didn't even try to dicker or talk cash with Mr. Hulon. He didn't particularly want to sell it in the first place, and Lord knows cash don't mean the first thing to a Gosset. Mr. Hulon's still got a nickel of the first dime he ever made. Now, there's somebody you need to work on, Preacher. I can promise you tithing has not ever crossed Hulon Gosset's mind.

"I got the deed drawed up real quick before he could back out, and that's another place I used my head. Did you know that lawyers charge you just for making a trip or two to the court house and filling out a little piece of paper? It comes from all that schooling. I tell you, education is driving prices up all over the country, and if somebody don't call a halt to it we may get bankruptured over education. The lawyer I got was Lester Creasey, who is good as any and better than most. On top of all that he was always one of Pa's best customers. About the third time I acted real cordial and told him I hadn't seen him since I left home and use to run into him and Pa in the corn crib all the time, he grunted and said by God, to hush, he wasn't going to charge me for drawing up that deed. Now, that's stewardship, too, Preacher, and I didn't cause him to stumble and use the Lord's name. Lester Creasey does that all the time anyhow. Did you know he's aiming to run for public office next fall? Everything helps, Preacher, if you're a good steward. Now, let's see. That leaves $33,905.50, don't it?"

Then I told him about the trust fund for the baby. I decided while Lester Creasey was in such an accommodating frame of mind I'd just have him tend to that too while I was at it instead of having to take time to work him up to it again, and besides it might be he wouldn't have his mind on it as good if it was any closer to election time. We put in initials, since we don't yet know whether the baby is a boy or a girl. R. J. Ruby Johnnie if it's a girl, which I hope it is on account of Ecclesiastes and all, and Reuben John if it's a boy. Either name gets in the daddy and the Bible, and you can't hardly beat that for anybody's name. Of course, what was of interest to Brother Whatever was that the trust fund was for twenty thousand dollars, which means that I can't ever again get at that money but it will be there for education when Ruby Johnnie or Reuben John needs it, whichever. And, of course, that sounds like an awful lot for education, but I believe on another one of them old sayings. It's, "If you can't lick 'em, join 'em," and I wouldn't write it in red or anything because it just don't ring right for that and I can't imagine Jesus saying it, but it is very true. By now me and the preacher was down to $13,905.50, and I declare he had broke just the lightest of sweats. His forehead was plumb shining.

"Ooh, Preacher," I said, "I was about to forget the headstone. It is not ready yet because they've got a three-month backlog, but that is going to cost me an even five hundred dollars. The reason it costs so much is account of the telephone. The letters and all worked out real good, for the Georgia Monument Company could carve 'Jesus Called' just as easy and a heap cheaper than 'Asleep in Jesus' or some such, but they're charging me plenty for that telephone with the receiver off the hook. I can't help it. I just had to have it. And if that's not good judgment I'll just have to answer for it later. Now, my figuring puts things at $13,405.50.

"That looks pretty good, but you know what, Preacher? There is such a thing as hidden costs, and a wise man and his money is not soon parted if he just keeps his head about him and thinks, and I am not talking about the Hulon Gossetts of this world who are rich because they never spent nothing. You know well's I do that the Gossetts don't even live in a brick veneer house, let alone solid. And they don't have a bathroom inside because Mr. Hulon says if somebody's too lazy to go outdoors to you-know-what, he's too lazy to live. That's stingy, that's not smart, because Jesus said, 'I have come that you should have life more abundantly,' and I am convicted that He certainly includes a commode and lavatory and tub and running water and all that. That is, if you can afford it. There is certainly nothing sinful about an outhouse, but Mr. Hulon Gossett is welcome to his. I can't imagine for the life of me Jesus Christ making a remark like that.

"Now, those hidden costs I was telling you about? I bet you hadn't for a minute thought about the premium John George paid out to the Prudential Company in the first place, but don't feel bad about it because I hadn't either. Not till I started adding it all up to see where I was and all, and all of a sudden I hollered right out loud, 'Why, that's a hidden cost.' And it was, Preacher. It's $826.50, and that balances out that other fifty cents that was on Luther and Son's bill, and I am glad to get shed of it because from now on we can deal just in round numbers and that's ever so much simpler. It's not that fifty cents is so hard to handle by itself. It's just that all of a sudden you remember that it's a half a dollar and a half of anything is a fraction, and as soon as I hear fraction it throws me back in Mrs. Barron's classroom, which is where I first heard of fractions and I have never to this day got over it yet. It was add fractions, subtract fractions, divide fractions, multiply fractions, and that old woman would yell and holler at you if you didn't learn 'em right till you had a headache and wanted to bust out crying and never hear of a common denominator again the longest day you lived. Mrs. Barron was a Christian and all and prayed real sweet every morning, but when them fractions hit at one-thirty in the afternoon, look like it brought the devil out in her. She hollered so mean I broke out in the hives. I did, too. And worse and still she locked Jane Dennis's bowels. Jane always was stubborn and had a temper herself, but nobody could stand up to Mrs. Barron, and Jane got that olive skin from her daddy's side the family and wasn't subject to hives. I've always felt like I'd rather put up with the bumps and the itching. Jane was in a real bad fix off and on for over two months and stayed constipated till summer vacation."

Brother Whatever was pretty restless. You could tell because he had begun to cross and uncross and recross his legs, so I settled back to business.

"Now, don't forget that we had saved up that money together, Preacher, me and John George, for that premium and that it had already been tithed on, so we get back to that double taxation again if we are not careful. And don't forget the ten dollars for double indemnity which I first added on back yonder when we started out. That comes to $836.50 and that brings us down to $12,569. Now that's the figure, Preacher, that my figuring shows that I owe the tithe on. And one-tenth of that comes out $1,256.90, and there comes them fractions at us again so I'm just going to round that off at $1,257 and forget about Mrs. Barron.

"Now, if you think I had forgot about the twenty-five thousand from Leon Talbott Sr. you are wrong. I have prayed over that too, Preacher. You know what that twenty-five thousand is? It's blood money, that's what it is. It's paying me for Leon Jr. Talbott cutting off my husband's head with a forty mile an hour fencepost and it rolling almost to the pitcher's mound before anybody could stop it. And Jesus Christ don't want any part of that money, I am here to tell you. Even if Leon Jr. is not quite right. What told me that was going back and reading about that poor, pitiful Judas Iscariot. You know he had sold out Jesus Hisself for thirty pieces of silver and got paid in cash, too, and then it turned out to be blood money. And what did Judas do? He hung hisself, that's what. They say it was on a dogwood tree but I can't find that anywhere in my Bible, and he laid the thirty pieces of silver there on a stump along side of him. It don't say that in the Bible either, but a stump would of been the logical place to lay it if you was going to do such outside instead of in a closet somewhere, which would of been more private and tasteful but Judas Iscariot probably didn't come from much to start with. Sometimes it don't hurt a Christian to use his imagination same as his head.

"Even the church back then wouldn't touch that thirty pieces of silver. And when you get to looking at my blood money it's really only twenty-five pieces of silver, but that's all right, for John George was certainly no Jesus Christ. I have got it in the bank at four and a half percent interest, and it looks like I'll never get away from fractions the rest of my life. I have not yet decided what to do with it, except I'm probably going to buy up some of this land around here for fifteen, twenty dollars an acre, but I know for sure and certain the Lord don't want no tenth of it. I know it down in my heart and that's where Jesus looks. So we'll say no more about it."

I could tell I was losing Brother Whatever. He was getting to his feet, and he opened his mouth and he said it. He came right on out with it. "Whatever," he said. It kind of croaked.

"Set back down, Preacher," I told him. "I am not done yet."

I reached down inside my shirtwaist and pulled out a check. That was where my grandma always kept her egg money, tied up in the corner of her handkerchief and stuffed down in there where it was safe because for sure and certain nobody ever messed with Grandma. She called it her titty bank, but of course I wouldn't even think of such a word in front of a man. He might read it in your eyes even if he was a preacher and get the wrong idea. I still had a little Evening in Paris bath powder left over from the last valentine that John George had give me, and that check sure smelled good. I sort of waved it at the preacher, and if he got any ideas besides clean and dainty from smelling Evening in Paris, then he's got a problem and I can't help him with it. Like Lurline used to say in the back seat, "I can hear you clucking but I can't find your nest." That don't even deserve to be wrote down, certainly not in red, but Lurline use to say it. And it worked, too. It cooled 'em off. Course I never looked in the back seat; that is not good manners. But you can tell a heap without having to see it and you can tell when things have cooled off. The way she talked helped, too. Lurline had a fancy accent to start off with and she kept on cultivating it, and that's why she's got such a good job with WGST now, and you can't listen at her and even guess where she was born at.

"Now, Preacher, in case you think this check is for $1,257, you are dead wrong and you have been misjudging me, the which Jesus tells us not to do less we our own selves be misjudged. Also it is my opinion that Jesus would of told us not to jump to conclusions if He had of thought to of said it. Even Jesus couldn't think of everything, Preacher, bless His heart. Sometimes we just have to haul off and do what we think is right out of our own minds and our own hearts, the which if you have got Jesus in there to start with then it's going to turn out all right in the long run, even if the New Testament is not always the rule book some say it is.

"For instance, I have never yet understood grace, no matter how much you preachers try to explain it. But I do declare I feel today like I am filled with it. Waldene Branscombe passed me yesterday when I was walking home with a sack of groceries. Montine would have delivered but the doctor says I need to walk. Waldene was in her brand-new bright red Packard coupe that her daddy just got her, and I hear it's the first one made since the War and old man Branscombe wasn't even on the waiting list. He's just got that much money and that much pull, don't you know? He had a little brass plaque mounted on the dashboard before he give it to Waldene what says, 'Seek ye first the kingdom of God and His righteousness and all this shall be added unto you.' The which I had heard about already because John Addison had told Montine that a fellow had told him about it, and that was even before the car was delivered. You can't get ahead of that John Addison. When Waldene offered me a ride, I climbed in because

I wanted to see it with my own eyes. Not to say I had doubted John Addison and a fellow, because I have lived here long enough to know he's right more often than your horoscope and a heap sight more dead on it. And, Preacher, it's there all right.

"The which I think sometimes you can misuse them mottoes of Jesus. I mean that what you think may apply to you, the person over in the next field may think you're puffing yourself up and giving yourself airs. And there is very few people in this town who think that old man Branscombe was seeking first the kingdom of God let alone its righteousness when he was short-changing sharecroppers and holding back wages on day laborers. Yes, sir, I had seen Waldene's car and I had heard about her plaque, and I had already acted on it. But I never said a word to Waldene about it nor told her what I've done. I'll just wait and give her a ride when my car comes. You see, Preacher, I've ordered a black four-door Buick touring car what's every bit as fine as Miss Lorraine's or Mrs. Vollenweider's. It's supposed to come next Friday, and it's got its own plaque on the front the glove compartment. My plaque says, 'In chariots some put their trust but my faith is in Thee.' I like never to found that verse but it's in Psalms, the which I am sure you already know chapter and verse, but the Bible is hard work for some of us. I can't wait for Waldene to see my plaque. But aren't you proud of me for not opening my mouth and saying a word about it, Preacher? When you know it's only human that I was busting to tell it? Now, if that is not grace, then I am not setting here."

That's when he said it again. "Whatever," he said. But he didn't move. To tell the truth, he acted like he couldn't.

"Now, Preacher, let's get down to business. And I do mean business, for that is what stewardship is all about, and just because you're a Christian don't in any fashion mean you're suppose to be a ninny about finances. Let us discuss this check which I had already wrote out and had ready before I seen you coming up the sidewalk, and I'm not telling how I knowed you'd be along this morning. You can wonder about that when you get around to it and have time to get over wondering about some other things. This check, Preacher, which you have already misjudged me about, since after all you're only human and jumped to the conclusion that it is for $1,257, is for $12,250. That is one-tenth of every nickel I got, including even the blood money what is in the bank and drawing interest at four and a half percent, the which you can be certain I aim to do better than that with it. If Little Hill Carstairs can buy them Hickory Freeman suits doing nothing but being president of the bank and paying me out four and a half percent, then I can do better than him, for he wasn't no better at fractions than I was and like to have drove Mrs. Barron crazy."

Brother Whatever was setting bolt upright like he had a wagon rod down his spine, and his eyes was bugging out so far they misted up his glasses. He didn't lick his lips, but he looked like he wanted to. He never said a word, and I believe "Silence is golden" is probably in the Bible somewheres, I'll have to look it up. If it is not there, then it soon will be.

"Preacher," I went on, and I had done put a firmer tone in my voice which you ought to do when you're really getting down to business, "this check is made out to the Faceville First Baptist Church and it is marked down in the corner 'the John George Higbee Higher Education Fund.' It is to be used to help poor children go off to college. Not a nickel of it is to be spent on sticks or stones or red velvet rope or pipe organs or stain glass windows or even yet on Lottie Moon. I have discussed it with Lester Creasey and he's already drawing up the papers."

Then I handed him the check and he stretched it out tight and looked at it real hard. If it smelled good to him, he never let on. The which I have never really and truly been able to make myself believe that when Elijah burnt all them dead bulls at Carmel it was a pleasing odor to the Lord. Land's sake, I can't even stand chicken feathers around the wash pot, let alone no burning bulls, and like it or not we are cast in God's image and that includes our noses.

The preacher said, "I don't know what to say."

I said, "Just say 'Whatever' and let it go at that."

He didn't ever take his eyes off that check, which makes me know the poor man don't even know he says that all the time.

"Now, Brother Laurens," I went on, "there is a catch in this love offering, the which that is what it is, since I have spent the last half an hour proving to you that I don't owe it. Not one penny of the $12,250 can be paid out, just the interest it earns. I mean, I been learning about principle and capital and all them words that sounded like Greek before. This is a present-day parable of the talents, Preacher. The good Master has give you $12,250. You gonna bury it? Or you gonna multiply it ten fold? Or better? I'm gonna increase mine, Preacher. So I can hear those blessed words, 'Well done, thou good and faithful servant.'

"Let's see what you and Jesus can do with yours. And I'm gonna be a watchful master over you. I'll ask a accounting of you every three months. Every quarter, don't you know, and there's them fractions again. Let's see what a educated man can do alongside a unschooled widow woman, Preacher. I'm gonna put mine in real estate."

Well, I thought for sure and certain I had give Brother Whatever more'n money. I thought at the very least I had planted the idea for a sermon in his head. And I did want to hear that one preached, too. Right out in the Faceville First Baptist Church with me setting on the front row right next to the Hammond organ. What I wanted was for him to preach a sermon on, "A good name is to be preferred above great riches," the which you'd think he would of tumbled to, but I be blessed if I was going to line it out for him.

Down in my heart that's all I wanted. A good name. That's all I've ever wanted, really. A good name.

Ever since Pa sold liquor.

Howdy Doody Time

I SAW IN THE paper the other day where Howdy Doody had died, and it put me to thinking. Of course, his name was not Howdy Doody. It was Howard Daudrill. Nobody but Bell and Buzz and me ever called him Howdy Doody and that not to his face. In fact, Buzz never laid eyes on him but one time. For a while there, though, Bell ran her mouth about him so much that we got sick and tired of just hearing the name of Howard Daudrill. Buzz nicknamed him Howdy Doody to get under her skin. She hated all those TV shows for children — Mickey Mouse, Captain Kangaroo, Pinky Lee, Howdy Doody, you name it. Calling her boyfriend Howdy Doody let her know what we thought about him and also about her for taking up with him.

What I got to thinking was that Bell and Buzz and Howdy Doody are all dead and I'm the only one left out of the biggest scam I ever got involved in. It could all come out now and nobody's left to get mad or get their feelings hurt or anything like that. But I'll never tell it. First place, I have not ever been one to spill my guts about somebody after they're dead and not here to defend themselves. In the second place there are just not very many people left who would even remember who I was talking about and few of them would care.

Bell and Buzz were two of the most unusual people I have known in my whole life. They certainly had one of the most unusual relationships. There's no doubt they were both what you'd call characters. The biggest thing they had in common was a sense of humor. I mean a true sense of what's funny, a real quick recognition of what is ridiculous in life. When you consider that as your definition, you know right off that sometimes folks that have it are going to laugh at things other people don't think are funny and lots of times they're going to appear cruel. And Buzz and Bell were. Most of the time to each other.

Bell was at least twenty years older than Buzz and me and maybe more than that; she was a fanatic about not telling her age. She took a nap every day and used Helena Rubenstein's Queen Bee lotion to keep down wrinkles. She had cataracts so that she couldn't see that the Queen Bee wasn't working. She had a blue Cadillac to match her hair and traded it every other year come hell or high water. Other than that, she was tight with her money like you wouldn't believe. She always claimed that she had been a flapper and had learned to drink liquor out of a fruit jar on the back seat of an A-model while me and Buzz were still in diapers. Said she was trapped between generations about tobacco, though, too old to smoke and too young to dip snuff. She washed her hair herself every Wednesday with that blue stuff in the water, then rolled it on bobby pins, tied it in a red bandanna, and went to town to buy a loaf of bread and a half dozen eggs. The bread, the hair, and the eggs all lasted until the next Wednesday. She saw to that by leaving off her egg on Sundays. "Who," she said, "ever heard of anybody walking in a store and buying seven eggs?" Like I said, she was a character.

It seemed like she and Buzz used to love to say things that would shock people; that went along with life being ridiculous. When they set out to shock each other, plain ordinary people had to hold their hats and their breaths and just hang on. It could get to be a wild ride.

I guess the worst she ever shocked me was once when she got a little tight and told me and Buzz about John Robert Anthony. She'd been going on about being a flapper and growing up in the twenties and then all of a sudden she put in and told it. She and John Robert were sitting in the front seat of the car waiting for John Robert's fiancee, who also happened to be Bell's best friend. Bell said they got to talking and poking around and first thing you know John Robert had unbuttoned his pants and pulled it out. I have never forgotten to this day how Bell told that story.

"We were sitting there, both of us admiring it. And it was a pretty good size, too. I've seen nearly every one in town, you know. All of a sudden John Robert looked up and said, 'Oh my God, here comes Laura! What in the world am I going to do with this?' And I told him just as cool as you please, 'Put it right back where you got it.' The very idea! He wasn't going to make me responsible for the damn thing and bust up a perfectly good friendship."

Buzz always said that was the most classical example of sang-froid he'd ever heard. I never went to med school; I just plain out thought it was scandalous and she would have done better not to have told it.

Bell may not have been as smart as Buzz, but she was every bit as quick. He used to wag his head and say, "Duke, try as I will I can't ever get the last word with that old woman." He didn't, either, except that last time with Howdy Doody, and I fixed it so that he died thinking Bell had got the last word with him on that, too.

The relationship started off sort of simple, at least as simple as anything could be with those two involved, but then it got pretty complicated toward the end. I'm sure that strangers we'd meet used to wonder how things all fit together.

Bell took up with me and took me under her wing, so to speak, after her husband died. She made a career out of mourning and still talked about Horace when he'd been dead for twenty years. Everybody in town got sick and tired of hearing her mention his name. Buzz's wife was as good-hearted a soul as I've ever met and a real lady, and she took to having Bell over for supper and then making Buzz take us all out to Atlanta to dance and party ever so often. Jeanne was the only one of us I never heard get on Bell about talking about Horace. Buzz and I both felt like when somebody's gone to the trouble and expense of dying the least you can do is let them be dead, but Jeanne would always be sympathetic with Bell and let her talk about Horace to her heart's content.

Bell took me in because she needed an escort. I'm not saying she didn't like me all right, but if there'd been another unmarried man in town who had more than one suit of clothes plus proper table manners and who would have put up with her ways, she would have liked him just as well. When Jeanne and Buzz finally convinced her she didn't have to spend the rest of her life lying in bed and crying about Horace, she got restless and wanted to go out at least three or four nights a week.

She liked to go to fancy restaurants, and she salved any guilt she had about throwing that money away by spending at least half an hour every time crying about Horace. She'd talk about how bad she missed him and how great he'd been to leave her so well-fixed, and then she'd spend ten minutes talking about how she'd helped him save his money. Then she'd touch a little on how much she still saved on groceries and fixing her own hair. By that time we'd be at the restaurant with the car parked and she'd get tipsy, order dinner, and be as funny and entertaining as anybody you ever saw. She loved to dance and I did, too. She needed me to drive on account of her cataracts bothering her after dark, and she needed a dancing partner and she needed a man around because she couldn't stand women. In fact, she needed me. That's the reason she liked me and I never was under any illusions about it.

Buzz didn't charge Bell for doctoring on her. That was because Horace had been such a good friend of his. At least I guess that's the reason. At any rate, it got to be a considerable service on his part because Bell was the world's worst hypochondriac and was fascinated with what she called her "innards." She was in his office at least once a week and sometimes more than that. She got to feeling obligated to him and because she felt it was unladylike to be beholden, she took to giving him expensive Christmas presents. Also fancy birthday parties. I was always included. It was fascinating to me to watch that woman giving Buzz Steuben glass for Christmas, shelling out cash money for dinner at Nicolai's, and driving a new Cadillac while still eating one loaf of bread and six eggs a week and doing her own hair up in a red bandanna every Wednesday.

One year she threw a big birthday bash for Buzz at Justine's. It was the first year after Justine's had opened and everybody was real impressed with it. It was the No. 1 place in Atlanta to go, provided you had the money. Bell had it. She was really showing out for Buzz that year. She had invited four of his doctor friends and their wives to meet us at Justine's. Jeanne spent a good part of the time we were driving into Atlanta telling Buzz not to get Bell stirred up and then telling Bell to be on her good behavior and not to relax and start talking nasty around these doctors' wives. That Jeanne was a long-suffering soul who endured much in the name of peace and good will. Ordinarily she just sat back and gave Bell her head, but she wanted a curb bit on her that night. Those wives had never been around Bell before, and Jeanne didn't want Northside Atlanta making fun of her friend. In fact, the last word she said as we drove up to the restaurant was, "Now, Bell, you and Buzz try to behave like Duke always does." There were lots of men who'd lie down and die for Jeanne. I was one of them.

I think Jeanne had Bell a little awed before we went in and then Justine's sort of overwhelmed her. It was Old South to a T. Restored antebellum mansion, old silver, candlelight, fine linen, waxed antiques, fragile china, family portraits, windows to the floor, high ceilings, wide boards, you name it. It was so Southern it made you ashamed all your ancestors hadn't died rich.

Here came the help. All black. I mean black. Not a mulatto in the bunch, not a one that your granddaddy would have called a "high yellow." Dressed in summer tuxedos and politeness oozing out of them. The most impressive thing about that flock of waiters was their diction. From the maitre d' on down, their grammar was perfect; you couldn't pick up a trace of a Negro accent. They were so formal and the setting was so grand that it automatically made you hold your shoulders back and mind your manners.

Bell herself was impressed. She was almost intimidated by our waiter.

"Is Madam comfortable?" he asked.

Madam was comfortable.

"Would Madam like to order a cocktail before her other guests arrive?"

Madam believed she would.

That waiter bowed and Madam-ed until Bell got so proper she almost quit being cute. She wasn't even trying to shock or scandalize the Northside doctors and their wives. Oh, she called the urologist among them the "little bladder man" and got him to dance with her twice, and she told the internist's wife that two drinks were her limit and she'd already had three, but for Bell she was pretty subdued.

Buzz ordered from the right-hand side of the menu like he always did when Bell was paying, but she didn't squawk as gratifyingly as usual. All in all, it was a very elegant party and everyone used perfect manners. Finally dessert time rolled around and everybody put their order in. Buzz got Bananas Foster; then the waiter bowed before Bell.

"And what would Madam like for dessert this evening?"

"Well, Madam certainly doesn't want anything that has to be set on fire at the table. I think I'll just have a little lime sherbert."

He bowed again. "Certainly, Madam."

Bell looked over her shoulder to be sure he was gone before she launched into a discussion with the surgeon's wife of Buzz's tastes and age. She was a little jealous of that wife, thought Buzz liked her more than he should. Suddenly the waiter reappeared at her elbow as polite and formal as could be. Bell almost snapped at him but not quite.

"What do you want now?"

"Pardon the interruption, Madam, but I regret to inform Madam that we are out of lime sherbert."

"Out of lime sherbert? At Justine's? Well, what do you have?"

That's when the veneer cracked and the whole evening fell apart. He bowed again, a little nervous at her attitude, and said, "We got aw-inge."

Bell leaped on it. "*Aw*-inge?" she almost yelled. "*Aw*-inge?" Everybody at the table and nearly in the whole room got quiet and looked at her. "You *got* aw-inge? Well, shit! Bring me aw-inge. Wanta dance again, little bladder man, hon?"

Things went steadily down hill pretty quick after that. Bell had another drink and wound up throwing up on my new suit while I was helping her to the bathroom. I mean I was a mess. She swore she'd buy me a new one if I wouldn't tell the Northside of Atlanta what she'd done. I didn't, but she never did. I haven't drunk wine since then. Every time I'm around it I can smell that suit.

She was some more sight of an old woman, I can tell you. When they brought the car around, she was still raising so much sand that Buzz opened the trunk and dumped her in it. He did it just to tease her and keep her stirred up, but she yelled and kicked so hard we had to stop half a block up Piedmont Road and let her in the front seat. It was quite a birthday party.

Bell got to where she was pretty possessive of Buzz, but she had more sense than to act like that even a little bit around Jeanne. Buzz gave her as good as she sent and put up with her, but Jeanne would have just put her in the road. One time Jeanne and Buzz had company. He was only a casual acquaintance but he came and stayed almost ten days. He was from San Francisco and had flown to Miami on business. He got his feet sunburned walking on the beach down there and got water blisters on the tops of them four inches high. He rented a Buick automobile and drove from Miami to our town close to Atlanta because, he said, he didn't know a doctor in Miami. Buzz said he wasn't in any shape to travel on to California but he also wasn't sick enough to go to the hospital. Private rooms in a hospital cost eighteen dollars a day back then, and Buzz just wouldn't put anybody through that unless it was an absolute necessity. Good old Jeanne said keep him at their house until he healed.

Well, sir, there he sat, barefoot and grinning, for the whole ten days. Yankees are funny. They've read all the crap about Southern hospitality and they believe it. They'll come and park on you and put you out and beam about how warm Southerners are. All the time they act like they think you're just a little bit retarded for not seeing through them. It's like telling a little kid he's a good boy so much that he's ashamed not to be.

Buzz ran into me and said, "Duke, for God's sake, come to lunch today and let me get a little rest."

Then he told me about their house guest. His name was Graydon Monk, and Buzz said he had about worn him down after three days. Said Mr. Monk was a leading authority on any subject you could bring up and would tell you everything he knew about it. Buzz said he was exhausted from listening because the guy was not a phony. He was really an authority. Said he knew he was because Buzz himself was an authority on a coupla subjects and when he'd brought them up, Mr. Monk knew more about them than he did. Said for me to please come to lunch because he needed a little time to be plain and ordinary and not have to wear himself out being the intellectual equal of a goddam yankee and that I could take the heat off him.

I said sure, I'd come. I forgot to find out which two subjects Buzz was an authority on. He had four kids in five years and used to spend a lot of time with the phone off the hook. Buzz used to say he was the only man he knew who had an emergency vasectomy; so I can imagine what one of them was. The second subject has always escaped me. I said, "I'll be glad to come by and meet Mr. Monk and talk to him for a while."

Buzz said, "You won't be talking, you'll be listening, but we'll sure be glad to see you."

Buzz was right. We ate on their big back porch which Jeanne had built right on the edge of the woods, and it's as pretty and restful a place as you could hope to find. Even with four children there. Everything was green and blooming, and after we'd howdied and shook, Mr. Monk commented on how pretty it was. I said, "Yes, this part of the country is always pretty right after a rain." That did it. He took off on rain. He knew the average rainfall of every county in California and every state in the Union. He talked about land mass, air currents, the Pacific Northwest, and Death Valley. By the time Jeanne called us to the table, he was talking Humboldt Current, Gulf Stream, and throwing around terms like "average precip." I decided he was California instead of yankee, but Buzz insisted there ain't all that much difference. "Shake 'em up in a sack," he said, "and you can't tell which one will fall out first."

We had soup. Jeanne prided herself on her homemade soup. She was finicky about all the vegetables being very young and very fresh and she put tomatoes, corn, okra, and butterbeans in it with a little celery and onions and seasoned it with nothing but chicken bouillon. I never saw anyone turn it down.

Buzz interrupted Mr. Monk's weather with the blessing, and we all tied in to the soup. Buzz said later that the yankee was eating his backwards, but Buzz was just cutting up. All of us knew to push your spoon away from you, but Mr. Monk was being extra precise about holding his shoulders back and bringing the spoon up to his mouth without bending over his bowl even the least bit. Never spilled a drop, either, for I was watching. So were all of

Buzz's little children. Mr. Monk might as well have been from another planet.

Just about the time he started in on the importance of rainfall to the level of Lake Okeechobee and the Everglades, the screen door opened and there stood Bell. She had on her thick glasses, of course, and had poked the little snap-on dark ones straight out so it looked like she was peeking out from her front porch. She was puffing a little from having walked around the house in the middle of the day. Bell didn't believe in exercise.

"Well, howdy," she said. "I didn't know you had company."

That was a lie. She knew it. Everybody in town knew that Jean and Buzz had a house guest who wasn't even kin. She also knew I was there, for I'd told her at the post office I was coming for lunch, and she'd for sure had to park that Cadillac by my truck in Buzz's front yard. She knew Buzz had company all right, and she was there to check him out.

"Come in, Bell," Jeanne said, "and join us for lunch. It'll be no trouble at all to set an extra place and pour you a bowl of soup."

"Oh, no, I won't do that. You know I never eat anything for lunch since Horace died and left me all alone, except two pieces of Melba toast and a glass of skim milk with a package of Knox's clear gelatin in it for my fingernails, and I've already had that. Don't mind, though, if I do sit and visit for a spell, it's been so long since I've seen any of you."

Buzz pulled her up a chair and did the introductions; then he made a social blunder. He asked Bell how she was feeling. She told us, for God's sake. Most of it centered around her back that day, and I was grateful she hadn't lately had what she chose to call a "gut spell." That's the worst organ recital she knew. All of us had heard the saga of the back before and didn't even listen to her, but Mr. Monk was a stranger and had to be polite and drink in every word.

". . . and that's it," she said, winding down. "It's been crooked all my life and it hurts like hell and I know for sure and certain I must have had infantile paralysis when I was a young'un, that being before we'd heard of polio, and it was sort of a social disgrace to have infantile paralysis and Mama was ashamed to take me to the doctor, not that it would have done any good." She glared at Buzz. "Not a one of you damn doctors has been able to do a thing to help me since. I think I'm just going to have to take up yoga."

With that, Mr. Monk stepped in. "Yoga? Yoga, Mrs. Moon? You know yoga?"

Bell blinked and sort of squirmed further into her chair, crooked back or no crooked back.

"Well," she said, "I know you're supposed to stand on your head and look at your belly button and it makes you feel better."

All Buzz's little children were watching Bell now. They were listening too. So were the rest of us.

"Nonsense," said Mr. Monk. "That's a layman's misconception. Yoga is a very beautiful and concentrated discipline when practiced by a dedicated participant."

Bell was out of her depth. "Do tell," was all she came up with.

"Yes. Can you believe that I once studied yoga in San Francisco for six weeks under the same swami who had instructed Pandit Nehru?"

Bell fidgeted. "You don't say." All Buzz's kids were looking at her. "Well, did you get to where you could stand on your head and look at your belly button?"

"Mrs. Moon, I've told you that has nothing to do with yoga. Unfortunately I had to leave San Francisco and interrupt my pathway, but I had a friend who began with the swami at the same time I did. He persevered and progressed eventually to the point where he could insert a marble into his anus and spit it out his mouth in ten minutes."

I was glad my spoon was down and empty. Bell jumped. Buzz's kids stopped eating. Everything was so quiet you could hear a joree scratching in Jeanne's fern bed. Buzz wouldn't look up from his soup bowl. Those kids swiveled their heads from Buzz to Bell and back to Buzz again. They knew exactly what an anus is because Buzz didn't allow anybody to talk nasty in front of his kids. You could tell they were expecting their daddy to do something to fix it, but I could tell Buzz was determined to let Bell get her own self out of the corner she was backed in to. She didn't let us down.

She blinked three times, jerked her stomach twice, and broke the silence.

"Well, personally," she said, "I never was the ath-a-letic type."

Everybody laughed, including Mr. Monk, and we broke up and left. Like Buzz and I always said, Bell was a character. Buzz used to tell that story and wag his head and say, "Nobody ever got the last word with Bell."

Buzz very nearly had her in church one time, though. Like I said, the two of them loved to shock other folks, and every now and then they'd try each other. Bell always sat by herself in church since Horace died, directly in back of her sister Turea and her husband. She said she placed herself just far enough from the aisle so nobody would sit on Horace. All the old-timers knew about it and wouldn't think of violating that holy space. The newcomers who every now and then would walk down the aisle and try to make her move over soon learned that there was at least one remaining honest-to-God character in the Methodist Church, for she wouldn't budge an inch, just scowl at them through those thick glasses and raise one corner of her upper lip like a snarling dog. Some of them never came back but went straight out and joined New Hope Baptist or Harp's Crossing.

Bell sitting in solitary splendor three quarters of a seat over from the aisle in the third pew on the left-hand side of the pulpit was a tradition. Nobody would have violated it. I sat with Mama till she died and then I moved to the balcony. I wasn't about to try to sit by Bell, and to tell you the truth I had no desire to. I've told you she was a hypochondriac. In church she was militant about it. Let somebody sniff behind her and she'd turn and stare him up and down like he belonged in the barnyard. If somebody sneezed or coughed anywhere within ten seats of her, she'd jump enough to shake the bench, snatch her mink stole real tight around her, and look like she was going to cry. Then she'd grab up her purse, take out her handkerchief, hold it over her mouth and nose, and ever so slowly turn her head looking for the offender. I wouldn't have sat beside Bell for all the tea in China.

Buzz usually sat in the choir. He said he couldn't sing, that they just needed warm male bodies on the back row. He was right, but everybody else was too polite to say it. On this particular Sunday the little children were going to sing and Buzz had to sit out in the congregation. Jeanne never went to church in the morning; so Buzz was by himself. He told me he decided when he walked in that he'd just go down front and sit by Bell.

He presented himself and she scowled. "Move over, Bell," he said. "I'm gonna sit on Horace's lap this morning."

"Well, I don't care if I do," she told him and shifted everything around on the seat. "That's not a suit you've been wearing to the office or on house calls and got all full of germs, is it?"

"I just came from a death call, Bell. Bad case of TB. Coughed all over me. Better hold your mink tight." Buzz was whispering, of course.

"You have not. All you doctors have got too rich to make house calls. I'm glad to see you, though. I've been sitting here in my widowhood every Sunday morning, half-blind and neglected, with people marching by me and the church growing up with rank strangers all around me till I hardly know a living soul. Who is that sitting across from Sister where Mr. Bert and Miss Ellie used to sit?"

"That's the Weatherfords. He works for Delta and she teaches fourth grade. We'd better be quiet, Bell. The organ is playing."

"I'll not be quiet. I've been waiting to find out who those people are and I aim to do it. Who's three seats behind them in that yellow dress and black hat and she ought to know better?"

"That's Mrs. Irene McNamee. Now, Bell, really. We've got to be quiet."

"Don't tell me about manners in church. For all you know I might be twice as old as you are, smart aleck, and you should be respectful. Who's that just squeezed in late over yonder on the second row?"

"Be quiet, Bell. Hush."

"I'll do no such thing. Who is it?"

"Mr. and Mrs. Barret. Shhhhh."

"Don't shush me. Who's that coming down the aisle now, so late Edward Fife is having to put them on the front row? They must have precious little children who are going to sing like tweetie birds and bore us all to death this morning. I've never seen them darken the doors of the church before."

"I'm not going to tell you. Please be quiet."

Buzz said he was getting desperate for her to hush because the preacher had already come out and it was meditation time.

"You are so going to tell me. Who is it?"

"It's Mr. and Mrs. Connors. Hush!"

She nudged him. "What does Mr. Connors do?"

Buzz put his lips right up against her ear. "He fucks Mrs. Connors. Now shut up."

Buzz said she jumped and sat bolt upright and real still. Said he thought he'd finally managed to get the last word with Bell for once in his life. But during the reading of the Scriptures, she nudged him again and slipped one of the Offering envelopes to him like a kid in study hall. Buzz looked down at it and it said, "All the time?"

"Hell, I can't ever get the best of that old woman," Buzz told me.

He never quit trying, though. Seemed like at times the worse he treated her the better she liked it. Every now and then she'd get her tail over the dashboard and give Buzz a hard time, but he got to where he felt responsible for her. Everybody in town would give out of patience with Bell, but Buzz always looked after her. In his own fashion. And she'd always wind up laughing about it and giving him another piece of Steuben glass for Christmas. She kept promising to give me a new suit for the one she'd ruined at Justine's, but all I ever got was a tie.

Every now and then I'd get pulled in on one of their capers. Like the time we got sewage in town. Of course, it wasn't anything but an oxidation pond, but we were all proud to get even that. The mayor had convinced everybody that the pond wasn't going to smell bad, and we all trooped down and voted a bond issue to build it. With the federal grant we got, it didn't amount to but a mil and a half added to our taxes, but Bell and a few die-hards still voted against it. In fact, Bell campaigned against it.

She went all over town squawking about taxes on widow women. That didn't go over so big coming from one of the widow women who was driving a brand-new baby blue Cadillac, even if she did have her hair in a bandanna and buy only six eggs a week. Then she took off on personalities.

"I remember," she told folks, "when Lafe Thompson and Mutt Atwater got in a big law suit over Lafe's building a chicken house in the city limits jam up against Mutt's property line. He put three thousand chickens in it. Mutt didn't even know it was there till he accidentally sobered up one time and smelled it. They spent all that money on lawyers and went to court and the only thing that happened was the lawyers proved that Mutt Atwater didn't drink and chicken shit didn't stink. Nothing else ever came of it. Lafe's chicken house is still standing and Mutt hasn't drawn a sober breath since the trial. I don't care what the mayor says, that pond is going to run us out of town. He's got the nerve to tell us they'll keep it aerated with propellers to keep it sanitary and odor-free, for God's sake, and ever since I've been born I've heard, if you don't want something to stink don't stir it."

Well, we passed the bond issue anyhow. Bell didn't give up. When they came with the backhoe to lay the sewer line across her front yard, she was taking her afternoon nap. She had sworn she would fling her poor pitiful little old widow-woman body on the bulldozer blade when it came, but she hadn't counted on a backhoe. Time she waked up good and ran out in the front yard, the workers had that ditch six feet deep and a pile of red dirt both sides of it at least waist-high and about four joints of pipe already in the bottom of the ditch.

They called me at city hall, since in those days I was the city manager and they didn't know who else to call. Said they had an old blue-headed woman in her night gown who was yelling and cussing a blue streak and had jumped in the ditch with the sewer pipe and one of the workmen. The workman had jumped out quick as she jumped in. I called Buzz, since even if I was city manager I didn't know who else to call. He came and got me in his little Ford Ranchero pickup and we went down to Bell's house.

Well, sir, I'll never forget that sight if I live to be a hundred. There were four Negroes and a white man leaning against the far side of the backhoe with their hard hats on and all of them smoking cigarettes. They had those hats pushed almost down on their noses and were as far away from that open ditch as they could get and still manifest possession of that backhoe. Buzz backed the truck right up to the edge of the hole and there was Bell. You couldn't even see the top of her head until you looked over the mound of dirt. That hole was so deep it made you wonder how she got down there without breaking a bone or at least pulling something out of joint. I never from that day on let her say a word to me about her back hurting.

She was in her night gown all right. Pale blue it was, cupped under her fanny like night gowns will do. Had strings over the shoulders instead of sleeves and her titties were perilous close to falling out. She was bare-footed. I mean she had really come as she was when she did get waked up. I was relieved to notice that she had on her panties under the night gown.

If Buzz thought there was anything unusual about an old blue-headed woman in a sewer trench at two o'clock in the afternoon less than a block from the court house, he never let on. He was as calm and dignified as he was at a death bed.

"What in the world do you think you're doing down in there?" he asked her, just as even and pleasant as if she were a child.

"I've told them and told them they weren't going to dig a goddam ditch across my front yard. I've told them I'd go back to a slop jar before I'd let them take me off my septic tank and hook me up to a pipe that carries everybody's filth all jumbled up together. What if something backfired in that sewer system's innards one day and blew those germs from God knows who all back through my commode and I sickened and died? Hell, no! I've sworn I'd throw my poor pitiful little old widow-woman body on the blade of the bulldozer. They come sneaking in here like a thief in the night while a lady's taking a nap and have this awful looking contraption with teeth on the end of a long arm eating its way across my front yard. I had to stop them, and there's no blade for my body to rest on; so I jumped in the ditch. That's what I'm doing in here."

Buzz never batted an eye. "Come out of there."

"I'll not do it. You can bring me some supper down in here if you want to, but I'm staying right where I am."

Buzz never raised his voice. "Bell, these men have to get back to work. You've proved your point. Now get your ass up out of that hole before I have them fill it up to your neck."

"I'll not do it. Fill it up!"

"Bell, you won't even take your shoes off in my office because you're afraid there are germs on the floor, and yet you stand down there barefooted where those black men have been spitting, and God only knows what all else they may do when they're down in a ditch where nobody can see them!"

She raised her arms straight up and got a cute tone in her voice. "Pull me out of here, baby."

It took both of us, but we hoisted her out. Then the white man came over and asked what we were going to do with her. Said his boys thought she was crazy and were scared of her. Said they wouldn't work no more if she was anywheres around. Then he told Bell, "Cover yourself, lady. You should ought to be ashamed."

That's when Buzz stepped over to the porch and got a chair and set it in the back of his pickup. He made me get in the chair and then he lifted Bell up and made her sit in my lap. Then he told the man to get his boys back to work, that the lady wouldn't be back until she had calmed down.

He got in the driver's seat and backed out the driveway. Bell was her old self by then and hollered, "Don't you dare drive around the court house with me like this! At least let me get in front!"

Buzz yelled out the window, "We're not going to the court house! Hold her tight, Duke. Don't let her kick loose."

Then, so help me, he drove to the cemetery. When he turned in, Bell realized what he was up to and began yelling, "No you don't, you little wall-eyed bastard! Don't you take me to Horace's grave like this. He'll rise up and kill me!"

That's right where Buzz drove us. He stopped alongside Horace's grave and said, "Now, Bell, you tell him yourself what kind of a fool you've been making of yourself. You know if there ever was a man in this town thought we needed central sewage, it was Horace. If you don't tell him, I will. Look there, I believe the ground's beginning to crack. I think he's coming out of there right now to get you."

That's when Bell saw how ridiculous it was. She commenced to laughing. Then Buzz started laughing. I can tell you I was thankful that nobody came along and saw me in the cemetery in the back of a pickup truck sitting in a rocking chair holding a blue-headed woman in a night gown with her laughing her fool head off at her husband's grave. I don't mind saying I was very uncomfortable, no matter how much she and Buzz had begun to enjoy themselves.

He crawled behind the wheel again and drove her to Sister's house. Bell was scared to death of Sister, wouldn't let her know she took a drink or anything and was always on her good behavior around her. She started begging Buzz not to stop and swore she'd do anything if he just wouldn't let Sister see her out in public in her night gown. So Buzz told her that he and I could come back and get her any time she was a mind to cut up and mess with the backhoe. Then he drove her home and she promised to leave the workers alone, and they finally got her sewer line in.

It was that Christmas that she gave Buzz the Steuben punch bowl and Horace's finger ring with the sapphire in it. She gave me a cruet set she'd found twenty years before in an antique shop in New Orleans. The stopper was lost to the vinegar bottle and it wasn't even real cut glass, either.

It was for a good long while after that Bell tried to hide things from Buzz, sort of like she had linked him up with Sister and was a little afraid of him in a way or at least of what he'd think. If Buzz had known about it from the start, she never would have got tied up with Howard Daudrill, and Buzz and I never would have got involved in what I still call the Howdy Doody Caper.

I met Howard Daudrill a pretty good while before Buzz did. In fact, I was there the night Bell met him. We had gone out to supper in Atlanta with Big Fat Frances and her husband, and they knew him from somewhere in business and introduced him. He was some kind of an insurance broker and it didn't take long to find out that he and Bell knew several people in each other's past, although he was at least ten years younger than she was. He had even met Horace and knew what a fine business he'd had, although Horace hadn't seen fit to buy insurance from him. Horace certainly had been a simply splendid person, he said, and it certainly had been a fine business and what had happened to it and would Bell think he was being forward if he asked her to dance? That was a lovely dress she was wearing. He could tell now that she had a strong family resemblance to her Melrose cousins who had all been famous beauties. The same bone structure and all.

All in all, he was so full of shit, as they say, that I kept waiting for his eyes to turn brown. Not Bell. I just assumed that as worldly-wise as she was and as cynical as she was about other people when she talked that she'd see right through him and laugh him down. I was wrong. She fell for it. Hook, line, and sinker. Howard this and Howard that was all we heard in the car going home until finally Big Fat Frances said, "For God's sake, Bell, you're simpering like a school girl. Howard Daudrill's been known all his life as one to turn a fast buck, and besides, he's married and got three grown daughters."

Bell said, "He's been separated from his wife for six months and they are going to get a divorce next year when the youngest girl finishes high school. We talked a lot on the dance floor. He's lonely and I am, too, and for your information we're going out Thursday night. He's a marvelous dancer!"

Big Fat Frances laughed and said, "Well, I've seen about everything, but this beats a hog flying sideways. Just remember, Bell: There's no fool like an old fool."

I could have told her ahead of time that would piss Bell off, and it did. She got pretty frosty and formal and that was the last Big Fat Frances saw of her for several months. I didn't see a whole lot of her myself. All of a sudden the need for my services was cut at least in half. That Howard Daudrill put a rush on Bell you wouldn't believe, and she cottoned up to him like you wouldn't even dream.

He really took her for a ride, too. First news you know she told me she'd loaned him five thousand dollars because, she said, his business was booming but his cash flow was tight. Back in those days, five thousand dollars was a lot of money. You could buy a Cadillac with it. He paid her back in a week. That was just bait so he could borrow more. He started telling her she ought to be more than a figurehead in Horace's business she'd inherited. Before you could scat a cat she'd got the business to switch its insurance over to him. Howard Daudrill turned her head plumb around. He got her to talking budgets, projected income, checks and balances, and ever and eternally that term "cash flow." About that time he'd got his foot so far in the door that he told Bell he wanted to meet those good friends of hers she kept talking about so much; so Bell invited me to go out to supper with Buzz and Jeanne and meet Howard at a restaurant in town.

Well, now, that was a show and it was short if not sweet. Be blessed if Bell hadn't talked about Buzz until Howard Daudrill thought he would be a fresh pigeon to pluck. He started talking to Buzz over dinner about accounts receivable, interest rates, and that everlasting cash flow. Buzz had sized him up in less than five minutes, and if you knew Buzz at all you could tell he liked Howard Daudrill about like he did chicken mess between his toes. He looked him in the eye and said, "I understood this was to be a social evening, sir, and I actually have little interest in the business world. There are two things I never discuss with other people, however, and they are my sex life and my finances. Have you read any good books lately?" Howard hadn't and it wasn't long till that meal was over and we were headed home.

Buzz gave Bell hell. She got to babbling and finally told her guts. He dug it out of her bit by bit that by now she had loaned Howard Daudrill over twenty-five thousand dollars. That's when Buzz tagged him as "Howdy Doody." Ridiculing him like that made Bell mad, and the reason was that she knew in her heart that Buzz was right and that she was making a fool out of herself. She was too stubborn to admit it, though, and she kept on defending Howdy Doody. He was a fine person, a lonely human, and a good business man. Buzz fired back with the ultimatum that she could prove it by getting Howdy Doody to at least sign a note for the money he owed her and that Howdy impressed him as being about as lonely as a fox stalking a rabbit. By the time we got home, he had Bell herself saying Howdy Doody instead of Howard Daudrill, and you could tell she was beginning to worry about her money.

She would probably have turned completely to Buzz after that and leaned on him for advice and sent Howdy Doody packing, but she told me later that Buzz made her mad and hurt her feelings, too. She told him with that sort of a little girl tone to her voice she could get sometimes that Howdy Doody had known her cousins down in Meriwether County and thought she had the same bone structure as the Melrose girls. Buzz snorted and laughed and said, "What a con artist! For God's sake, Bell, you know you look like the Harbuck side of your family. They've got noses like Irish potatoes and their ears keep growing till they're eighty. We love you for what you are and like you are. Not for your looks. Don't you lend that Howdy Doody any more money!"

When we left, Bell turned to me and did a little squawking. Said Buzz favored the Taylor side of his own family and by the time he was fifty his dewlaps would be hanging down until you couldn't tell him from a goddam Boxer puppy. Then she said, "Tell me the truth, Duke, does my nose really look like an Irish potato?" I tried to smooth things over by telling her Buzz had probably meant a little fresh, new-dug spring potato and wasn't thinking about an Idaho baking potato, but I could tell she was still in a snit. I couldn't help it. There's just not much way to comfort somebody about a Harbuck nose.

Bell took to calling me instead of Buzz. Not for advice. Just for somebody to talk to because Buzz and Big Fat Frances had cut themselves off. You see, she still couldn't give Howdy Doody up. She told me with triumph in her voice that Howdy Doody had signed that note in a flash when she finally brought it up and for me to be sure and let Buzz know. Said she wasn't going to call him herself because she was still pouting with "the little son of a bitch." Then she told me that Howdy Doody borrowed another five thousand on account of his cash flow and brought her a note all ready to sign before he even asked for the loan. And later another two. And then three. And she told me not to tell Buzz about those notes. No collateral but his signature. So I didn't. But I agreed with Big Fat Frances about no fool like an old fool.

I guess Howdy Doody would have inched along a few thousand at a time and drained Bell of every nickel Horace had left her plus everything the plant was still earning if he hadn't gotten over-confident and showed up at Bell's house drinking one night. She had actually invited him for a home-cooked meal. That was something she hadn't done for any of her other friends since Horace died. Said it made her sad to use the dining room furniture Horace had bought her just two years before he died, but that didn't make any sense at all to any of us. Horace had bought every stick of furniture in the whole house. Bell just didn't like to cook and wasn't going to put herself out that much for any of us.

It sort of shocked me when I found out she had invited Howdy Doody for supper at home. I kind of wondered if Bell was getting a romantic interest in him and maybe she thought that he was in her, but of course I never mentioned that to her. Anyhow, she never told any of us about the home-cooked meal until it was all over. Then she only told me.

Howdy Doody showed up for it all right, but like I said, he had liquor on his breath. That wasn't as bad as what he had on his arm, and that's what really got Bell's dander up. He brought another woman with him and told Bell she was an old friend he had run into unexpectedly and that he was sure Bell wouldn't mind setting just one more place for supper.

Bell was fit to be tied. She called me that very same night as soon as they were gone. "Duke, can you believe it? Marched her peroxided self in my house twisting her tail like a bitch in heat. She plopped down in my living room for me to wait on her. Didn't even offer to help with the dishes after supper, either. God knows where she came from, but she's got to be a tramp. Didn't know who her grandparents were on either side and couldn't carry on a conversation about anything. Her name was Byllye Teale with two y's. She told me three times, and she didn't even know her mother's maiden name. Said she'd been raised in West End and she thought her mama was born in Texas. I never heard of any Teales anywhere, and if she didn't know the name of her grandparents you can be sure she's no lady. On top of that, I never had a speck of use for any female who insists on putting a y in her name where an i would do as well and was there in the first place. She probably started out as plain old Willie Jo. On top of that, she didn't eat grits and whined that the country ham was too salty. For God's sake, if it's not too salty it's not country ham, and that's what I'd invited Howdy Doody down here for in the first place.

"He kept nipping and when they finally left he was so drunk that Byllye had to drive, two ys and all. I'm so mad at him I'm going to kill him when I see him again. Don't you tell anybody about this. I ought not to be telling you, but I just this minute got my hands out of the kitchen sink and I had to tell somebody. I've never had a fuss with Howdy Doody before but, boy, is he in for a stem-winder!"

She told me four times before she hung up that whatever I did, don't tell Buzz. She told me so many times I decided that she really wanted him to know. Monday morning I stopped by his office on my way to city hall and told him. I told him about the last three notes, too, which of course had no collateral and were plain old promissory, on-demand notes. Buzz looked at me real solemn for a minute.

Then he said, "Don't let her ever know you've talked to me, but be sure you keep her talking to you. This has gone far enough. I'm going to have to step in there and get that sucker's feet out of the trough. If I approach her head-on, she'll just dig her heels in and get butt-headed. First thing you know she'll deed old Howdy Doody the house and that five acres she and Horace built on. We can't have that. She's promised to will me that house." He laughed. "Not that I need it, but she keeps saying I've been good to her and that Horace loved me and Jeanne, and she'd like for me to have the house when she's gone. Says if she left me money I'd just fritter it away. Well, Horace would have a fit if he knew how she was frittering it away with that Howdy Doody pimp. We've got to save her from herself, Duke, and I know how to slip up on her blind side and do it. But it all depends on her not ever knowing that I've found out about the dinner party for Byllye with two y's."

He started grinning and I asked him what he was going to do.

He said, "Just keep the telephone line open with her. I've got to wait till Wednesday to fix Mr. Howdy Doody's clock."

I asked him if he was that busy that he had to wait till Wednesday or why couldn't he go on and do it before Howdy Doody got his fingers in the till again. He just grinned and said, "Bell's a suspicious old soul, and if you're going to fool her you'd better have it down pat. I need at least three days for incubation, you know."

I called Bell Monday night. She had quit being mad; she had come down to being bewildered and hurt. Couldn't understand how a fine man like Howard Daudrill with his family background and all, and especially one who had known the Melrose girls, could stoop to associating with the likes of that Byllye woman. Let alone bring her into her house for grits and country ham. The very idea. On top of that, Byllye had on a tacky dress and the nicest thing you could say about her, even on a Sunday morning with the sun shining bright and the birds singing, was that she was common.

On Tuesday night she called me. She was walking on air. Howdy Doody had called her. Now she understood everything. "That woman didn't mean anything to him. She'd been married to an old friend of his once and he ran into her unexpectedly when he came out of the Commerce Club on his way down here. He'd been entertaining some important accounts and they were heavy drinkers, and of course he had to drink along with them, and when he got downstairs he realized that he was in no condition to drive. He got to thinking how embarrassing it would be if he got stopped in our town on his way to my house, and on impulse, him not thinking a thing about it on account of the drinks muddling his perception and all, he asked Byllye if she'd mind being his chauffeur for the evening. That's all it was. He swore to God she didn't mean anything to him. He kept on drinking after he got here because when he got that girl in my house and started comparing her with me, he realized what a social blunder he'd pulled and he needed to drink."

I couldn't believe my ears, but I swear she was saying it. It was obvious that she also believed it. I just listened.

"I forgave him everything. After all, Horace was a heavy drinker when I first met him. I had to put him in Brawner's for his honeymoon while I went home and told Sister I was married. And look how good I got him straightened out. Howdy Doody needs me, and I'm going to kill that Buzz for hanging such a name on him; I'm afraid I'm going to slip and call him that to his face some day. But it really is Howdy Doody time. He's coming down to see me Thursday night. He's having a little cash-flow bind again and is bringing another note with him. He'd come tomorrow but it's Wednesday and the bank's closed, and I'm going to have to go into savings for this one. He's feeling better. Said he got so sick they had to pull off the road and let him throw up the other night."

I couldn't help it. I asked her how tight his cash flow was binding him this time and she said, "Just ten thousand. You know, Duke, you don't walk in and out of the Commerce Club with important clients on chicken feed. He's got a deal coming up in June and he'll pay me back everything he owes me then."

I got off the phone and called Buzz. He whistled and then he laughed. "The timing's perfect," he said. And that's all he'd tell me. Buzz was still laughing when he hung up but I was nervous as a hen on a hot hoe.

You'd never guess in a thousand years what Buzz did. Wednesday night, when he was sure she'd be started on her favorite TV program, he called her.

"Bell, do you know anybody named Willie Mae?"

"Who?"

"Willie Mae. Calls herself Byllye with two y's, but her real name's Willie Mae. I don't know her last name, Peale or Seale or something. I've forgotten."

"Hell, no. Why would I know anybody named that? Never heard of her."

"I thought so. That all sounded like a big lie to me anyhow. I'll let you go. Sorry I interrupted your show."

"Wait a minute. Wait a damn minute. Why are you calling? What big lie are you talking about?"

"I won't bother you with it. It was something I heard professionally anyhow, and I've got no business repeating it."

"Don't you dare hang up, you little wall-eyed bastard. You've got my curiosity up and you damn well better tell me what you're talking about."

"Well, Bell, it was nothing. And you must promise not to tell a soul because it does involve professional confidence and all."

"I'll never breathe a word of it. Tell it!"

"Well, I just now had to get out and go back to the office to see the worst case of clap I ever saw in my life, and . . . ."

"Who was it?"

"There you go. You know I'm not going to tell you, especially since you know him. Anyway, he was really in a fix. Said he'd had clap a dozen times and he'd have waited till morning and not bothered me, but this was the worst dose he'd ever seen and it came on him so quick he was afraid it'd rot off if he let it run like that overnight."

"I wish to hell you'd use medical terms! The way you talk makes me want to put on gloves to hold this telephone receiver. Who was it?"

"Bell, you know I'd die before I'd tell you. Besides, that's not the point of me calling you. The only reason I'm talking to you at all is that he mentioned your name."

"My name? Whatever for?"

"Said he'd been up to the Farmers' Market late Saturday night and ran up on a car parked behind one of the sheds. There was a good-looking blonde in the back seat with some man with his breeches down who'd passed out cold. He talked her into getting into his truck and he rode off a ways and she gave it to him twice right away, and he took her back to the car and her boy friend never even woke up. This fellow said she really was a good looking woman. Had the cutest little nose you ever saw, he said, and the prettiest titties and was sweet as honey. They got to talking while they were smoking cigarettes between rounds and she told him her name was Byllye with two y's and he told her he never could spell worth a toot so it didn't matter about the y's, and she got to laughing and said she'd started out as Willie Mae. He gave her his best friend's name instead of his own, but he did tell her that he lived in Roopville."

"Buzz, my God, you're making this up."

"Bell, how in the world could I make up a tale like this? Just wait, you're coming up next. This fellow said Willie Mae hollered out, 'Roopville? Roopville? I ate dinner at a lady's house in Roopville not three hours ago.' Of course, he wanted to know where, and she told him a Mrs. Bell Moon had her and her boyfriend down to her house to eat. And this fellow knows you and he said, 'Doctor Buzz, that woman was just not the sort Mrs. Moon would have in her house and her with the clap and all, and she had to have been the one give it to me cause I hadn't had a woman in two months before Saturday night.' And I agreed with him that she had to be lying because it was well known that you hadn't served anybody a meal in your home since your husband died and you certainly wouldn't start out with anybody except old and dear friends."

"You're exactly right! The very idea! I never heard of such a thing! Tell that fellow she was lying, or better still tell me who he is and I'll tell him. On the phone, of course. I don't want even to be in the same room with anybody with the gonorrhea. Why, I don't even sit down when I'm forced to go into a public rest room, and I've always taken Lysol in my bag to scrub the tub and toilet when we used to go to hotels. The very idea!"

"Calm down, Bell. I've already told the fellow that the girl was lying. He nor I either one believed that story. I'll let you go."

"No, you won't! You've ruined TV for me tonight, and you keep on talking."

"There's nothing more to talk about. I gave the fellow penicillin and he'll be all right by morning, but I bet he gets his produce somewhere besides the Farmers' Market from now on."

"What'd the girl look like?"

"Bell, I never saw her. The fellow said she was blonde and had pretty titties, but that's true of nearly all pickups I should imagine, or they couldn't get picked up. The fellow did comment on her nose, but that doesn't tell you much either."

"Well, how'd she get my name, I'd like to know? The very idea! What'd she say my house looked like? Where'd she say I lived?"

"Bell, I was only treating clap and I'd gone out after dark to do that; I wasn't running a tourist bureau. The fellow and I both knew she was lying, so I didn't press it too far. Remember, you must never tell I've even mentioned this to you, for I just don't gossip about my patients."

"I've already told you I won't breathe it to a soul. You want me to sign an affidavit?"

"O.K., O.K. I just can't be too careful. The fellow did say, come to think of it, that Willie Mae said Mrs. Moon was an old lady and had a real pretty house. The girl giggled and told my patient that God had made Mrs. Moon ugly and then He'd turned around and made her mad. Said she had the biggest ears she'd ever seen on a woman, but her boy friend had warned her about that ahead of time and told her not to stare at them. Said Mrs. Moon was all right but she sure couldn't cook worth a shit; her ham was too salty. Look, Bell, I've got to go now; I have some other calls to make. You just relax."

"That goddam blonde slut! Whoever she is! And wherever she may be spreading her filthy diseases! To whom! Thanks for calling, sweetie, and thanks for stopping that lie in its tracks. But I may never relax. Not ever again. Anywhere. Bye, now."

Thank God Buzz had told me to deny having talked to him. The minute he hung up, Bell was on the phone to me. She hadn't told anybody but me about Howdy Doody and old two-y-Byllye, she said, and I just had to have told Buzz. I swore that I hadn't, and then she told me all about Buzz calling and the fellow with the gonorrhea, and then she got a panicky tone in her voice and hollered, "Oh, my God, it must all be true then," and slammed down the phone.

I called Buzz and filled him in, and he said to get off the phone because he figured she'd be calling me back. He was right. She kept calling me back all night. It got to where I wished I didn't have a phone.

First off, she called and wanted to know how long it took to catch gonorrhea after you were exposed, and I told her I wasn't a doctor and also I'd never had gonorrhea and for her to call Buzz. She said she couldn't do that because she didn't want him to get the faintest notion she was worried because then he'd know two-y-Byllye really had been in her house and just be damned if she'd ever cook country ham for anybody again the longest day she lived. Then she hung up.

Thirty minutes later she was back. She'd got out all the dishes they'd used and washed them again and scalded them real good, and did I think her ears were really all that big?

Next time she called, she'd scrubbed the commode and the floor in the powder room with Lysol and flushed the toilet six times, and did I know how long a gonorrhea germ could live outside the human body?

An hour later she'd vacuumed the rug and sprayed the sofa with Lysol and was trying to remember everywhere two-y-Byllye had sat and couldn't, so she just sprayed all the living room chairs. Said she had cussed the lazy whore on Saturday night for not helping with the dishes but now she was thankful that at least she'd never set foot in the kitchen.

She called back in fifteen minutes and said everything smelled so strong of Lysol that she ought to feel clean but didn't, so she'd scattered moth balls all over the living room rug. By now her sense of the ridiculous was coming back to life and she giggled a little.

I made the mistake of giggling, too, and in another half hour here she was again. She'd quit saying "Hello" after the second time she called. "I just want you to know how far this has gone. I got on my nightgown ready for bed and I still felt like there were germs all over the house and no telling where they might have crawled or floated or whatever the damn little things do to get at you. So let me tell you what I did. I took a douche! Hadn't had one in years and like to never found all my paraphernalia. But maybe I can sleep now. Bye."

At one-thirty the phone rang and she started talking soon as I took the receiver off.

"I was lying here and couldn't go to sleep and I got past worrying about germs in my house and started getting mad. And of course the only one to be mad at is that son of a bitching Howdy Doody. And I thought, why should I lie here awake and let him sleep? Then I thought I couldn't tell him about two-y-Byllye and the gonorrhea without bringing Buzz into it, and the more I thought the madder I got. Then I realized that no matter what happened I never wanted to see the goddam dead-beat bastard again the longest day I lived, and I'd just break it off and leave him wondering what had happened. So I called him. I told him not to bother coming down here tomorrow with any note for me to sign and to pay up those old ones as soon as he could. I told him to pay them to the bank and not to me because I never again wanted to touch anything he'd handled if it hare-lipped Hell and half of Georgia. I also told him that I hoped his cash was the only flow he was having trouble with and hung up. He's called back three times and I've slammed the receiver in his ear every time. I'm fixing to leave the phone off the hook, take two phenobarbs, and go to sleep. I know I have worried you to death this evening, Duke, but I didn't have anybody else to talk to. I'll make it up to you. I really will. Bye, now."

And she did.

I never did get a new suit out of Bell, but I did a lot better. I got the house.

It was a stroke that finally got her and not anything even remotely related to germs, which would have been a comfort to her; she'd dreaded them all her life. Buzz didn't know she'd changed her will till she was dead.

He never knew that I helped her change it. Like I said, I got the house. All I had to do was tell her Buzz had laughed and said he didn't need it. Buzz got the thirty-five thousand dollars worth of notes that Howard Daudrill owed Bell. I told her Buzz already had a collection agency that he used and would probably enjoy digging that money out of Howdy Doody.

I can hear Buzz laughing now. "Duke," he said, "nobody ever got the last word with that old woman. Talk about worthless paper!"

My conscience didn't hurt me at all; Buzz never got puked on at Justine's. I never told him that it was my idea for her to leave him Howdy Doody's notes, either. Buzz had a good sense of humor, which as I have repeatedly stated is nothing except a well-developed sense of what's ridiculous, but I wasn't quite sure how far it'd take him in this case.

I hardly ever think about all that anymore, but when I saw Howdy Doody's funeral announcement, it came flooding back. There wasn't any two-y-Byllye mentioned in the paper as a survivor, and I also noticed he never had got divorced.

Buzz got killed two months after Bell died. Deer hunting, and fell out of a tree and broke his neck. I've never been as surprised in my life as when Jeanne told me he'd left me all his Steuben glass.

It looks real good in Bell's house. Every now and then I get down one of the red wine glasses. I fill it plumb full of bourbon and water and drink a toast to Howdy Doody. All by myself.

Judgment

I HAVE BEEN going to church at
least once a week all my life. Been singing in the choir ever since
I was thirteen and turned out to be an alto. After all that religion
I've been exposed to, the hardest thing yet for me to do as a
Christian is to judge not lest I be judged. Mr. Bazemore Hubbard
told old man Oscar Plunkett one time that the hardest thing for
him about being a Christian was to love his neighbor as hisself,
that being the way Mr. Bazemore talked. Old man Oscar told
him straight out that'd be easy if he'd just quit thinking so much
of his own goddamn self, that being the way old man Oscar talked
and no words of my own. All that is between Mr. Bazemore
Hubbard and old man Oscar Plunkett, and they do say it broke
them up from playing checkers together down at Langford's Store
for nearly three months. But the hardest thing for me is judging
not.

It seems to me that if you don't judge in your own mind and
always leave it up to God to judge, then you also don't punish but
leave that up to God, too. Then it seems like that'd lock you into

putting up with just about anything from just about anybody, and that is stretching Christian tolerance too cotton-picking thin, and I can't do it. I judge my fellow Christians' actions in spite of myself and I just can't help it. I do. I accept it. It's like race prejudice. They all preach against that nowadays. When I first started listening to sermons they were against liquor and sex. Nowadays it's race prejudice. You can pray all you want not to have it, but if you got it, you got it. You can pray from now to Kingdom Come for it to be removed, but it sets there just like a rock that's bedded in the waters and it shall not be moved. The best you can do is accept it and pray without ceasing that you don't ever let it make you do anything that's unpleasing to the Lord. That's the way I am about my judging. I accept it. And I pray.

To tell the honest truth, there are times when I enjoy it. I enjoy wondering how the Lord is judging some things, since it's all to be left up to Him. Then I enjoy speculating on how close the Lord and I are on our opinions about some things and some folks. I go ahead and do this because I can't help it, and then I pray for forgiveness.

Thank God we have a forgiving God, I always say. I used to offer up my prayer for forgiveness during the meditating moment before the preacher prayed. Since I have grown older and quit feeling like I'll go to hell if I don't shut my eyes every time there's a word of prayer, and especially since that Ben Baxter was sent to us by the Conference, I have been saying my prayer for forgiveness during the Benediction. Lord knows I've said it so many times I've got it down short and sweet, and Lord knows the Lord's used to hearing it. The Benediction's plenty of time for it, and it's sure the most appropriate time since I notice I do a lot of my judging while I'm sitting in the choir loft looking around and not listening to the preacher.

I never was in any peril about judging preachers before the Reverend Baxter was visited upon us. Except maybe when the Conference had sent us that old fool Hamilton Holt, and there I go getting into the judgment thing again because the Bible plainly states that he who calls his brother "fool" is in danger of hell fire. If that's true, and I'm not saying one minute that I'm doubting it, that's just the way I talk, the whole church was pretty well in danger of that sort of hell fire before Brother Holt had been here three months. He was a punitive appointment. I know he was, for I heard out of my own ears Mr. Tritt say so, and like him or not, there was never anybody knew more about the business end and the politics of the church than Mr. Tritt.

The Bishop and the Cabinet were ticked off because our church never gave the preacher a raise and the Bishop's salary is figured on percentage of the salaries of the local preachers. Well, come to find out, the total our preacher was getting was right on up there with the best of them, but what Mr. Tritt was doing was putting just a little bit in salary and the balance of it in a travel account. Travel account didn't add one thing to the Bishop's salary. It did give us more control of the local preacher though. The District Superintendent tumbled to what we were doing and brought it before our Commission on Finance, that being the same as Mr. Tritt, since he had been chairman of it ever since I can remember and sometimes they didn't even call meetings, just asked Mr. Tritt on the sidewalk after church what he wanted done about this and that and the other.

Mr. Tritt never denied it one minute. He just got black around the eyes like he does when somebody challenges him about something he's dead set for certain going to do anyhow and has already figured out a way to do it, him being a lawyer and all. He told the DS he was mighty right about our givings and that it wasn't any oversight on our part, it was exactly what we intended to do, "we," of course, being Mr. Tritt. Then he went on and gave the DS what I call Mr. Tritt's bishop speech and lined out to him that it was the Bishop that had led us into the American Council of Churches, racial integration, deletion of the word *heathen* from our missionaries' vocabulary and was even now pushing to join us up with the United Brethren. Then he gave him his famous viewpoint that the local congregation still owned our own church property because there weren't any deeds recorded to it anywhere except in the name of the American Methodist Episcopal Church South, and we'd be in a sight better shape if we hadn't ever unified back with the North in the first place.

The which all of us had heard Mr. Tritt get off on that track a hundred times and none of us paid any attention to it. That was just Mr. Tritt. We didn't judge him, just went on to morning worship and choir practice and Circle meetings and Sunday School and let him have his way. I secretly agreed with him about that word *heathen*. I looked it up in my Webster and it says, "Any unconverted member of a tribe or nation who does not believe in the God of the Bible. One who is neither Christian, Moslem, or Jew." The Methodists won't let the missionaries use that word anywhere now for fear of hurting someone's feelings or their delicate sensitivities. It sounds hypocritical to me. If you aren't going to tell them what they are, how are you going to convert them? And if you don't aim to convert them, why in the world are we spending money on missionaries in the first place? We could just send it to the United States Public Health Service and be done with it. I don't care what the National Conference says, we still have heathens.

Mr. Tritt was the biggest giver in the Church, and the older I get the more I think it's a mistake to let one person give more than another to a church. It's better to do with a heap less and have everybody equal in their own sight as well as the Lord's. I've watched big givers all my life, and it's just human nature for somebody to want to run something they put a lot of money into. Where a man's treasure is, there is his heart also, you know. Mr. Tritt was forever giving to the church, like the carpet, the organ, the light bill if it was coming past due, college tuition for preachers' kids, you name it. Whenever he loved something, Mr. Tritt ran it. That involved his children's and his grandchildren's lives and it certainly included his church. Everybody in town knew that. Maybe the IRS didn't, but it wasn't our business to tell anything to them in the IRS.

So here came the DS at budget time and picked a fuss and butted his ecclesiastical head against a stone wall. Mr. Tritt didn't give an inch. He told the DS that if the Bishop would get us out of the National Council of Churches, which in his opinion was nothing but a Communist front organization, he'd guarantee our preacher's salary would be tripled in two years. We wouldn't give him any more automobiles under the table either, that being the way the DS talked and not an admission on Mr. Tritt's part of what we did, him being too smart a lawyer for that. The DS had been a fraternity man at Emory and thought he was as good as anybody and better than most, and that's not judgment, that's observation. He fumed up and told Mr. Tritt that appointments were coming up and he'd see to it we got a preacher that suited our mind-set and personality level.

After Conference time, sure enough, we got Hamilton Holt. He would have been punitive anywhere he was sent, and I personally think that the Cabinet just didn't have anywhere else to send him. He'd already been to nearly every other church in North Georgia and nobody would ever take him back. It was just our turn to get him, to my way of thinking, but then I'm not nearly as judgmental as Mr. Tritt. Of course, I didn't have a guilty conscience about cussing the DS out, not to say that Mr. Tritt did either, but I would have if I had have. You see what I mean about putting our own values on things?

At any rate, Hamilton Holt moved in and things got lively. He was an old man, and I would sure have hated to endure him any younger. He smoked cigars and you could smell him coming a block away, which as far as I was concerned was better than having a bell on the cat. I personally was the one that stopped Mr. Tritt from complaining to the Cabinet about our preacher smoking, even though it was against the rules for ministerial conduct. I told Mr. Tritt that he never was in a position to have to drop what he was doing and visit with him. Brother Holt's cigar smoke gave every housewife in the church ample warning; she could head out the back door and be gone before he even had the chance to ring the front door bell.

Hamilton Holt was like something out of the past. He stomped and hollered and beat his fist on the pulpit and waved his arms about till the candles on the altar flickered like the windows were open, which they hadn't been since we got air conditioned. In fact, most of them were stuck tight, but that preacher made you think you had stepped back thirty years. Hamilton Holt just wasn't cut out for a church that had gotten dignified enough to have acolytes and lighted candles.

On top of that, he was theatrical as all get-out. He vaulted the altar rail one morning and grabbed the collection plate from one of the ushers. Then he hollered, "Let me show you how a real servant of the Almighty harvests the vineyards of the Lord." He ran in a half crouch up and down the aisle, looking for all the world like Groucho Marx, holding the plate and shaking it under the noses of folks till they gave what he thought they should. Then he preached a sermon on temperance and actually turned his head up like a dog at the moon and sang in this horrible falsetto, "Lips that have touched wine shall never touch mine," mocking, he said, an old maid school teacher who thought liquor was the worst sin in the world. She died, he told us, as a perfect example of the steward who buried his one talent. I didn't have to judge on that one. Everybody in the church said it was the strangest temperance sermon they'd ever heard. Even Miss Phronie Franklin, who prides herself on not ever criticizing anyone, said it was thought-provoking. The Lord Himself knows that Miss Phronie may have been provoked into a heap of situations in her life, but thinking sure never was one of them. I think I can safely say the Lord and I were right together on Miss Phronie.

Hamilton Holt used Madame Curie as an illustration one time. He jumped from behind the pulpit, went down to the Communion table, blew out one of the candles, and pretended the candle stick was a microscope while he hollered about the wonders of science not being a circumstance to the glories of God. At Easter he pantomimed nailing Christ on the cross flat on the floor out in front of the altar rail. He flailed and grunted till he hammered all the nails in. Then he huffed and puffed until he hoisted the loaded cross upright into a hole and stomped the dirt around it. Of course, that was a new idea to me. For some reason I'd always just assumed they nailed Him to it after it was in place. Hamilton Holt was dripping wet with sweat when he finished that morning, and he did have everybody's attention. I say again, though, that he just did not belong in a church with candles.

He got to the mayor one Sunday. I'll never forget it, for I was on the very front row in the choir loft and felt like I had to be extra dignified and set a good example and all that, and it nearly killed me not to be able to laugh. Buck Betsill was the mayor and the youngest one we ever had. He was a stomp down good one, too. For years and years. That office fit him like a glove and he worked as hard at it as if it paid more'n fifty dollars a month. It was like he was born to be mayor and it had finally happened. Buck was always dignified in church, as we all were, on account of the choir director, who was the straight-backedest young woman you ever saw and put up with no foolishness whatever, and I mean none.

Buck had a streak of fun in him. He tried to hush it up and live it down, but everybody knew he was the one who had decorated Santa Claus. It was the year before Buck ran the first time, and of course the town didn't have any money at all. Jim Brissendine was president of the Civic Club that year, and they set out to get decorations for the Courthouse Square, being as we were the only town in Georgia that didn't have any. Jim worked up at Fort McPherson and they were getting new decorations, and he begged them out of the old ones and put them up on our Courthouse Square. One of them was this great big Santa Claus made out of plywood. He was nine feet tall, standing there on the lawn spraddle-legged with his hands on his hips. Second night after he was installed, somebody sneaked out with two coconuts that had been spray painted red and hung them right between his legs. There they dangled for two days. Everybody was too embarrassed to take notice of them, let alone be caught taking them down. First time I saw them, I had the kids in the car and I had to speed up and go through the intersection on yellow before they could ask a bunch of questions. I took them to Mama's and left them so's I could drive back real slow and get a good look and a good laugh.

Finally Jim Brissendine put on an overcoat and hat and some dark glasses and removed those coconuts himself. Seemed like that sort of took the Christmas spirit out of the Courthouse Square. The Civic Club itself kind of petered out after that. Buck didn't aim for it to get out on him, but everybody knew he hung the coconuts, and if it hurt his race for mayor, nobody could tell it. In later years some of his political enemies did try to lay it on his doorstep that he was the one who killed the Civic Club. I always thought myself that it was due to them taking Pearl in as a member and everybody being scared of getting some of her food at the covered dish suppers. It was easier not to go than it was to worry about getting hold of something with cat hair in it. Again, I will point out that is not judging. It is a statement of fact. There is no way even the strongest Christian can tolerate banana pudding if it's laced with cat hair.

Anyhow, the Sunday after the Easter that Hamilton nailed Christ on the cross and lifted Him up, he preached on the little lost lamb. He even talked the choir director into doing "The Ninety and Nine" as our special. That was when she was trying to be a Christian and cooperate with him, no matter whether it matched up with what she called good taste or not. Toward the end of the sermon he had really got into it. His old lanky hair was hanging in his eyes and his coat sleeves had ridden halfway to his elbows so that his cufflinks sparkled, and he was sweating like a bull in a ginger mill. He began pacing the pulpit, back and forth, one side to the other, holding a hand above his eyes like he was shading them from the sun and looking way off out yonder somewhere. He took to calling that lost lamb. "Oh, where is the one that strayed?" he hollered. "The one that left is dearest to my heart! Where is my little lost lamb?" Back and forth, back and forth. He'd crouch down and take a look under the Communion table and flicker the candles and holler for the little lamb. "The ninety and nine are in the fold! Where are you, little lost one? Answer the plea of your master, oh little lamb! Let me find you and bring you safely home!"

Then from Buck's seat on the back row of the choir it rang out plain as day. It sounded so real everybody thought for awhile it was part of Hamilton's show. "Baaaaaaaa," Buck said, "baaaaaaaa," and I personally will vote for him for mayor long as he sees fit to run, even if he didn't finish high school. After all, he went all the way through World War II without ever even tasting alcohol in any form, and it's not every day you can find a mayor who doesn't drink liquor. Hamilton Holt opened the doors of the church that morning and got two new members, which were the only ones who came in while he was our preacher.

I never felt like I was judging Hamilton Holt lest I be judged. He was like a thunderstorm — you weren't responsible for it and you couldn't participate in it. It's a waste of time to judge a thunderstorm. There wasn't anything to do but watch it and set your business aside while you waited for it to pass over.

Which it did. Thanks to Baby Earl. Hamilton all of a sudden took leave of his senses. He decided to put a lock on the preacher's study. Nothing in our church, including the front door, had ever been locked before. Hamilton said he had important books that might be stolen, but everybody thought he was just being contrary. It wouldn't have mattered except that was where the telephone was and all of a sudden little children couldn't call their mamas to come and get them, and the church was isolated like it was before we ever got a telephone.

Baby Earl's wife came home from choir practice on Wednesday night fuming and fussing because she hadn't been able to call Baby Earl and tell she was on her way home, like she always did. They lived way out in the country. She had to cross Whitewater Creek and might get raped or robbed or have a flat tire or something like that. Baby Earl wasn't about to take all that fuming and fussing setting down. He was so relieved his wife was honing in on somebody else besides him that he set out to fix it. He drove into town, parked his car in some bushes to hide it, marched into the church in the middle of the night, and took the study door off its hinges. Carried it on his back slap across town. Where he took it nobody knows, for it has not to this day been found, but it was flat out gone when Hamilton Holt came in the next morning. Just a gaping hole leading into the hall.

Hamilton Holt flung a stomp down fit. He raved and ranted and used words like *varlet* and *knave* and *dastardly*, such as none of us has heard since we got out of Mrs. Cole's Shakespeare course. He stormed around and said if that door wasn't put back within twenty-four hours he was going to leave this town and shake the dust of it from his feet. Mr. Tritt's wife said she ordinarily didn't open her mouth about church business, but if anyone put that door back he'd have her to answer to. Miss Lizzie Graham made a special point in her Circle that day of reading the Psalm about "Be ye lifted up, ye everlasting doors." Miss Lizzie has got a lot of dry wit about her.

Hamilton was as good as his word. He had worked himself up to such a frenzy that the next day he called the Bishop, who was in a meeting way off in Seattle, Washington. He called him long distance, person-to-person, and retired himself not just from our church but from the whole Methodist ministry. Then he started flinging books into boxes, and that afternoon he was gone. He was quick but he was thorough; he shook the pecan tree in the parsonage yard and hauled all the nuts off with him, too. We had One-eye Jack as a janitor, and he went into the study to see if he could help, but Hamilton was cussing so that Jack told me there wasn't no dealing with him, that being the way Jack talks. Everybody in town will tell you I've got a good ear for accents and can mimic just about anybody to a T. One-eye Jack was a nice, gentle soul, one of them that tries to smooth rough spots over by acting like they don't exist, and he said, just as soft and polite as you please, "Are you going to another church, Preacher?"

Hamilton Holt slammed a leather-bound book in a box and yelled, "Another church? Another church? Hell, no. Goddamn another church!"

You know what? Not only did we have to get another preacher in the middle of a Conference year but we had to hire another janitor. One-eye Jack left us and went to sweeping up out at Ebenezer Baptist. He was a man of some principle.

I can truthfully say that I never sat in judgment on Hamilton Holt. In fact, I have never even judged Baby Earl. If I did, I can tell you right now I'd give him first place. We all know that the Lord moves in mysterious ways His wonders to perform, but moving through Baby Earl to cleanse the Methodist Church of Hamilton Holt was a piece of divine maneuvering that amazed everybody in our congregation. To my way of thinking, it ranks as a minor miracle — a good ways behind raising Lazarus from the dead but in my opinion a sight more entertaining. We did lose One-eye Jack to Ebenezer Baptist in the process, but you can't have everything in this old world.

The most trying time in my religious life was yet to come up. I very nearly fell completely from grace when Ben Baxter was minister of our church. That was when I got to judging so bad and so quick and so continuously that I shifted my prayer for forgiveness over to the Benediction. I'd judge Ben Baxter through the opening prayer, the announcements, the responsive reading, the Apostles' Creed, and certainly through his sermon. I would judge him to a faretheewell. The only way I could feel forgiven and not be judged myself was to wait till the very last minute every Sunday and pray all through the threefold Amen we sang after his benediction, so's he'd have time to get to the back of the church and shake hands. Then I'd be slow getting out of my choir robe and leave through the other door so I didn't have to touch his hand or look him in the eye.

That man hit our town knowing more about it than any stranger had before and more than most people could have learned in a year of living there and watching close. By that I mean he knew about the people. He knew who were the big shots in the church and he knew all about everybody's faults. He even knew who was kin to whom, and that is a pit that most newcomers keep falling into for years, saying things in front of folks without knowing they're kin to who you're talking about. Not Ben Baxter. He knew the Tarpleys didn't get along with the Smiths even though they'd married sisters. He knew the Haygoods drank a lot of liquor but that she was an alcoholic and he wasn't. He knew Walt Turpin had fallen out with the Board of Stewards and dropped out of the church and he knew why. He knew the Caldwells and the Ramspecks had fallen out over the new church building forty years ago and that both families still gave heavily to the church but they didn't socialize with each other and always voted on different sides about anything that came up. He knew who gave the most in the church and he even knew that one of the Caldwell grandsons was supposed to be a little funny about other boys. He knew things that none of us would have told an outsider for years and years. I mean he stepped into town knowing all those things. Lo and behold, come to find out, he had known the newspaper editor's son at the University of Georgia. When he found out he was coming to our town, he'd looked him up and spent a whole week of afternoons with him. Not only asking questions but taking notes. He hit town ready to change committees and shift folks around so's he could run the church to suit himself. He came very near to doing it.

You got the feeling that the whole world ran to suit Ben Baxter. You got the feeling he arranged it that way. He was a pretty boy but I didn't hold that against him. A man can't help the looks he was born with. He had wavy hair and blue eyes and red lips and dimples just about everywhere you could put one. He was real fair-skinned and looked like he bathed more'n once a day. He was a little too tight in his skin for comfort. My husband called him

"Chunky-butt," but my husband's an irreverent man and doesn't go to church no matter who the preacher is. He says as far as he's concerned religion is like sex — them that talks about it most is practicing it least. He doesn't mean any harm by that, that's just the way he talks. I make him come to the Easter Cantata every year and sit in the balcony with the boys. He's good to baby-sit while I'm at choir practice, but it doesn't hurt him to go in person once a year and see why he's been baby-sitting.

It wasn't Ben Baxter's looks made me dislike him the minute I laid eyes on him; it was his winning ways. He could break out with winning ways thick as chicken pox, and he shifted into them as smooth as velvet breeches on a two year old. He'd tuck his head down on one side into his shoulder sort of, look at you underneath his eyebrows, and smile and dimple like a Baptist virgin. Then he'd crinkle his eyes up when he smiled at you, and even twist his foot on the floor. You could tell he thought he was loaded with what some folks call "charm," but it's been my experience that you'd better be mighty careful or it comes across as being put on. It was the crinkling his eyes that bothered me most. I tried it in front of the mirror when I was by myself once. The only way you can crinkle your eyes on purpose is by smirking real silly. That's exactly what Ben Baxter was doing. I figured his grandmother had told him over and over when he was three years old that he was simply precious. You could tell he still believed it. He had enough winning ways to make you sick to your stomach.

He wasn't in town a month till he'd hunted out all the rejects and the malcontents, like the Bible says David did when he raised his army. He had them coming back to church and serving on committees. He knew just what to say against whom when he went calling on any particular person. He swelled attendance all right, but some Sunday mornings I felt like we were sitting there just waiting for Bastille Day. When somebody's got a lot of hostility in his heart about the way the church is being run, I personally feel like everybody concerned is better off if they just stay away. We sure don't need to hang out our dirty linen and get everybody all stirred up.

He even got Walt Turpin back in the church. Walt had been on the Board of Stewards and a faithful member till his wife died. He got mad at Moody Cunningham, who was our preacher at the time, because he wasn't at her bedside when Mrs. Turpin passed, although Moody had been faithful as a hound dog for the six months she was bedfast with her cancer. Started in her pancreas, they said, and when she died she was yellow as a gourd and had lost ninety-six pounds. Didn't know her own children. Even her teeth had dried out. Moody had called on her the day before she died, but when the time finally came he was in Atlanta visiting Mr. Bob's wife who had just had an operation. It was a hysterectomy and we never have been sure if they took both ovaries or left them because Mr. Bob's crowd always tries to clam up and be real secret about family business. Anyhow, Walt Turpin let it get out that he was hurt with the preacher and felt like he was paying more attention to Mr. Bob's wife than to his for a condition which, after all, was not even malignant. He went on to say that probably the reason for that was that Mr. Bob was a member of the Commission on Finance and gave more to the church than Walt did. So Walt quit coming to church because he was mad at Moody Cunningham. He said.

When the Cabinet moved Moody out at the end of four years, the Committee on Stewardship and Evangelism called on Walt, but by that time he was used to laying around on Sunday morning. He said now he was mad at Mr. Bob for having been such a pet of Moody Cunningham's and couldn't stand the thought of seeing him setting up there with all them other hypocrites. Nobody in town paid a lot of attention to it because we all knew that Walt Turpin's mama was a Peavy. The Peavys are bad to hide their real feelings and also to hold a grudge, and the Turpins are the butt-headedest bunch in town, and when you crossed them you wound up with Walt. It's called genetics. I learned that at GSCW. I for one felt like Walt wasn't really mad at Mr. Bob or

Moody Cunningham. He was mad because his wife had cancer. He just had to take it out on somebody he could see. When Ben Baxter got him back to church, I knew he'd been down there feeding him a lot of trash about Mr. Bob. That is not judgment, now, that is deduction. I was not born yesterday.

Within three months Ben had Mary Lou Jimmerson coming back steady. She'd had her nose out of joint because Mr. Tritt had said at a Steward's meeting that her husband didn't have no sense. That was just Mr. Tritt's way of talking. Sooner or later he said it about everybody and what he meant when he did was that somebody disagreed with him, but Mary Lou took it personal and had been sulling for five years. Ben had Marvin Seagraves and Lon Dodson and the widow Bottoms and Marshall Drawdy and a whole bunch we never saw in the church, except for funerals, coming regular. Within a year he had shifted committees around to a faretheewell and had about got himself a majority on the Board of Stewards. You could tell that he thought he had our church by the tail on a downhill drag. He'd duck his head and twinkle at the ladies, and the world was his oyster.

It wasn't his politicking that got me to sitting in judgment on Ben Baxter. After all, everybody in our town was teethed on politics. We grew up without a moving picture theatre in town and before television, so politics had always, one way or another, been our favorite form of entertainment. I looked around at Mr. Tritt and Buck and some of the other old-timers and figured Ben Baxter was up against a bunch of pros and his time was coming. I just felt like he was going to keep on messing around and get himself taught some sure enough politics. I never get involved in criticizing a preacher. To me one of the nicest things about the Methodist church is that every four years they move the preacher on out. If you don't like one, all you have to do is wait and he'll be gone and the waters will close over him, so to speak, and the church goes on forever. I firmly believe that God is behind the Methodist church because looking around from the front row of the choir loft leads you to realize that if it depended on the assortment of humans out there in the congregation, it would have failed years ago. I'm not judging, just musing.

What started me to judging the way I did on Ben Baxter was his preaching. Not the way he did it but what he said. Although the way he did it was a caution. He'd grab the top of the pulpit with both hands and lean on it and then throw his backbone out and put his hips to swiveling, and it was something else to behold. You couldn't see it from the congregation but you couldn't miss it from the choir loft. It was for all the world like that scene in *Gone With the Wind*, which I have read the book twice and seen the movie six times, when Scarlett is at the Armory ball in black, leaning on the counter with her elbows proper as you please, but dancing around with her feet fit to kill. Ben would swing his bottom from side to side and round and round and then rub up against the pulpit all in a plumb rhythm that put you in mind of Elvis. It was somewhat of a distraction if you were trying to listen to his sermon.

I made Earnest come one Sunday when it wasn't even Easter and sit on the front row way over to one side where he could see. He said later, "Ruthie Lee, you're right! Old Chunky-butt is plain hunching that pulpit. No wonder you've been so sweet to me on Sunday afternoons lately." And I told him that if he didn't hush his mouth I'd quit leaving the kids at Mama's after church and he could just play golf or softball or whatever after dinner like all the other fellers have to do. Of course, I was just teasing. Lord knows Earnest is too tired during the week when he gets off that bulldozer to even look at me, and I have to get him rested up and tend to him on Saturday nights and Sunday afternoons or he'd never get tended to, and that does make a husband ill. Earnest has the name in town of being real good-natured and even-tempered. I'd die before I'd take the credit for it. There is good judgment and there is bad judgment. But there is also such a thing as modesty.

The trouble with me in church is I listen to the sermons. When we were children, Mama was Methodist and Papa was

Baptist. I guess that's what some would call a divided home. Papa carried all of us to the Baptist church and Sunday school except for the baby, who went with Mama to the Methodist. First thing Mama did when Papa passed was slap us all in the Methodist church and send us to Epworth League instead of BYPU. I still kept a lot of Baptist in me, though, and I was scared not to listen to every word of a preacher's sermon for fear that'd be the time I got slated for hell-fire or something. A lot of Methodists say Hell is here on earth and that may be partially true, but I still believe in it as a sinner's comeuppance when he's dead and gone. I listen.

It didn't take me long to pick up on that Ben Baxter. He was saying things like "the legend of Adam and Eve" and "the fable of Jonah and the whale" and "the story of the Virgin Birth." He even said "the myth of the loaves and fishes." Then one Sunday I heard him say, "We are told in Matthew that Jesus rose from the dead on the third day." It hit me like a bolt of blue lightning that we had a preacher who didn't believe himself a single solitary thing we stand up and proclaim in the Apostles' Creed every Sunday morning.

I like to fainted. The director doesn't like for us to fan in the choir, but that Sunday I had to, front row or not. This wasn't too long after that Altizer fellow had made a fool of himself at Emory by saying that God is dead, and they had politely eased him on off up to some yankee school, where He may be for all I know. Dead, I mean. I'd sure die if I had to become a yankee. I figured some of that had rubbed off on Ben Baxter, and after a few Sundays I asked Bittie Baker if she reckoned our preacher was one of those secular humanists we'd been hearing about. Bittie wasn't much help but I'll never forget what she told me.

"I don't know for the life of me what a humanist is, but I'd sure say he's secular from the way he keeps frigging that pulpit. It makes my vertigo worse just to watch him. It's going to be a long four years." Bittie sings lead soprano and she sat directly behind him, so I guess it was pretty rough on her. She is also outspoken.

The more I listened, the worse it got. He'd use a little Scripture and then we'd get thirty minutes of pure old sociology like they used to pour down us at GSCW. I finally hit the absolute bottom in judging another fellow human. I came to the conclusion that Ben Baxter had never been saved in the first place. It's all right not to be saved. It's a free country, and there are as many of them wandering around out there unsaved as there are unwashed. That's his own personal business. But he didn't have to haul his overwashed, dimpled up, unsaved self into the Methodist ministry and descend on us, tearing our church apart and pitting folks against one another. I tried to understand it.

I knew that his daddy had been a Methodist minister. One of the retired preachers told me that his daddy died bitter because he'd never made DS. I've seen a heap of preachers' kids over the years who grew up to be lawyers or doctors or school teachers or bankers, but I haven't seen a whole lot who grew up to be preachers. I had sort of figured out for myself that they grew up with what you might call an overdose of religion. They were around it twenty-four hours a day and it just wasn't important to them like it was to the rest of us, if you know what I mean. Then, too, maybe some of them just didn't believe as strong as some of the rest of us do. They didn't believe because, number one, here again they'd been around it so much they were bored and unimpressed, and number two, maybe they'd seen their daddies as just ordinary human beings when the glamour of childhood wore off, and they'd rejected everything they stood for while they were rejecting them.

Now, we're getting down into some deep rock-bottom judging here, but I decided that Ben Baxter's problem probably was that he loved his daddy and had the family pride we all have in us deep down and all that, but that he despised the church and the system that had made the old man bitter. He was also probably a little ashamed of his daddy. As who isn't now and then? And so what? It all goes with being a daddy. He'd spent all his teen years being a loyal preacher's son and fooling his daddy and letting him think that he believed same as he did. Then he hit the University of Georgia and sat in with the beer drinkers and went to some fraternity parties and got a little taste of being free to believe and do what he wanted to. He decided to go into the ministry himself and make the Methodist Conference do for him what it had never done for his daddy. And here he was in our midst. Using us for a stepping stone, and never mind whose feelings he hurt in the process.

If all that sounds far-fetched, let me tell you that it would make a blame good college paper at GSCW in either sociology or psychology. It's got love and hate in it, plus that teen-age rebellion everybody is so concerned about right now plus father-son conflict, plus sociopathic manipulating and I don't know what all. It's a darn good theory and I bet I could make an A on it.

When the kids grow up, I just may go back and finish college. Not that I've ever been sorry I dropped out. Earnest came along fall of my junior year and he was ready to marry right then and there. If I'd delayed it I'd of lost him. I talked to old Aunt Membus about Earnest and she told me, "Chile, when you find one make yo ovaries flutter like that, drop whatever you doing and go with him right then. You'n always step back in the row where you left off." I listened to her. I've never been sorry. I wouldn't trade Sunday afternoons for ten years at GSCW. Of course, I dressed it up for Mama and quoted Proverbs about there being three strange things. In fact, I used Naomi and Ruth in my wedding vows. I had more sense than to quote Aunt Membus to my mama.

On top of everything else, Ben Baxter was an actor of the Method School. I think that's what they call it, that one where they take lots of dramatic pauses and sort of understate things and mumble about them. Between the hunching and the method style and his politicking, he nearly wore me out. After two years he had Big Earl off the Board of Trustees, Buck rotated off the Board of Stewards, and the doctor off the Pastor-Parish Relations committee. He laid his sights on Mr. Tritt, and Buck Betsill chewed him out about it. The only reason Ben Baxter had said anything to Buck in the first place was that he knew from his sources that Mr. Tritt and the Betsills had quarreled a lot in the past. What he failed to comprehend and what his sources hadn't explained to him was that this is a small town and we don't appreciate any outsider meddling in our spats and feuds, and there was no way Ben Baxter could ever be anything but an outsider in our town.

He went to Buck and told him he thought Mr. Tritt was too old to be playing such a prominent part in the church and that he was just very quietly going to delete his name for nomination to the Board of Trustees and the Board of Stewards. Buck told him that despite the differences he and Mr. Tritt might have had in the past, Mr. Tritt had done things for this church nobody even knew about and that he was not going to stand by and see some newcomer smart aleck do anything to hurt Mr. Tritt's feelings. He told Ben Baxter that if he left Mr. Tritt's name off, he would personally nominate him from the floor and would raise a ruckus that would be heard plumb to the Bishop's office.

We all knew that Ben Baxter was scared of the Bishop. He knew the Bishop, not the Lord, held his future in his hand. He had even taken a leave his first year at our church to go on a trip the Bishop was leading to England just so he could get to know him firsthand and show off his winning ways. Ben Baxter was born politicking and jockeying for position, but his twinkling and charm didn't cut any more ice with Buck than it did with me. He backed down in a hurry. Made some snide remark that it must be great to be mayor of the town so that people would be afraid to oppose you in anything. Buck laughed in his face and said, "What you need, you overstuffed smart ass, is a conversion experience." Next Sunday Ben Baxter preached a sermon on misplaced loyalty. I would have completely missed the point of it if I hadn't been in the side room and overheard that little altercation between him and Buck. Ben Baxter kept right on loading committees and Boards with neglected newcomers and disgruntled widows, but he never put his mouth on Mr. Tritt again.

By the time he'd been with us for three years, I had taken to hitting the Benediction real quick and routine, sort of like saying the blessing when you're late for work. In fact, I had mired so deep in sin that some Sundays I'd be praying for forgiveness for judging Ben Baxter and would catch myself saying, "But I told You so," to the Lord. It doesn't take any great theologian to know that when you get to that point you are in a plumb fix. I kept laying off to have a conference with Ben Baxter to sort of purge my soul and clear the air, but every time I'd get almost worked up to it, he'd pull another caper that just confirmed my judgment.

On Palm Sunday of his fourth year, he hit an all-time low in his morning prayer. He closed his eyes, grabbed the edge of the lectern, turned his face to the ceiling, commenced to swiveling his chunky-butt, and started off. "Our Father and our friend," he said. Now, I'd got to the point where every time he tried to be buddy-buddy with the Almighty it set my teeth on edge and made me feel like it was just one more instance of him being sly and deceiving about not believing what he should have done. Who wants a father for a friend anyhow? Only reason mankind had to search around and find that human name for Jehovah in the first place was that a father is supposed to be a guide and a judge and a source of wisdom. If you want a friend, join a club, I say. Don't get any more roles mixed up than you can help.

"Our Father and our friend," he said, "we thank Thee this morning for the warm sunshine that is filtering down from the heavens to warm the cold and fallow ground. We thank Thee, our Father and our friend, for the green grass and the little flowers that are peeping through the warming soil to herald the symbolic rebirth that we are about to celebrate. We thank Thee for the little birds that are singing so beautifully as they make their nests in the budding trees in assurance that spring has come. We thank Thee, our Father and our friend, for the little squirrels that are chasing each other round and round the tree trunks, helter-skelter, faster and faster, scaling off bark as they go; up, up, until they reach the topmost branches and bask in the sunshine of Thy love."

Well! I had had enough. That was the biggest bunch of sentimental and trite hogwash I'd ever heard in a pulpit, and that is an intellectual criticism, it is not judging, and I did not ask forgiveness for thinking it. Front row or no front row, I raised my head and opened my eyes. Everybody in the church had their eyes shut or at least their heads bowed so it looked like their eyes were shut. I sneaked a sideways look over at Bittie without moving my head. She was wide awake and looking square at me. We communicated for a minute without saying a word. I bowed my head and didn't think any more about Bittie Baker. I was busy thanking God I hadn't had my conference with Ben Baxter to tell him how I felt, for if I had it would now all be to do over again. Our choir director tells us that the Lord doesn't like sour notes any better than anybody else, and I suspect He feels the same way about silly prayers.

When I walked in from church, the phone was ringing off the hook. It was Bittie. She didn't even say hello, she just started right in. "You know and I know what those squirrels were up to," she said. She paused just a minute to let me catch on and catch up. "I didn't hear another word that fool said the rest of the service. I sat right behind him and prayed those squirrels wouldn't catch each other, for my woods are et up with the little bastards already." And with that she hung up. If anybody thinks that was rough talking, I am here to tell them that's not a circumstance. Bittie is a character and so was her mother before her. The whole family always says just exactly what they think.

Well. It was coming up Conference time and we had patiently served out Ben Baxter's four years. It looked like freedom was right around the corner. The church was still holding together and hanging in there. We got wind that the Bishop and the Cabinet were planning to send Ben to Griffin. Ben Baxter himself told it to some of his favorites and was as smug as a fresh-dressed mama's boy. That would have been one whale of a promotion, and those in the church who were maddest at Ben said it looked like the Bishop had really been sucked in by Ben's sucking up.

Nobody faulted the Bishop. He was not of this world. He was an old bachelor and a scholar. In addition, he was so forgetful and vague it'd make a dog laugh. When he was Dean at Emory long before he made Bishop, they tell it that one of his professors asked for the afternoon off to go buy a new car downtown. The Bishop said come to think of it he believed he needed a new car and just to bring him one, too. The professor asked him what kind he wanted and the Bishop said, "Bring me a green one." I always believed every word of that myself, for I had heard him preach when I was a girl. It was an unforgettable experience.

It was well known all over the Conference that the Bishop couldn't stand to deal with plain ordinary people. Unhappy congregations drove him up the wall. They are made up of nothing in the long run except plain ordinary people if you stop to think about it. If a congregation was dissatisfied with a preacher that was the one thing the Bishop would never forgive. He'd lay that sin to a preacher's charge quicker than adultery. After watching the Bishop most of my life, I privately think that he only had the haziest notion of what adultery was anyhow, but keep in mind that's an opinion, not a judgment. Even a saint who is ignorant of adultery knows an unhappy congregation when he sees one.

Buck was friends with the mayor over at Griffin, who happened to be a Methodist. They weren't close buddies or anything, but Buck had met him two or three times at some mayors' meeting and they passed and repassed. We're not supposed to know until it's announced where a preacher is going or who we're going to get as a replacement, but the Cabinet can let things leak same as most grand juries do. Preachers are almost as bad to talk when they ought to be listening as just plain ordinary walking-around folks.

In other words, most of them are more like their congregations than anybody is prepared to admit. Buck got on the phone long distance, person-to-person, and called the mayor of Griffin. He told him it wasn't any of his business, but . . . . That is a good way to start a conversation because it makes whoever is saying it look real concerned about your welfare and just automatically makes you feel like they're on your side. Especially, I should imagine, if it's long distance, person-to-person.

Buck went on to tell the mayor of Griffin that he didn't know for certain but he had it on good authority that the Cabinet was planning to dump Ben Baxter on Griffin. Then he lined out Ben Baxter's personality to a faretheewell. Within two days the DS had a delegation from Griffin breathing fire and brimstone. Two days after that Ben Baxter wasn't doing near as much twinkling. It's hard to keep your winning ways sparkling when you're having to go around and tell your friends you were mistaken about something. Especially when it doesn't make you look very smart.

You couldn't squelch that Ben Baxter though. First news you know there's a rumor that he might get sent back to us for a fifth year. His little groupies acted like Santa Claus was coming, but most of us were sick to the bone. We didn't want to raise a stink and tear the church up, but it was distressing to think about one more year of Ben Baxter.

Buck Betsill was what saved us. Most folks don't know it to this day, but he did. It started off innocent enough. Buck said out loud after choir practice that he believed he'd just get up a petition about Ben Baxter to keep him from coming back, and he wanted to know would any of us sign it. Bartholomew Boggs, who sings tenor when he concentrates on it, said, "I'd sign it in a New York heartbeat. I'd sign it so big King George could read it without his glasses, and him dead over two hundred years." That's the Boggs way of talking. You have to pay attention because they gather things from all over and throw them in a conversation. Everybody heard him and Buck, but it was Mary Lou who told Ben Baxter. Mary Lou quivers her voice when she sings and is a holy terror on "His Eye Is on the Sparrow." She is a classic example of the old saying: "A dog that will tote a bone will carry a bone."

When she told Ben, here she came toting back again with the news how upset he was. He sure didn't want any petition going to the Bishop; said it would be a black eye in the district. Buck told Mary Lou deadpan that it was too late, he already had over two hundred names on it. He also told her the black eye would be bigger on Ben Baxter than on the district. Bartholomew Boggs chimed in and said nobody'd even brought it around to him yet and he hadn't had the pleasure of signing it. Here went Mary Lou. Carrying back and forth, back and forth. Within three days Ben Baxter knew for certain that Buck already had over three hundred and fifty names and that Bartholomew Boggs was hunting him so he could sign it.

It was only a week till Conference and Ben Baxter nearly went crazy. He had been quit speaking to Bartholomew Boggs for about eighteen months and to Buck for longer than that. He'd had a serious falling out with Bartholomew over Ben Baxter running his mouth about Bartholomew's daddy, and of course Buck was hot about not being a steward any longer. Ben Baxter went to the president of the bank and told him to talk to Bartholomew's brother-in-law and have the brother-in-law tell Bartholomew that if he'd just tear up that petition when he got his hands on it, he'd promise to leave our town. The brother-in-law is a lawyer, and he looked Ben square in the eye and wanted to know if he would put that in writing.

Ben gave up and left. He took Douglasville, which wasn't but a two-hundred-dollar-a-year promotion. It was certainly no feather in Ben Baxter's cap, but it beat having the Bishop's attention drawn to a petition, and Ben really had run out of time to do any more manipulating. The choir director told me confidentially that Ben Baxter told her husband Buck was a GD SB. That's her way of talking. She's such a lady she won't just come out with things. I don't doubt for a minute that Ben Baxter said it, either. Without the initials.

The funny thing about the whole situation to me was that there never was any petition at all. I know. Buck, himself, told me. When I told Earnest, he grinned and said, "I hope Chunky-butt has learned that dealing with Buck is like trying to pee off the back of a moving pickup without getting wet." Then he tweaked me on my behind and said, "Ruthie Lee, have you noticed how some preachers describe a church by calling it a ten-thousand-dollar pulpit instead of a six-hundred-person congregation? Quit expecting them to be any different from the rest of us." You do not have to have a college degree to be blessed with good sense. Like I heard Mr. Tritt say one time, "You can educate a fool but he'll still be a fool." I am proud of Earnest. He may not be educated, but he is sure no fool.

You had better believe our church was packed for Ben Baxter's farewell sermon. Buck tried to get the choir director to sing the "Hallelujah Chorus" for the anthem and Bartholomew Boggs promised her he'd concentrate, but she chose "Be Still and Know That I Am God." We never had a choir director with better taste. It was a day I will never forget.

First off, Ben Baxter was under pretty good control in his lower parts. He held the pulpit tight, but he also held his chunky-butt tight. Shifted his feet back and forth a little but never did put his rear end into overdrive.

He didn't even read a text that morning. He just said, "I want to tell this congregation a story." I could feel Buck Betsill and Bartholomew Boggs behind me getting still and quiet as church mice. They thought they were really fixing to get it.

Then Ben Baxter set in and told about Trapp Godfrey. He'd just that week found out about Trapp Godfrey's daddy's will and what Trapp had done about it. He told it straight and he told it simple. He used some of his dramatic pauses but he had left his winning ways at home. I felt like there was a stranger in the pulpit.

I knew very well who Trapp Godfrey was. His daddy was Mr. Lum Godfrey. You can count on anybody from that generation who was called "Lum" to have the initials C.C. Folks were bad to name their children Christopher Columbus back then. The child, of course, didn't think too much of that and always wound up being called "Lum." Mr. Lum was born during Reconstruction, and when he was thirteen his daddy died with the typhoid fever. There were seven or eight children, I forget which, although I had heard my grandmother say. They buried Mr. Lum's daddy and came home from the funeral all stunned and moping. The family was by itself again, all let down and at the end of the world like you are when a funeral's over. Mr. Lum rounded them up and told them to change their clothes, including his mama. Then he said, "Let's go to the field and get to work like Papa would want us to do. Crying ain't going to help a thing and somebody has got to pick the cotton."

That has always been a saying in our family: "Somebody's got to pick the cotton." We used it whenever folks got to goofing off or there was an extra nasty job that nobody wanted to do, and I'd always known that it had come down to us from Mr. Lum Godfrey when he took on manhood at age thirteen.

I never laid eyes on Mr. Lum, but he and my grandaddy were friends and I'd heard of him all of my life. He worked hard and got married. Then he worked even harder. He accumulated a hundred acres of land and went to the Presbyterian church all his life. He was a righteous and respected man. He lived to be ninety years old and was said not to have an enemy in the world. They say that about a heap of folks when they're dead, but it may have been true about Mr. Lum.

He had three children, a boy and a girl of his own and the daughter of one of his wife's cousins who had died and left a little girl. Mr. Lum and his wife raised her the same as their child. She grew up and married a Methodist preacher and moved around from pillar to post and had an afflicted child that was a constant care for all of its life. Mr. Lum's boy was Trapp, and he married and prospered moderately. He wasn't what you would call real well-off or anything like that, but he accumulated a little land and paid all his bills and held his head up. The other girl married well and lived in Atlanta. Joined those clubs and all.

Ben Baxter didn't know all that background and he started his farewell sermon with, "There was a certain man who had three children, and he was full of years and it came time for him to die." Now that's a dramatic sentence if I ever heard one, and the church got quiet. Plain ordinary people do love dramatics. I can't remember all Ben Baxter's words, but I already knew what happened on account of Grandaddy and all. Mr. Lum got to be around eighty and lost his wife. That brought him to realize that he was going to die someday, too; so he made a will. He called Trapp in and explained it to him.

"Son," he said, "I've thought about my estate, what little I've accumulated on this earth during my time on it. I've made a will and I want to explain it to you while I'm still at myself and so's you'll understand. Lorena's married to a preacher and they've got no prospects of retirement and have never owned a home. I'm leaving the house and four acres of land to Lorena. So she'll have a home. I'm leaving you and Little Sister the rest of the land between you. Now I know the land's not worth as much as the house, but I know what's fair. This doesn't mean I love Lorena any better than I do you and Little Sister; it's just that I want all of you to have a home and she's the only one who doesn't. You've always been a good son, Trapp."

Time dragged on, and Mr. Lum was out of his head the last two years he lived. He had a stroke and had to be waited on like a baby, which it fell to Trapp and his wife to do because they lived the closest. While Mr. Lum was declining and withering, prosperity came to that part of the country and laid waste to it. They put an interstate highway slap through the back of Mr. Lum's property. Time he died, developers were pricing it by the front foot instead of the acre, and it'd make your head swim to think about it.

Trapp went on down to the courthouse the week after Mr. Lum passed and probated the will. Lorena got the house and four acres. Trapp and Little Sister got all the rest in joint ownership. Trapp signed the deeds as administrator and they got everything filed in the Clerk's office and Trapp got dismissed as administrator, all official and everything. Signed, sealed, and delivered. That Trapp was one more organized and orderly Presbyterian.

First news you know here came a Japanese firm wanted to put in a manufacturing plant and a shopping mall with a Rich's and a Sears and a Penney's and a Davison-Paxon's and I don't know what all in it. The Japanese won World War II to my way of thinking. We can just forget Pearl Harbor as we have the Alamo. What they couldn't take by fighting, they're buying right out from under our noses. By this time Little Sister and Trapp are sitting on the interstate and Lorena's house is way in the back waiting for her husband to retire so's they can move into it. It came down to something over a million and a half dollars the Japs offered for the land, and Little Sister hollered, "Sell!"

Trapp was agreeable and Lorena said that wouldn't make her home a fit place to live, so she'd sell too. The Japanese wouldn't give her but twenty thousand for the house and her four acres because it was way on the backside and not attractive to them. They all three met in the lawyers' office and signed over and sold out.

That evening Trapp Godfrey called Little Sister in Atlanta. By that time it wasn't long distance anymore. We had direct dial and could even pay extra and get push-button. He told her that this had not been what Mr. Lum intended at all, and he proposed that they divide what they'd got equally with Lorena. Little Sister had the same upbringing as Trapp, and agreed about respecting their daddy's wishes. They met at the bank with the lawyers again and worked it out so taxes wouldn't mess it all up and each one of them gave Lorena two hundred and fifty thousand. The Presbyterians got no more use than the rest of us for the Federal Government and the IRS.

Ben Baxter didn't put in the part about the taxes. He just told it straight and from the moral viewpoint. It was beautiful the way he did it. You could have heard a pin drop. That is, if somebody had got off the carpet and dropped it on the floor. We got the carpet two years before we got the candles. He put in a long dramatic pause and everybody was hushed. Still waiting.

"How hard," Ben Baxter said, "it is for some of us to do the will of our earthly fathers. How much harder then is it to do the will of our Heavenly Father? How much more beautiful? Who among us can turn his back so finally on Mammon and choose this day whom he will serve? He who has ears to hear, let him hear."

You could tell he wasn't through yet. The church was still quiet. Then he stood up tall and his robe hung straight, wasn't any sign of chunky-butt. His face turned real white and his voice got as sincere as a hog on ice.

"My fathers," he said. I swear that's what he said. I heard the s.

"My fathers, I believe. I believe." He took a deep breath. "I believe in God the Father Almighty, Maker of Heaven and Earth, and in Jesus Christ, His only Son, our Lord, Who was conceived by the Holy Spirit, born of the Virgin Mary, suffered under Pontius Pilate, was crucified, dead, and buried. The third day He arose from the dead. He ascended into Heaven, where He sitteth on the right hand of God the Father Almighty. From thence He shall come to judge the quick and the dead. I believe in the Holy Catholic Church, the communion of Saints, the forgiveness of sins, the resurrection of the body and the life everlasting. I believe. Forgive me, Father!"

That was it. I felt like it was Genesis again and God was moving out from the formless and across the deep.

Ben Baxter wasn't crying, but I was.

It was the sweetest judging I have ever done.

EARTH

Fulfillment

IT WAS THE DEEPEST front porch in Byarsville, Georgia. If noontime gloom in the parlor was a midwinter nuisance, it was more than mitigated by the delights of living on that porch in summertime. The house faced due north and the sun never shone full under the porch's overhang; just enough rays slanted in to make the sultanas spectacular. If there was a breeze anywhere in town, it could be found stirring there, slowly twisting the baskets of ferns on their chains and cooling the perspiration on a visitor in tantalizing welcome. The porch was so deep that Miss Addie did not even need to turn the rocking chairs up against the house when it rained; she just pulled them back from the railing. It was a livable porch, a lovable porch, and Miss Addie presided there in queenly serenity.

The neighbors came every day in good weather. Most of the time they came in shifts, or dropped in one at a time, but sometimes they all wound up being there together. Then Miss Addie's rockers would be full and also the two iron chairs that were painted green and bounced instead of rocking. Hospitality in Byarsville was guaranteed when the front porch of a house sported more rocking chairs than there were members of the family.

Mamie Kate was Miss Addie's most frequent visitor and the most constant occupant of the porch. Many times she installed herself there while Miss Addie hoed in the garden or squatted in the flower border pulling chickweed and blue devil out of the violets and Sweet Williams. Mamie Kate always sought a particular rocker, one that had been painted white once and green twice, as could be attested by the thickened scabs of color scaling from its arms. It had a low seat that was hollowed out by so many Baptist bottoms that it reminded Mamie Kate of a giant hen nest. The height of the seat, the chair being what her mother called a "nursing rocker," made it easier for young Mamie Kate to mount. If she sat far enough back in it and turned it a little toward the corner of the porch, her left leg was not likely to trip anyone as it protruded straight and rigid. She hated the two iron chairs. They were hard to clamber into; they swayed erratically and unpredictably on their curved-back legs; and her leg braces made fearsome clanking noises every time she shifted weight.

Mamie Kate objected to the noise of stainless steel clanking against sheet iron only because it called unwanted attention to her. She was accustomed to the burden of the braces and to her legs that looked like broomsticks covered with desiccated skin. She was not sensitive about her crab-like appearance when she walked, twisting from the hips, balancing on her crutches, and slinging her rigidly braced legs from side to side. On her regular trips to Scottish Rite Hospital in Atlanta, she had long since realized that she was one of the luckier spina bifida patients in Georgia, and she accepted the hungry eyes of other children confined to wheel chairs as acknowledgment that she was superior and special to the Lord. Neither did she mind the acknowledging eyes of the public. Everybody in Byarsville knew everybody else and nobody in town was infamous enough to be unkind to a crippled child. In truth, they favored and petted her.

When she was on Miss Addie's front porch, however, Mamie Kate wanted to be as inconspicuous as possible. She came early and she stayed late. When no one was with her except Miss Addie, she chattered like any six-year-old, but the minute another visitor appeared she was stubbornly silent. She had discovered that if she sat very still and pretended to be overly shy, people soon became no more conscious of her than of a piece of furniture and conversed among themselves as though she were not present. If she stared at an open book in her lap with her hair falling over her face and delayed answering a direct question until it was repeated at least twice, people assumed that she was lost in another world and talked with delightful adult frankness that she never encountered elsewhere. Mamie Kate had taught herself to read, but Miss Addie's porch was a stage and the actors there taught her about life.

Mamie Kate was on stage the afternoon Miss Sally got the telephone call. Miss Sally lived with her two widowed sisters in the biggest house in the neighborhood. It had been built before The War, and the lots for all the other houses around it had been sold off piecemeal as the years advanced. The big house was left to Miss Sally as long as she lived because she had a gimpy leg and her papa had assumed she would never get married because of it. Her sisters and all their children had spent her lifetime treating her as though the leg was not her only affliction, and she entered her seventies with a scatterbrained innocence that all her relatives nurtured and protected. She puttered in the kitchen but only with teacakes and jellies; her sisters did the heavy cooking. She puttered in the flower yard but never to much effect because of her leg; they let her cut the roses and re-pot the geraniums, but that was about the extent of her gardening. She had puttered in the welfare office as a file clerk, putting charts in the wrong folders, catching and correcting her errors with little self-deprecating shrieks, until mandatory retirement.

If her sisters had been home the day she got the phone call, they would never have let her tell about it on Miss Addie's front porch and Lutie Carmichael would not have heard it and told it over town. But that day Miss Sally was late getting home from Mrs. Bowen's, where she went every Wednesday to get her hair set and rinsed with blue, and the widows had gone visiting without her. Lutie had dropped across the street to Miss Addie's to catch her breath, she said, and to get away from her mama and brother for just a minute. She was helping Miss Addie snap a mess of pole beans while she visited. They were engaged in a discussion of Lutie's mama's bowels and consequently Mamie Kate was really reading *The Princess and Curdie*. Miss Sally came hopping across the lawn, stabbing her gimpy leg up and down like a pogo stick. Mamie Kate knew she was excited because she was tearing up more grass with that one bad leg and walking cane than Mamie Kate would have with two legs in braces plus a pair of crutches.

"Addie! Lutie! I declare. Just wait till I tell you about this odd call I got on the telephone. Mandy and Sister weren't home. They've gone to play Scrabble at Mattie Lena's, and I thought one of the nephews was just pranking around. So I called Bob and asked him the question because he's the biggest tease of all Beulah's boys, and he acted real strange and told me to keep quiet until I talked about the call with Sister and Mandy, but they're not home and I saw you all sitting on the porch and thought I'd come ask you."

Lutie regarded a bean to see if it was a shelly or still worthy of being snapped. "Sally Strickland, calm down and quit talking so fast. Land sakes, nobody can make heads or tails of what you're talking about. What did you call Bob and ask him? Take everything one step at a time and tell it as you go."

Miss Sally pulled her lips in and pushed them out real quick several times as if she had been eating fig preserves and wanted to get the little seeds out of her teeth without using a fingernail. "Well, I called Bob and he like to never answered the phone. Was out in the yard at his dog pen, I guess. When he said hello, I said this was Aunt Sally, and he said, 'Yes, ma'am;' all of Beulah's boys are real polite, you know. And then I asked him, 'Bob, what's a ten-inch dick?' And he dropped the phone. I know he did, for they've got theirs hanging on the wall in the kitchen, and I could tell it had fallen all the way in the sink. And from the amount of racket it made, Anne had gone off to play bridge and left the dinner dishes dirty again. I declare, I believe girls that smoke are the sloppiest housekeepers in the world. Bill's wife plays bridge now and then, but she doesn't smoke and her house is neat as a pin; you could eat off the floor."

Lutie still held the shelly in her hand but she was not looking at it. "Mamie Kate," she said, "what are you reading, honey?"

When no answer was forthcoming, Miss Addie assured Lutie, "She's lost to the world and a thousand miles away. She taught herself to read when she was four and keeps her nose in some book all the time." Miss Addie had let the newspaper in her lap slip and some of her beans and strings fell on the floor. She leaned over the arm of her rocker to retrieve them.

Lutie pursued the subject. "Land's sake, Sally Strickland, I don't blame the boy for dropping the phone. Whatever in the world made you ask a question like that in the first place and what did poor Bob say?"

Miss Sally was twisting her rings. Mamie Kate made a silent vow that when she got that old she would pass her rings on to somebody young and pretty who would enjoy them. Miss Sally always had old teacake dough crammed in between the prongs, and her diamonds looked dulled.

"Well, I thought the line had gone dead or something, for he was such a long time answering; so I asked him again. 'What's a ten-inch dick?' I said. And he took a long breath and said, 'Aunt Sally, I don't know and that's the God's truth.' Then he told me not to ask anybody else that till his Aunt Mandy and Aunt Sister got home. But I didn't want to wait that long. So I called Sister Maude's son, Wade Hampton, who's ten years older than Bob, and knows everything. He sounded real gruff and said, 'There ain't no such a thing. Get off the phone!' Will you two ladies please tell me what's going on around here?"

Mamie Kate carefully turned a page in *The Princess and Curdie* just in case Miss Addie might be watching her. She could always go back and find her place.

Lutie said, "Tell us exactly what happened on the telephone, Sally Strickland! Then maybe we can help you."

"Well, like I told you, I was all by myself and the phone rang. And I said, 'Hello,' and this man said, 'Is this Sally Strickland?' You know the phone is listed in my name because I own the house, at least till I'm dead, although Mandy and Sister split the bill with me and everybody in town knows if they want to call Sister or Mandy they have to look under 'Miss Sally Strickland.' So I get all the calls about the specials or photographs and what not, and so I said, 'Yes, this is Miss Sally Strickland.' Then he said, 'How would you like to have a ten-inch dick?' I thought either I'd won something or he was selling something; so I said, 'What's that?' And he said, 'Aw, you know what it is.' I said, 'Well, I certainly do not or I wouldn't be asking. What do you do with it?' Then he said, 'You put it in the hole.' Then, of course, I said, 'What hole?' and he said 'Now, come on! You know what hole.' I thought maybe he was trying to sell gardening tools or something, so I said, 'Is it a chrysanthemum or a lily hole?'

"And then he said that awful BM word and hung up. That last word he said really upset me. It's so uncouth and anybody who says it anywhere is vulgar and common, let alone in front of a lady. I remember that from my mama when we were children and the colored maid stepped in cat mess and said that word."

Lutie put her newspaper of string beans on Miss Addie's porch railing. It was obvious that she was done with chores. "Sally Strickland, my stars alive! If you weren't such a goose you'd have sense enough to know you've just had one of those obscene phone calls. I've heard of folks getting them in Atlanta but I never heard of one down here before. Comes from them doing away with long distance. It lets just any trash come in on our telephones. We'd be better to go back to operators and party lines where everybody recognized everyone else's voice. I'd kind of like to have one of those perverts call me sometime though; I believe I could straighten him out for sure and certain. But that's what happened. You got an obscene phone call, Sally, and if you weren't such a ninny you'd have sense enough to know it!"

Miss Sally was working her lips, twisting her rings, and jerking one shoulder. Mamie Kate sat very still.

"Lutie, I guess I've got sense enough to know that call was obscene. I'm not as dumb as some folks think just because I haven't buried a husband and have five grandchildren, one of whom — as we all know — has never been anything except what somebody would call slow. I told you already about old Sudie and the cat mess when I was a little girl; I know obscene when I hear it. What I want you to tell me, since you know so much, is what's a ten-inch dick?"

Lutie put her hands on her hips. Her face was a little flushed. Miss Addie cut her eyes at Mamie Kate and put a cautioning finger to her lips. "Sally Strickland," Lutie said, "the only thing I'm going to tell you is what your nephew said, 'I don't know and that's the God's truth.'" She paused and glanced at Miss Addie. "I'm glad I don't know and probably Bob's sorry, men being what they are. For all I could tell you personally, Wade Hampton may be right; there ain't no such a thing. You can wait and get your information from Mandy and Sister when they come home from Scrabbling at Mattie Lena's, and far as I'm concerned you can just hippity-hop your way back up the hill to your house and wait. But before you go let me tell you one thing. It's better to have a feeble-minded grandchild than to be dried up on the vine and never have even had the prospects of one. I wouldn't trade places with you and your diamond rings for all the tea in China."

Miss Sally rocked back and forth on her bad leg and caught the back of a chair to steady herself. "Lutitia Carmichael, I didn't go to hurt your feelings and I'm not going to get mine hurt over anything you say. We've been neighbors all our lives, and everybody knows you come from a long line of high-strung, sharp-tongued folks. All y'all act like you can't help what you say, you just open your mouths and out it comes. I love your whole family and I love you, and I want you to know that I'm not going to fall out with you over any ten-inch dick. Whatever one may be. Bye, now."

The silence on the front porch as Miss Sally left was total. Mamie Kate was graven in stone, staring sightlessly into her book. Miss Addie gave a murmuring ripple of inconsequence about the dry weather making the beans a little tough. As soon as Miss Sally's door closed up the street, Lutie collapsed into her rocker again and began laughing.

"Just wait until Mandy and Sister get home! They're not going to know either. I dated Mandy's husband before he started courting her, and he was sure no candidate."

Miss Addie gave a little warning shake of her head. "Lutie, I suspect we'd better let this conversation drop. Little pitchers, you know."

Lutie reached for her paper of beans and put them back in her lap. "Mamie Kate! Mamie Kate, honey! Do you think your mama is home yet and looking for you? . . . You can quit worrying, Addie. I never saw such power of concentration. Land sakes, I doubt if the child even knew Sally Strickland was on the porch. You know, Addie, whoever made that call ought to be hung, but for him to get a hold of Sally Strickland out of all the ladies in town is the funniest thing I've ever heard of."

Miss Addie was not laughing. "Miss Mandy and Miss Sister are going to be upset."

"I know that, Addie. But let me tell you one thing. It's not going to be so much over the insult to Sally as it is they don't want folks in town knowing their business."

"Well, I don't think you and I should tell anyone. If it gets out, it should come from them."

"That's well and good enough for you to say, Addie. You're always better to everybody than they deserve, but I'm going to tell Mattie Lena just as sure as Jesus Christ had the measles. That Sally Strickland has been a scatterbrained, over-protected ninny ever since Mattie Lena went to school with her, and Mattie Lena will enjoy this like you wouldn't believe."

Miss Addie snapped her left palm full of beans and tossed them into the pan. Her gentle voice was calm. "Lutie, I don't think Sally is necessarily a ninny. She is what I would call an unfulfilled woman, and I don't think it looks nice for two widows with a long tail of grandchildren behind us to be too hard on her."

"Well, it's her own fault. She had a chance to marry three years ago right after she left the welfare office, and you remember it as well as I do. Bobby Lee Swanson's wife died with that stroke, and after three years his comb turned red, or whatever happens to men, and he was courting Sally hot and heavy. They even got engaged. You remember that. He gave her a diamond bigger'n anything he'd ever even thought of giving his first wife. And Miss Sister flung a plumb hissy fit. Crying and wringing her hands and saying she'd have no place to live if Sally married and brought her husband into the family house. You remember how silly that was, what with Miss Sister having enough money in the bank to build three houses and enough bank stock to buy them back if she wanted to. She was just trying to break up Sally's only romance. And she did, too. Land sakes, Addie, you're obliged to remember that!"

Miss Addie watched as Mamie Kate shifted a little in the rocker and tugged abstractedly at her dress tail while turning another page.

"Oh, I remember all that very well. It's the only time I've ever seen Miss Sister cry, including thirty years ago when she buried her husband."

"Well, I guess you know I've always felt it was my fault for Sally not marrying Bobby Lee Swanson."

Miss Addie looked up from her beans. "You, Lutie? What did you have to do with it?"

"Well, Miss Sister had been weeping and wailing all over town, and you can't help but get your sympathy up for a seventy-year-old virgin who's got her first crack at romance and has to buck family disapproval and all. Sally came over to our yard late one afternoon when I was hanging out Mama's sheets. That was before the doctor put the catheter in and I was washing four to five times a day. We stood by the clothesline and she said she had to talk to me and wanted to know if I thought she ought to marry Bobby Lee or not. Now, ordinarily I'd just say a flat no to anybody who was enough in doubt to have to ask somebody else that question, but Sally was a special case and I told her I sort of favored the idea. Even if it was causing more ruckus in the neighborhood than anything since Mr. Will's afflicted grandson cut off some of his own private parts back behind the Strickland barn. And she said, 'Well, I think I love him, but Sister says I don't know what love is, what with this being my first fellow and all.'

"I snorted and told her I didn't think Miss Sister was any authority on the subject, for her husband had been forty years older than she was and the only sign of affection I ever saw pass between them was her helping him in and out of the car and wiping his chin at church dinners. And I asked Sally if she thought she would enjoy living with Bobby Lee. And I'll never forget what she said. 'Oh, I know I care about him, and I know that regardless of what they say I could keep the house clean for him and cook for him. I can cook better than they think I can, and I can do a lot of things better than they think I can if they'd just have the patience to let me instead of jumping in and doing it themselves. Oh, yes, I think I could be a good wife to Mr. Swanson and share his life.'

"And that's when I stepped in it, Addie. I said to her, 'And his bed? You think you can share his bed with him?' And she hopped around on that little game leg of hers with the curled-under toes and grabbed one of the bed sheets to keep from falling. 'Lord, Lutie, I hadn't thought about that!' she said.

"I told her men don't give out diamond rings just to get their floors swept and have fried eggs and grits at their own table. I furthermore told her Bobby Lee was four years younger than her and that put him at sixty-six, and from what I'd heard of the

Swansons he'd be expecting a heap more out of her under the covers than just a warm spot on a cold night. And Sally got to teetering back and forth and pulling on that sheet till I thought she'd jerk it off the line. It was the next morning she gave the ring back, and Miss Sister changed from tears to sway-backed virtue and was real sweet to Sally for three months. That's why I've felt like I'm the one who ruined Sally's only chance."

Miss Addie's hands were still. "I never knew that, Lutie."

"Well, I'm not proud of it. I've felt like a meddling old busybody ever since. But I was right about the covers. You know three months later Bobby Lee did get married, and he told somebody down at John M. Jackson's when he got back from the honeymoon that a man could get the furtherest behind on that and catch up the quickest of anything he'd ever seen. Soon as Bobby Lee Swanson got married again, Miss Sister got back to her old self."

"Lutie, that wasn't altogether what I meant when I said Sally is an unfulfilled woman."

"Well, I don't know what else you could mean, Addie, and God knows I agree with you about unfulfilled. Let me tell you what she said to me not six months ago. I was sweeping our front porch at sunup and Sally was across the street puttering around their front steps with a silly little hearth broom like a four year old in a play house. She came gimping and stumbling across the road and says to me, 'Well, Lutie, what sort of night did your mama have and how is she feeling this morning?' That was before Mama went into the coma and she was sleeping all day and hollering all night. I'd had the doctor out at three o'clock, and why the dumb doctors can't just give somebody a shot and put the whole family out of misery when somebody gets like Mama I'll never for the life of me understand. Like the darkies say, 'Mama's lived out her time and now she's working on mine.' Anyhow, it had been a devil of a night, if you'll pardon the expression, Addie, and I was right short with Sally. I said to her, 'I don't know about Mama, but I feel like I'd slept with every man in Byarsville last night.' You know how I am when I'm upset.

"Sally said, 'Oh,' and see-sawed her way all the way back to the ditch using that hearth broom for a walking stick before she stopped and yelled back at me, and it was loud enough for the Pendergrafts to have heard if their windows had been open, 'Tell me, Lutie, do you feel good or bad?' It plain got off with me and I hollered out, 'You'll never know now, Sally. Since you let Bobby Lee Swanson slip through your fingers, it's too damn late for you.'

"I was so mad I slammed the door going in, and that woke Mama up again and she started hollering and pulled her tube out and peed the bed. I had to strip the sheets and get another catheter put in, and that ran the doctor's bill up some more. I got to thinking about the Strickland girls across the street with all that money they're too tight to spend and us without enough to hire even one darkie to help tend Mama, and I was sick as a puking dog all day. If Sally Strickland is an unfulfilled woman, it's her own fault and I've got little enough sympathy for her. She's still a ninny. She's a rich ninny, and the devil with being fulfilled."

Miss Addie stood up with the dishpan of beans balanced on one hip. "Lutie, I wasn't talking only about what you seem to think being fulfilled means. I can think of a dozen maiden ladies who've never had a date in their lives but have led a full life. What made me say that about Sally was her listening to that awful telephone call and being so innocent and sheltered she didn't even know what that terrible man was talking about. The very idea of a woman who's spent all her life in this little town with that great big yard to work in and her family has kept her so hemmed around that the only holes she can think of are ones for chrysanthemums and lilies. Anybody with any gardening sense at all would know that the two aren't alike at all. She's been kept in a little box all her life, wrapped in tissue paper. That's what I call being an unfulfilled woman."

Lutie was standing at the edge of the step. "Addie, you're too close to being a saint to be true. I still feel like if you'd put a man in that box underneath the tissue paper you'd take care of fulfillment. Let me go see about Mama; it's past time to turn her."

"Thanks for helping with the beans," Miss Addie said. "I'd better get them washed and put on with the fat back, or they won't be done when the girls get home from work. You think about it before you tell Mattie Lena about Sally's phone call. We need to be good neighbors."

When Miss Addie came back to the porch, Mamie Kate was also departing. She had made it halfway to the street, her book tucked securely into the little bag her mother had made of unbleached domestic and affixed to one of her crutches. She had carefully left a red balloon and her last piece of bubble gum on Miss Addie's chair.

"Good-bye, Mamie Kate," Miss Addie called to the swaying figure. "Thanks for the gum and balloon. You come back any time you want to."

When her mother came home from the law office, Mamie Kate sat in the kitchen watching her prepare supper.

"Did you stay all afternoon with Miss Addie, darling?"

"Yes, ma'am."

"What did you do?"

"I almost finished *The Princess and Curdie*. I think I'll start *The Little Colonel at Boarding School* next."

"Mamie Kate, you amaze me. I wasn't reading any of those books until I was in at least the fifth grade. I'm so proud of you. Did Miss Addie have much company?"

Mamie Kate pushed a little roll of biscuit dough across the oilcloth. "Not that I remember. I was so interested in Irene and Curdie that I didn't notice. I believe I like Curdie better than I do the princess."

"Honey, it's not nice manners to get buried in a book to the point you don't even pay any attention at all to other people. Miss Addie's awful sweet to let you come to her house in the afternoon while Mama works. You thanked her, didn't you?"

"Oh, yes ma'am. Miss Addie's my best friend." She paused for a long moment. "Mama?"

"What is it, honey?"

"What's an unfulfilled woman?"

"Whatever makes you ask that?"

"I was just wondering."

"That's not in that book you're reading, is it? I can't remember anything like that in there, but to tell the truth I never did completely finish it. You just don't worry about things like that, honey. There's plenty of time later for you to learn what an unfulfilled woman is."

"Yes'm. I'll wait. But I can tell you I'm not going to be one. I've made up my mind to that."

Her mother put the biscuits in the oven. "That's nice, darling."

Mamie Kate leaned both elbows on the table. "Mama."

"Yes, pet?"

"Did Jesus have the measles when He was a little boy?"

"Mamie Kate! I never heard of it if He did! It's sure not in the Bible. What you won't think of next!"

"Yes'm. Mama, do you think I could learn to work in a garden? Just a little one? So's I could at least learn to plant lilies and chrysanthemums?"

Her mother was busy setting the table. "Mamie Kate, darling, I've told you that I want you to do anything you possibly can in this old world. I don't see why you couldn't have a little flower garden. What brought all this on?"

Mamie Kate shrugged her shoulders. "I don't really know. I just want to learn all about gardening tools, and like I said, I sure don't want to grow up and be an unfulfilled woman."

Saba

(An Affirmation)

Dear Natalie and Matthew,

For four years I have loved your father. It has been more than
the love one feels for a friend new-found in late life, although that
is beautiful enough in its own right, an event to be cherished for
the rarity and purity of it. It has been, rather, the feeling I could
have only for another son, were it possible to have a son borne by
a woman I never met and nurtured in a land I never knew, one to
spring into my awareness all grown and fully formed, fierce and
proud and beautifully intelligent, polished into grace in his pro-
fession, a son to watch with pride no matter from what distance.
No ties of blood have I with him but rather a deep current of
awareness that transcends such ties.

That current is fed by something for which and on which blood
has been spilled since there have been humans who walked erect
and knew the thick, hot fluid of life coursing through resilient
flesh and exulted that there was something in the world worthy of

that blood and that flesh. A man of worth, having nothing to which he can sacrifice himself, will soon or late find something worthy of sacrifice or he loses his worth. Even the basest of beasts will defend its lair.

Your father and I are bound by love of the land. My land, of course, is Georgia, here in the United States of America, beginning now its third century of the greatest exercise the world has ever known in brotherhood. Your father's land is Lebanon, millennia older than Georgia. I know little of Lebanon. I know that the cedars for King Solomon's temple came from there, for all Georgia boys are familiar with the Jewish history recorded in the Old Testament. I remember that much was made of those trees, and they must have been beautiful indeed because they are lauded in the Song of Songs itself. I know that Lebanon, because of its location, must have known Nebuchadnezzar and Cyrus and Darius and Alexander and Caesar and Mohammed and Ataturk. Lebanon was aware, I am sure, of Saul and Samuel and David and Daniel and also Saul of Tarsus, who changed his name to Paul and traveled extensively. Somewhere along the way Lebanon heard of Jesus of Nazareth and many believed. Of course, many also did not believe, a statement that applies equally to Georgia.

Regrettably I know little of the autonomy of your father's land or of the physical characteristics of it. I know that in the mid-twentieth century its capital of Beirut was the financial center of the Mediterranean and the Near East and it was regarded as one of the most civilized capitals of the world, an example of political harmony for all to emulate. There was a prestige about the American University in Beirut that spread even to Georgia and had something of the same ring to it as the Capital City Club in Atlanta. I know that in the last ten years Lebanon has gone to hell in a bucket and that the city of Beirut has been trashed into a wasteland and that no one in America fully understands the politics there or the age-old reasons that neighbors are killing each other, that Moslems and Christians are at each others' throats, that even those two religions are divided into sects that war with one another.

In America, in Georgia, we read the papers and we watch television. We listen to commentators with different analyses, and we get the impression that these men are pretending to a learning about Lebanon that they do not possess. In Georgia we shake our heads, as men do when their minds cannot fathom something, and say, "Those people are crazy." There is much human blood soaking the soil of Lebanon today, and the land is littered with chunks of flesh and random, unidentified bits of bone, for the weapons of terrorists are messy, explosive, and often indiscriminate. We do not understand.

Into this atmosphere your father chose to carry you two children and his blonde, Carolina-born wife in August of 1986. I understood why he did it, but I was fearful.

In 1982 a novel I had written was published. In this book I had set down as well as I could not only the description of farm life in the Georgia of my childhood but also the feelings that a child experienced growing up in that era in that place. At that time I had not personally known your father. I had referred patients to him, as a general practitioner does to specialists, for I had been told by professors at Emory Medical School that Joseph Saba was a most excellent neurologist. I had been delighted with his care, his diagnoses, his compassion, but I am a busy man and so is Joseph Saba, and our relationship had been limited to an exchange of letters about patients, objective, clearly-typed missives crammed with cold facts and nothing more. His were always signed with a scrawl that was not only indecipherable but resembled a cipher or an exotic monogram, threatening at any moment to open out into an incomprehensible Arabic phrase.

If I failed to send a letter along with a new referral, which I more often did than not, this man would call me before he saw the patient and bluntly ask, "Dr. Sams, what do you want me to do for this patient?" The first time this happened I was taken aback, for specialists are not usually that open or that direct, and I am afraid

I stammered a little with confusion and surprise. Then I learned just as bluntly to reply, "Prove to me he does not have a brain tumor," or, "Tell me she is having migraines," or, "I am worried about multiple sclerosis and need you to confirm or deny it," or even, "She is a crock and forgive me for dumping on you."

We were two busy men, both of us busier than we should be and both of us determined to look after sick folks and to do it as thoroughly and economically as possible. It was professional teamwork that was as mutually satisfying to us as intricate plays, when they work, must be to those athletes whom we in America reward with millions of dollars to cavort in sweat and physical perfection across our playing fields and television screens. I never said a personal thing to Joseph Saba, nor he to me, but I wondered occasionally what he looked like and from which country he had acquired his accent. Our relationship was good, and there was no need to tamper with it.

One day I received a different sort of letter from him. It was fat with many pages and it was written in perfectly legible cursive script. "Dear Dr. Sams," it began, "I have stayed up all night and have begun this letter many times. Your oldest son had told me about your book and that it was very good, and I had passed this off indulgently to family boasting. Then I was walking through the mall and saw the book and on impulse bought it. Last night I finished reading it. Dr. Sams, I have never been so homesick in my life. I travel to market with my grandfather again, except the mules are carrying loads of olives instead of cotton. You have transported me from Georgia to the hills of Lebanon, to the land of my childhood, and I have been flooded with memories that make me laugh and make me weep. My grandfather is a very strong man and I have never felt so secure as when he took me by the hand down a row in the field or a street in the village and said, 'Look you here; this is thus and so,' or, 'This we do and this we never do, in this family. You are a Saba.'

"The book made me remember the body being the temple of the soul, Dr. Sams, and how I defiled it daily. And on Saturday I would repent and walk in glorious righteousness all day on Sunday only to begin my sin anew each Monday. I remember the Baptist missionary coming to our village and arguing with our priest. My grandfather's brother-in-law was converted from the ancient faith, and I can remember my grandfather snorting when he came to our house and saying to my grandmother, 'Here comes the holy one. He has been saved,' but later he accepted the change and would visit in the village with him in harmony."

There was much more, and then the letter ended, "Oh, Dr. Sams, your book has made me want to return to Lebanon and my grandfather, and I dream that in this crazy world some day I might lie in peace in my native village in the common grave of our family under the watchful eye of the statue of the Virgin Mary. Thank you, Dr. Sams, for taking this Lebanese boy home once again."

I tell you children this so that by the time you read these words you will have some idea of the bond between your father and me; that you may understand the love of Land; that you may know the importance of person and place. Your father is forever in my heart.

The following summer I developed a monstrous weakness in my right hand. I could write only if I held the hand with my left for added strength and control; I could not cut a slice of tomato with my fork. I could not grasp a piece of paper with any firmness between my fingers. I noted that the muscles in my calves were so beset with little involuntary fibrillary twitchings that they seemed to harbor beneath the skin a multitude of spastic worms. When I fancied that my left hand was also becoming weak, I made an appointment with your father and drove myself to his office.

I felt uncomfortably pretentious when he said, "You honor me, Dr. Sams, with your presence and your trust," but he was so busy with his hammer and his needles and his machine that delivers electric shocks that I was caught up in admiration of his absorption, his thoroughness. He moved in his long white coat as lithe and lean as a swimming eel, the muscles and tendons of his fingers under absolute control of directive intelligence. When all was done, he invited me to dress and wait in his office. Closing the door on me, he said he would return as soon as he saw his next patient. I had not heard nor seen another patient but thought little of it. "You can sit in this chair behind my desk and make yourself at home, Dr. Sams."

It is almost embarrassing to be closeted alone in the private place of another. One feels sneaky about indulging idle curiosity and looking with more than casual interest at anything other than photographs or framed documents hanging on the wall. One averts one's eyes from opened correspondence lest one be accused of prying into personal things not of one's concern. I looked at your father's diplomas, his record of residencies in prestigious hospitals, the certification that he had achieved Diplomate status in his subspecialty. I roamed the small room restlessly, resistant to the idea of sitting in his chair. This was his domain. I had no desire to usurp his throne, even if on invitation and only for awhile. The silence grew until I was aware of the singing of cicadas in my ears, herald of incipient deafness announcing the approach of age. I moved to Joseph's chair and sat. The desk top was clear of litter and I thought of his horror could he see mine.

There was one book on the desk, its linen covers frayed with use, its pages softened by frequent thumbing. It was a textbook of neurology and it was small as such tomes go. I fancied that it might snug itself into one of the larger pockets on Joseph's coat. It lay open and there were focusing lines of red underscoring some of the sentences. Obviously this was an old companion from Joseph's student days. I drew it to me.

"Amyetrophic Lateral Sclerosis"

The heading startled me and gained my total attention. Lou Gehrig's disease. Yes. The terrible, inexorable, progressive affliction that creeps over a man until he drowns in his own juices, unable to swallow any of them and too paralyzed to expel them. I read of demyelinating the lateral horn cells of the central nervous system, a process I could describe to you children as similar to stripping the insulation from multiple electric wires until the current in an entire circuit is shorted out. It cannot be repaired. It is a permanent loss. The lights supplied by those particular wires will never shine again. I read that the disease usually begins on one side and rapidly spreads to the other. Underscored in red was the statement: "It is always associated with muscular fasciculation, primarily in the legs." Then another statement emphasized by heavy red lines: "Unfortunately death always ensues, never more than three years after diagnosis."

I was caught by the word *unfortunately*. It is rare to find a hint of compassion in so clinically explicit a textbook of diagnosis.

I had attended a patient once with ALS, a vibrant tower of manhood brought low and humiliated by the slow extinction of all his lights. He was the spinoff of specialists and hospitals, set loose to die in his own home at the pace of his marching conqueror, but not of his own will. The hands were the first to go and he could no longer use the releasing pistol, and rapidly he could not even spoon food into his mouth. I made calls and observed a saint of a neighbor bathing him like a child, turning him constantly, freeing his airway of secretions, listening to his words, pressing his hand. He adored her and rapidly refused to have his daughter in the room. He only tolerated his wife. He clung to the neighbor. She was his death partner, and only she made him comfortable with his shame. When his speech failed him, she could understand him long after others looked mystified at his guttural explosions. When the current to his larynx finally sputtered out, she helped him to communicate by going through the alphabet and letting him blink his eyelids to spell out a word of direction. Soon that failed. The last light to go out was the rage within his eyes. I remembered him as being a tyrant, a despot who had fought and flailed and ranted and would have drowned in hate had he not had an angel for a neighbor.

I moved from Joseph's chair to the window. My head was as clear as sunup in January, my emotions just as frozen. I wondered how the specialist would handle this one, how much range of feeling would be exhibited from doctor to doctor, how he would handle the onerous burden of announcement and how I would bear the weight of listening.

He walked rapidly across the room (a redundancy, since I never saw him walk any way but rapidly) straight to his desk, his legs scissoring so vigorously they threatened to leave his long white coat. He reached over, closed the textbook and then turned to me. He neither invited me to sit nor gave any indication of seating himself. Not three feet apart we faced each other, shoulders squared, heads erect, as formal as soldiers in dress review.

"Dr. Sams, you have either a spinal cord tumor or amyetrophic lateral sclerosis. You need a spinal tap and a myelogram to rule out the former. I would rather a neurosurgeon do the myelogram, since, in the unlikely event it is a cord tumor, it is quite high." His voice was rigidly calm.

Rising to the challenge, following his lead, I was also calm. "I am grateful for your candor."

"Dr. Sams, is there anything else I can do for you? Do you have any questions?"

"Yes, Joseph. I have some questions. Have you heard from your grandfather? How is he faring through this mess in Lebanon? Are you worried about him?"

His smile cut through in flashing white beneath his glistening brows and through the blueness of his close-shaven face. "He is well, Dr. Sams. I heard from him two weeks ago. He is in no danger, really, for our village is high in the mountains and very isolated. He says that I should not worry. He says there is nothing to do but let the crazies all kill themselves. When that is over, he says, there will still be the land and he will be on it and then we can rebuild Lebanon. My grandfather is a very strong man, Dr. Sams."

I held out my hand. "Thank you for everything you have done, Joseph. You are making this easier for me. I shall try to be like your grandfather."

He moved rapidly to escort me to the door. As I stepped over the portal he said, "You are already like my grandfather, Dr. Sams. Very like."

"Now it is you who honors me, Joseph."

"No, Dr. Sams. Not in one hundred years could I repay the trust you have shown in me today. Are you all right?"

"Joseph, I am fine. Thanks to you. And thanks to your grandfather. I will let you hear."

Well, there I was — full of Anglo-Saxon and Celtic genes, all of them programmed for caterwauling histrionics. I remembered my father being so grandly mysterious about his Peyronie's disease that the family went into frantic speculation every time he sighed and distantly proclaimed that he had "an incurable disease." I thought back to my aunts and uncles and my grandparents and how they dramatized physical complaints; how even a head cold could become the axis around which the attention of the clan revolved. Here I was driving home alone, praying that I had a spinal cord tumor because at least there was a chance, however slim, of curing that, and my behavior was being totally manipulated by a Lebanese immigrant who was less than half my age. I resolved that I would be as matter-of-fact and controlled with my wife and family as your father had been with me. Suddenly I laughed. To pray for a spinal cord tumor is the ultimate in the unexpected and the height of optimism. A line of verse flashed through my head.

> "The Assyrian came down like a wolf on the fold,
> And his cohorts were gleaming in purple and
> gold...."

I wondered why this had come up to remind me of your father. Then there came to me the concluding line of another poem and I said aloud,

> "For there is neither East nor West,
> Border nor breed nor birth,
> When two strong men stand face to face,
> Though they come from the ends of the earth."

The resolve to be like your great-grandfather carried me through the next two weeks with an absolute minimum of self-pity, fear, or dramatization. My wife was quickly on the telephone with her nephew, The Neurosurgeon, to ask who he thought was the best man in the United States on spinal cords. "Or England, for that matter," she told me. "You know, he did have that fellowship over there." My wife puts slightly different values and use on shared genes than I. The upshot of all this was that I wound up at Ochsner Clinic in New Orleans with a specialist who was a giant of a man with the gentlest hands on earth. The lumbar puncture and the subsequent myelogram were entirely normal except for a few more cells than usual in the spinal fluid. I did not have a spinal cord tumor.

I lay for twenty-four hours with head perfectly flat to avoid any post-manipulative headache, succored in that foreign city by the presence of my oldest son and The Neurosurgeon and comforted by the nursing skills of an angel of a daughter-in-law. As I considered Lou Gehrig's disease and my possible interaction with such an entity, I realized that my weakness had disappeared. The grip in my hand was strong. I could grasp objects once more with surety and use my hands with precision. Those marvelous appendages adorned with opposing thumbs, which have elevated us above all our viviparous suckling brothers, were restored to the marvel of their complex and wonderful perfection.

Cautiously I asked the specialist about amyetrophic lateral sclerosis. Plateau, yes. Remission, occasionally. Improvement, never. ALS was ruled out. Consensus impugned a low-grade virus, something like Guillain-Barre, and the giant in New Orleans predicted complete recovery.

I asked my oldest son to telephone your father. Back came his answer: "Never in my life, Dr. Sams, have I been so happy to be wrong."

I tell you all this only to show how strong the bonds are between me and your father. I did progress to complete recovery. I was busy, your father was busy, we had interchange primarily about patients and saw each other only on rare occasions. In August I went to your house to meet a neurologist your father was thinking of inviting into his practice. We were around the swimming pool when I said, "Joseph, what's this I hear about you? Are you really going back to Lebanon?"

"Yes, Dr. Sams, all the arrangements are made and we leave next week."

"We? Who?"

"My wife and children and I, Dr. Sams."

"Joseph, you are crazy. You cannot take these babies into Lebanon! They look like you and maybe you could get by with them, but what are you going to do with a blonde American wife? She'll be a hostage in five minutes."

"Dr. Sams, we will be perfectly safe, I promise you. We are going into Syria and my family is going to join us there. The village is quite near the Syrian border and it is no problem. All arrangements have been made and there is no danger."

I looked around his teasing grin and into his eyes. He wears that grin all the time except when talking about amyetrophic lateral sclerosis and spinal tumors. "Joseph, I don't know why you are going and it's none of my business, but you cannot take those two children with you. Helen and I will keep them until you get back."

The grin faded. The eyes deepened. "Dr. Sams, the reason we are going is because of the children. My grandfather is eighty-five years old and has never seen them. I could not bear it if something happened to him and he had never seen my children. Natalie is three and Matthew a year and a half, and my grandfather has never beheld them. I promise you they will be safe, and

119

I promise you the person would never be safe again anywhere in the world who harmed one hair of their heads. Do not worry, Dr. Sams. I promise you."

Someone else came up and I went to the kitchen and served my plate and made small talk with the young neurologist. Your father is about to kill himself working and desperately needs help, and I thought perhaps we might, between us, teach this young doctor about medicine in the real world.

I don't for the life of me know why the older generation worries about the younger generation killing itself working, since all of us with any perspicacity should look around and realize that we have seen many more people die from playing, or its complications, than from working, and that our longer-lived peers are more frequently those who have worked hard than those who have frolicked with excess leisure. A person who has disciplined himself to hard work more easily disciplines himself to good health habits; ergo it boils down to a matter of discipline. Nonetheless, your father does work too hard and has little time with you children, and he needs help.

Joseph escorted me in departure with hospitality that would shame a Southern Colonel. At the door he assured me again that his family and he would be absolutely safe during the upcoming sortie to the Middle East. I assured him in turn that I would worry until I heard of their return.

"What do you want me to bring you from Lebanon, Dr. Sams?" His mocking smile was stilled, his voice had the timbre of sincerity in it. "I mean it. What would you like to have more than anything else from Lebanon? What can I bring you from my country?"

I searched his eyes and thought about it. "Joseph," I said, and I also was very sincere, "bring me the blessing of your grandfather."

I looked back as my wife and I drove away. Your father was waving to us, but abstractedly, as though in deep thought.

Over the next three weeks I thought often of you all. I prayed frequently, but I did not worry, since there is absolutely no logic whatever in a Christian doing both. It was with relief that I heard you had returned. Since neither of you was old enough to have any detailed or permanent memory of this trip, let me tell you what I have heard of it. Much of my account comes round about from my son talking with your father in the hospital, for neither I nor Joseph has yet had the time to sit down leisurely and visit with each other, dropping those little inconsequential details into our conversation that are the delight of both a good friendship and a good story. I am hoping that visit will come, but I want this letter written to you in case it does not.

The four of you flew into Damascus. I've had no details of that trip except that you two, at ages three and eighteen months, took over the airplane until your foresighted father finally sedated you. You children right now are beautiful, loving, and bright, but you are also possessed of an energy level the suppression of which I fancy caused a gaggle of flight attendants to rise up and call your father blessed. Unanimously.

In Syria you went to the designated rendezvous, but there was no word waiting from the contact with Joseph's grandfather's village. Apparently there was no way to telephone. After a day and a half, Joseph piled you two dark-haired, olive-skinned babies and your blonde, blue-eyed mother into an automobile and simply drove across the border into Lebanon. I am glad I learned of this only post facto or else my prayers would certainly have degenerated into worry, for your mother's skin is as white as milk. She had no visa for visiting Lebanon and she must have shone in that land like a barrel of spilled flour. At any rate, you traveled without incident to your native village, to your ancestral hearth, and found nothing amiss. No one in the family had received your father's last message about where to meet. Your father's grandfather was well and in good spirits. It was a joyous reunion; the old man adored you children and you, in turn, were in your happiest and most winning form for him. Joseph felt fulfilled.

On the second or third day of your visit, things had calmed
down enough for Joseph to idle some time with his grandfather in
relaxed conversation, a time I fancy that was synchronous in more
than pure coincidence with the first afternoon nap that you two
had been induced to take in Lebanon. He told his grandfather of
his friend in America, the Georgia man who loved the land, the
country doctor who enjoyed reciprocal love with his people, the
author of books that had spoken to a Lebanese man and made
him feel homesick for his childhood. I have no idea how much
detail he recounted, but he ended with, "I asked Dr. Sams what
he wanted me to bring him from Lebanon, and he said, 'Bring me
the blessing of your grandfather.'"

With this, I am told, your great-grandfather jumped up and
went into the important room of his house, what we Southerners
call the parlor, the supreme repository of both memorabilia and
relics, the emotion of acquisition leaving only posterity to dis-
tinguish indifferently between trash and heirloom. He returned
to Joseph and said, "Give these to Dr. Sams."

Joseph looked down at the objects. He had seen them all his
life, ensconced high above the reach of children, admired and
revered.

"Grandfather! I cannot possibly take those to Dr. Sams. How
do you propose that I get them out of the country?"

"Joseph. I am placing these in your hands and I am telling you
to place them in the hands of Dr. Sams. How you manage to do
that is your concern. Do not bother me with it. Tell him that he
has the blessing of your grandfather."

The family had another feast and celebration that evening, for
everyone in the village was glad that you and your parents had
come. Lebanese blood is warmed by kin, and the heart of a friend
beats with steady devotion. The following afternoon your father
and his grandfather were once again having a quiet visit. Of a
sudden, the grandfather stood up.

"Joseph, my heart is hurting fiercely. I am dying."

And so he did, children. That moment. In your father's arms. Your father attempted resuscitation, but he told me later he knew in the beginning it was futile. He was glad he was there to make arrangements, to summon his uncle from Paris, to arrange the funeral, to be the leader of the family in the last rites for the man who had meant so much to him. He was glad that you children were there.

There were many anxious times on the way back to America. First off, you were apprehended by the border patrol in Lebanon. Your father had a visa, your mother did not, a fact which produced both concern and agitation among the patrol. After several hours of interrogation and lectures, you were permitted to depart. It turned finally on your mother's giving a solemn pledge that she would never again visit Lebanon without a visa, a demand she met with such alacrity and enthusiasm that a more insecure man than your father might have felt his very background being disapproved.

You were barely out of this predicament when you crossed the Syrian border and were detained by the patrol there. Your father said that he used all the personality and persuasion he possessed and still the guards became ever more obstinate and obstructive.

"Why do you want to live in America," one asked, "where crime rules the streets and you are liable to be beaten or killed if you set foot out of your house?"

When the man discovered that your father is a physician, and an American-trained one at that, he insisted on describing some symptoms he was having and asking your father's advice. Another guard heard and wanted a consultation about his brother who was gravely ill. Then another. Joseph said that soon he had gathered a roadside medical clinic there on the border between Syria and Lebanon and that he was pushing himself to his limits of graciousness and geniality. He dared do nothing else. Among other concerns, I am sure that he was conscious of his grandfather's blessing to Dr. Sams, concealed God knows where. When he told me of it, I thought of Rachel smuggling away the household gods of Laban for Jacob, spiritual insult added to the economic injury of the dappled herds, but I refrained from query. There is a slight distance of dignity between your father and me and we both respect it.

The cars lined up behind you, and still your father dispensed professional concern and consult on the Syrian road bank. An impulsive driver several cars back had the temerity to blow his horn in impatience, and a guard went rushing back to him, snatched open the door, threw the driver to the ground and began kicking him in the head.

"Control yourself," he shouted, "you donkey dung, you roadside scum! Can't you see that we are very busy with important matters the likes of you could not be expected to understand? We do not look with favor on anyone who interferes with our duties or interrupts our routine. Get back in your car and behave yourself or it will not go well with you. Do you hear me, disobedient dog of a driver? Do as I tell you!" He delivered a final kick and rejoined the group around your father. "Tell me, doctor, about back pain in old women. Just here, and here. I know an examination would be better, but my mother-in-law would never forgive me if I missed the opportunity to ask an American doctor who understands Arabic so well."

When all of you were finally permitted to leave, this same guard leaned through the window with a final admonition. "Guard yourself and your loved ones well on the violent streets of the United States, doctor." Your mother was not required at this point to make a pledge about return visits, but I am sure she would have been willing. I understand, however, that she fell in love with Damascus. She liked the Grand Mosque and the shops, and your father gave her an extra day or so to compensate for the Lebanese and Syrian patrols. You children have the genes of courage from the Celtic side also.

Back in the United States, Joseph called me and came over. As usual, he was in a hurry. He told me about his grandfather and about the blessing he sent to me. Then he placed in my hands the two most unlikely objects I could imagine to have come forth from Lebanon. They were tusks of ivory. Each was about two feet long and most gorgeously carved. At the base was the head of a crocodile, jaws gaping wide, pulling on the trunk of the first in a string of six progressively smaller elephants. I was reminded instantly of Rudyard Kipling's tale of the great gray-green, greasy Limpopo River all set about with fever trees, and I must find the occasion to read that story to you children.

The tusks were beautiful, but in addition there was an aura about them, a command of one's attention that emanates only from true art. Of course, being primitive, there was also something phallic about them.

"Joseph! These are lovely!"

"I am glad you like them, Dr. Sams."

"But, Joseph, these are not Lebanese. These are African. I am certainly no expert, but this is primitive African art of a superb quality. These pieces should be in a museum. This is a treasure, and I cannot possibly accept it."

"You have no choice, Dr. Sams. I am only a delivery boy, and I have performed my function."

"But, Joseph, these pieces are family heirlooms and should stay in your family. Truly, I feel most uncomfortable accepting these from you."

"You are not accepting them from me, Dr. Sams. They are from my grandfather. You are accepting them from him. You can someday discuss your discomfort with him, but for the present you have no choice." His smile brightened my tears.

"Joseph, I am overwhelmed. I shall guard these for my lifetime and I shall specify in my will that they go to one of your children at my death."

"Not so, Dr. Sams. They are now in your family. I must go now. I am pleased that you like them, and my grandfather would be pleased. He thought I needed an American grandfather."

Half an hour after his departure I had a thousand questions to ask. Some are still unanswered, and I await the leisurely afternoon or evening, the slow comfort of a good bottle of wine, the languid coursing of friendship so frequently dreamt and so rarely attained. To the pressing question of how Joseph's grandfather acquired these carvings, however, I have learned the answer. It amazes me, and I must share it with you.

The grandfather was one of two sons in his family. They were very close in years although not so close in other ways. His older brother was what we in the South euphemistically label "slow;" he was good with his hands and had a strong back but he required a great deal of direction and was noticeably lacking in imagination. He was equally loved and nurtured in the family as the grandfather and had the same emotional and educational opportunities, such as they were. Lebanon was very poor.

When your great grandfather was twelve years old, his father sat him down for a talk. He delineated the boundaries of the family land that he owned, which had been handed down to him from his father and in turn his father's father and so on back beyond the memory of the family. In America we are so accustomed to vast acreage and the history of homesteading that we have to gear down our concepts to comprehend the situation in older, more densely settled countries. Land was the life source, the raison d'etre, when the grandfather's father ushered him into manhood.

He told him that the family holdings would support one son but not two. They considered this for awhile and then the grandfather's father said to him with the gruffness that insulates love too intense to manifest itself without burning the speaker, "You have the brains. You leave. He gets the land."

When I heard this, I remembered Reading Gaol.

"Yet each man kills the thing he loves;
By each let this be heard.
Some do it with a bitter look,
Some with a flattering word.
The coward does it with a kiss,

The brave man with a sword."

The grandfather emigrated. He had no choice. He could read and write but the only means of livelihood in his village lay in the land, in farming, and he no longer had any prospects of sustenance at home.

He made his way to Marseilles and hired on board a ship that went up and down the coast of Africa. He soon settled in a country called the Ivory Coast and became a peddler. Carrying trinkets and notions in a pack on his back, he walked into the countryside and jungles, selling for a profit and living off the land. He learned the language and saved his money. Before long he bought a horse. Then from the chieftain of one of the tribes out in the brush he began buying cows.

In a scenario reminiscent of the American West, he herded the cows across the lower reaches of the Sahara Desert and sold them, fighting rustlers and bandits along the way. He prospered and hired others to help him. Always he traded and always for profit; there was suspicion that he had Phoenician blood in his veins. Carefully he saved his money, never carousing or wenching as he saw other white men doing in this alien land. The chieftain also prospered.

The young Levantine sat with dignity in the councils of the men, and when he departed Africa he left behind no wife nor black babies. He left a reputation for fierceness, fairness, and honesty, and he departed as a wealthy man. He was nineteen years old.

At his farewell meeting with his friend and business partner, the old African chief presented him with the carved ivories, family relics that had been given to the chieftain's grandfather when he assumed leadership of the tribe. The young man was reluctant to accept them but there comes a time when a strong person must face the ceremonies of honor simply and with poise. It was from his African experience that he developed the pronouncement he later gave Joseph. "A Saba will always be first, even if on the road to Hell."

When he returned to his Lebanese village, there was great rejoicing. He bought land. He bought ancestral land and looked after his older brother for the rest of his life. His father said to him, "I do not know what happened to you in Africa, nor do I want to know, but you have returned as a person of great substance. You are nineteen years old and you should have a wife. She must be chosen carefully. I have in another village a distant cousin who is known far and wide as a virtuous woman. You journey to that village with gifts for the mother and ask for her oldest daughter in marriage." (This, little children, is the Lebanese version of the old Georgia saying, "Salt the cow to catch the calf.")

The grandfather did his father's bidding and was welcomed most graciously. When he asked about the older daughter, he was told that she was absent on a visit to some cousins. The virtuous woman assured him that if he would wait a week, her daughter would return and be most happy to marry such a fine man. Your great-grandfather said, "A week? I cannot spare a week. I have things to do. Don't you have somebody else?" The lady thereupon presented her younger daughter and he carried her back to his village as his wife. She became your "Grandma Linda." From what we Americans would regard as a most unlikely beginning there evolved a very long and happy marriage and a marvelous family.

The grandfather never quit trading and never quit being fierce and honest and fair. He was obsessed with the importance of education. At one time there were one hundred and twenty children from his apartment complexes in school and one hundred eighteen of them were on the honor roll. He saw to it. He demanded to see report cards. For B's and C's he administered spankings, for straight A's he awarded five dollars. The children were not kin of his; they were his responsibility because they belonged to his tenants.

He paid well for educating his own children. One he sent for seven years to the Sorbonne in Paris. The other son was Joseph's father and he sent him to Rio de Janiero forever because he did not approve of his behavior. Joseph and his mother and sisters remained in the village under the eye and beneath the wing of the grandfather. He was indeed a very strong man. He understood Reading Gaol very well.

The elephant tusks, most magically and artfully carved, had been carried from the jungles and savannahs of Africa to the hills of rural Lebanon. The grandfather placed them in a hallowed spot in his house and there they rested for the duration of his life, an everpresent reminder that trust does indeed attain fulfillment between men of honor, that virtues are not relative but absolute, that good on occasion triumphs beautifully in replacing evil, that a good name is more to be sought than great riches. They were even testimonial that the sword, be it one of truth and justice, does not always kill, but sometimes prunes and invigorates.

Now the ivories are similarly enshrined in my house, their beauty magnified a hundred-fold by what I feel about them. I am in awe of two men I have never met, an African lord and a Lebanese patriarch. I marvel at events the skeptic would label coincidence and the believer would call choreography. The carvings are symbols to me of the ascendancy of innate ability over material inheritance, but they are more. They have a luster about them of the love of one's land; the story of Anteus no longer seems a myth.

I hear a voice that never reached my ear saying, "Leave them alone. When the crazies all kill themselves the land will still be here and we will rebuild."

And another: "You have the brains. You leave."

And the voice of Joseph: "You either have ALS or a spinal cord tumor."

And my own: "Bring me the blessing of your grandfather."

The ivories tell a story. A story of brave men face to face. A story of courage and a sword. A story of continuity, of love, of the importance of the land.

I, being of sound mind and disposing nature and in acknowledgment of a flow of events that has to be divine, do will and
bequeath the elephant tusks I hold in trust from the mountains of
Lebanon and the plains of the Ivory Coast to the children of
Joseph Saba, my adopted grandson.

Go always with God, little children.

Ferrol Sams

Big Star Woman

I AIM TO SUE. I'm going to sue me a doctor! Everybody else is doing it and I can't see any reason why I shouldn't? Do you know it had never crossed my mind until lately what all you could sue doctors for? And I mean collect big bucks from them, too, like that OB man in New York, New York, who has got to educate that mentally retarded baby and he didn't have a blessed thing in this world to do with that child being afflicted?

When all that doctor suing first started I was kind of shocked at it, but here lately I'm getting in sympathy with it? There is no sense atall in them Cadillacing and cocktailing all over the countryside, playing golf and putting their wives in mink coats and bridge clubs and the like, while those of us who put them there can hardly get even nodded to in the Big Star? I'm talking about the wives, because doctors don't go to the Big Star, don't you know?

That does not apply to my doctor? I'm not just talking about the Big Star but also about the Cadillacs and the country clubs? As far as I know his wife is just fine as she can be and may not even play bridge, but I bet you a dollar she's got herself a mink coat? I know that Dr. Glass doesn't do golf or belong to the country club they just started in our town? I asked about why he didn't play golf one time and he said he hadn't ever been that bored. He is next to God as far as I'm concerned, even if he does spend a lot of time remembering the good old days, as people call them? He even got to talking one day about when the Big Star used to be called the A&P, and that stood for Atlantic and Pacific Tea Company, which had got started as a little bitty family store except it was owned by yankees, and when it was successful, of course it spread all over the country? Yankees are bad to spread, don't you know, and you can just expect that out of them?

I get wearied with hearing about merging and what yankees bought out what other yankees and how this county looked before the roads were paved and all that? Every time I say something to Dr. Glass about his office calls going up to twenty-five dollars, he just smiles and gets to talking about the good old days when you got a Co-Cola for a nickel and on Saturdays Krystal would have a special of two hamburgers for five cents and you could see a double feature for a dime? Then he wags his head and sighs and says he doesn't know what the country is coming to if we don't whip inflation, but we just have to ride with the tide and keep up with progress and scratch each other's backs or else the whole house of cards will fall in?

When I was helping my daughter with her eleventh grade English, she had to do a paper on clichés, and I listed a whole page full for her just from remembering my last visit to Dr. Glass and she made an A? He'll talk you to death but I love Dr. Glass to pieces, and nobody in their right mind would ever try to sue him, for he'd talk you out of it before you could get lined up behind a mean lawyer to save your life? On top of that he will still get out at night to sew up a cut or for a child with an earache? If anybody ever did sue him they'd for sure have to go out of town to do it? They'd never get a jury here where he hadn't birthed a baby or raised a youngun or treated a cancer, and he has several times given me good medical advice in the Big Star, too, which is a place he goes to a lot, almost as much as me? I remember once it was in the produce department he advised me about my daughter Sally, and he was a real comfort, you know?

He said, "Myrtice, I know how you feel and certainly abstinence is the best policy, but if you've lost control of her and you're reasonably sure she is sexually active, then I personally think it is better for an unmarried girl to be on birth control pills than it is for her to experience the trauma of either an abortion or an illegitimate child." I love the way Dr. Glass talks when he's being medical; he can make the worst things in the world seem so detached and faraway like? Like it's happening to somebody you've read about and not a cliché in sight? I told him that I had worried and fussed over the wet dog hairdo and the sunrise eyelids, but when Sally came home with three earrings in each ear I knew I had lost the whole battle? I do not believe there is a virgin in the whole state of Georgia who has more than one earring to the side; it is like a notice on the bulletin board? When a teen-ager comes home with her ears looking like something out of National Geographic, you just might as well make arrangements for birth control pills or else an obstetrician, you can take your pick?

Dr. Glass patted me and said he knew I'd done my best, but that was water under the bridge or yet over the dam and no use to cry over spilt milk? And he was right. If I'd named her Brandy or Tiffany or Crystal, I'd have been asking for it and encouraging fast behavior when she got in her teens, to my way of thinking? But I'd named her Sarah Martha after both her grandmothers, and how proper can you get, for pity sakes?

I sure don't agree with Dr. Glass about everything? He can have those good old days and the A&P grocery store and all like that, but I am a Big Star woman myself? As far as I'm concerned the Big Star is real progress and I love to get my cart and push it around and just look? They've got live lobsters and live trout swimming around in tanks, and I have even seen such as octopus and squid laying out on a bed of ice next to shrimp and pompano? Over in produce they've got papayas and mangoes and kiwi and star fruit and I don't know what all? I would never think of buying anything like all that, but I enjoy watching the people that do? Most of them are newcomers who haven't been here more than four or five years, and they talk funny and you'd be hard put to pronounce their names, let alone spell them, but folks who were born in this county are just not papaya buyers? I tell you, the Big Star is a trip without a suitcase, as they say?

Another time Dr. Glass ran into me in Big Star right after little Wallace Junior's funeral. He was looking in the pastry case at all the bagels and croissants and what not that none of us natives had ever even heard of till Big Star opened up? I think he was just about to buy some of those croissants, too, till I came up, although they're not near as good as biscuits, especially Mrs. Winners, and certainly not worth what you have to pay for them? He never said a word, just put those big old long arms of his around me and pulled me into a tight hug and then walked off? We both cried; I don't mean we boo-hooed in the Big Star, but I heard him sniffle and I for sure and certain had to get my Kleenex out? Anybody sue that man? I'd kill the one what tried.

The only time that Dr. Glass has ever been sued was not about anything he'd done wrong in the medical field, and in fact it wasn't about anything he'd done wrong about anything? It was over a property line? I like to laughed out loud right in front of the judge when they were picking the jury? First six folks that got called up the lawyer asked them if Dr. Glass was their doctor and they all said "Yes," and he struck them, as they say? Then he turned around to the courtroom and asked if all the jurors who had ever used Dr. Glass would please rise, and be blessed if every person in the place didn't stand up except old man Pat Conroy, who was so deaf he hadn't heard the question?

I got picked. That's the first and only time I've ever actually served on a jury, although I have been called to jury duty many times since only to get struck the minute my name is called and almost before I can even stand up and smooth the back of my skirt good? I learned a lot about the actual court process through that experience, and it is helping me a lot in my plan to sue a doctor? Most folks think that all they have to do is get a lawyer and put their viewpoint before the public and then the judge and jury pass out justice like a hired hand grading eggs, all impartial and grade A extra-large sitting in a carton ready for Big Star customers, uncracked and clean? Well, I am here to tell you that is not the way it is at all? If you want to win a case, you had better plan and plot and scheme and be braced for anything the other side can throw at you and have a few surprises for them, too?

Justice is blind, you have always heard? And they have that statue of a woman holding a set of scales in one hand and a sword in the other? She is fairly flat-chested with one of them hanging out and a blindfold over her eyes? And if you'll notice she's got on sandals, too? Any Southern woman could tell you not to trust another female who's wearing a high-waisted evening dress with flat-heeled sandals and no hose with one shoulder bare and no bra? Justice is not blind; Justice nowadays is what they call a travesty, to my way of thinking? You can tell by the way she's dressed if nothing else?

Like I say, I learned a lot when I served on the jury that time, and one of the main things I learned was how much the verdict you get depends on little nit-picking details? First off, you want to get the right lawyer and that's important, and it's not just a matter of how much law they know, it's also important how they look to a jury? I've watched a hundred lawyers while I was sitting in court waiting to be called, and you don't want one with an old-timey short haircut who comes in to argue a case with a whole batch of books under his arm? That's like going to a doctor who brings a textbook in the room and thumbs through it to find out what medicine to give you with you sitting right there able to read good as he can if that's all he's going to do, for pity sakes?

Dr. Glass like to have got off on the wrong foot about hiring his lawyer, but he caught it in time and changed over before his case

went to trial? First time he ever mentioned it to me was before
the trial got started, and he didn't tell much that time? It was
right there in the fine wine section of the Big Star, the which we
both tried to make like we were just passing through to the
cheeses but we weren't, because he already had a bottle in his
basket and I'm sure he caught me bending over to check the price
on one of those French Burgundys? It has got to where the
grocery cart in the Big Star is like the back seat in an automobile
used to be when you were dating — it is just not good manners to
look in it?

Dr. Glass was innocent as he could be, sitting there in the
middle of his life, minding his own business and practicing his
medicine, when one of those newcomers hadn't been here but
about ten or twelve years slapped a law suit on him? His name
was Scratchyouvinskyvich or some such nonsense as that, but
he'd had it changed, after three or four years of nobody being able
to pronounce it, to Screven? Mr. Screven had come in here early
before the county had got eaten up with all that progress and land
prices were still real low and bought himself a land lot just north
of the old Glass home place? The deed said two hundred acres
more or less, and also the deed to the old Glass homestead said
two hundred acres more or less, and the land had been farmed and
cultivated right up to the line between them for over a hundred
years and nobody thought a thing in the world about it except in
the old days how hot it was and how long those cotton rows were?

Keep in mind that "more or less," because that was important?
Dr. Glass went down to his farm one Sunday and found survey
stakes all over his cow pasture because nobody had raised cotton
around here since World War II and the hands all moved off to the
cities? He called Mr. Screven up on the telephone and asked real
pleasant like what was going on, and Mr. Screven said he was
fixing to sell some of his land if it was any of Dr. Glass's business?
And Dr. Glass told him the surveyor had made a bad mistake and
had come across his pasture fence some six hundred feet with
those stobs with little red flags on them and he thought maybe

that did amount to being his business? And who was his surveyor anyhow because if he'd hired Esric Lee it never would of happened, since Esric has been surveying here all his life and before that his daddy, Mr. Omar Lee, and if Mr. Screven had hired him, the mistake would never have happened because Esric had more sense than that in the first place? And with that Mr. Screven flared up and said, "Dr. Glass, I'll tell you one thing right now: I don't want an inch of land that belongs to you," and Dr. Glass told me later that it was the nasty tone in his voice that got to him? So he fired right back, "Mr. Screven, you and I are going to get along just fine because I am here to tell you that you won't get an inch of land that belongs to me," and he thinks that he slammed the phone down before he said, "You yankee son of a bitchkyvitch," but he's not real sure?

At any rate, in a month or so here came the law suit? Mr. Screven had this fancy new surveyor hadn't been in the county long as he had even and also hired himself a fat, prissy lawyer from Newnan wore a green coat to court every day of the trial with a yellow tie and just didn't make a good impression at all? Dr. Glass had to hire a lawyer too, of course, and he decided he might as well get modern and all and go with a specialist in that field of law? So he looked around and got one from out of town his own self and set out to explain his case to him?

Dr. Glass told me all the details when the trial was done with right there in the Big Star where they sell the fancy coffee from all over the world and grind it for you? I never buy anything myself, don't you know, but plain old Maxwell House, but it sure is a good smelling place to meet up with somebody and talk? Dr. Glass was expecting any lawyer with bat brains to just listen a while to him tell how his family had farmed that line for a hundred years and he himself has had a pasture fence on it and cows everywhere since they quit cotton thirty years ago and then tell him not to worry but to go on and tend to sick folks and he'd tend to the land line?

But that specialist leaned back in his swivel chair under his diploma from the University of Illinois School of Law and said he reckoned he better research it out at the State Archives Building in Atlanta and could Dr. Glass come back in a week? So Dr. Glass did and the lawyer said he might be in a lot of difficulty since all the maps at the Archives Building showed those land lots to be square and to have two hundred acres in them? More or less? Dr. Glass took a long breath and explained to him that Esric Lee said there was a whole string of land lots across our county that were long and a whole string right next to them that were short? And the reason for that was that when we took over this land from the Creek Indians the Army surveyors were tearing through here with chains and rods and what all and laying it off rough and folks was settling it and clearing it and farming it fast as the Army laid it off? And Esric always went by established lines because if you changed one, you'd have to go slap across the county from Flint River to Whitewater Creek, and the court-house wouldn't hold the paper work, let alone the mad farmers and their lawyers?

And then that specialist tapped his top teeth with a yellow No. 2 lead pencil and said, "Tell me, Dr. Glass, what year was Georgia admitted to the Union?"

Dr. Glass said he couldn't believe his ears? But he asked him what did he mean, and the specialist repeated the same question? Dr. Glass said he just couldn't help it, that he said, "Georgia *was* the Union, you yankee bastard," and fired him on the spot? Dr. Glass is getting a little franker in his old age than he ought to be, but you can't talk dignified and medical-like all the time, and I'm sure he was under a strain by then what with being plumb set about by yankees and worried about his cow pasture and his homestead? After all, it wasn't just property to Dr. Glass, for pity sakes. Homestead is family land and that's worth dying for, you know? You're looked down on forever if you let that get away from you. Nobody else heard him but the coffee-grinder lady, and I'm sure she had heard worse? I was so tickled and so proud that Dr.

Glass was confiding in me and I was the one comforting him for a change that I bought a pound of Blue Mountain coffee beans from Columbia and had it ground, but it wasn't really any better than Maxwell House and cost twice as much?

Well, after that Dr. Glass had to find him another lawyer pretty quick because Court Week was coming on us, and he hired Mr. John Wesley Hodnett, who was eighty years old if he was a day and talked even franker than Dr. Glass but who knew everybody in the county who'd been born there and not just moved in and for sure and certain had known Mr. Omar Lee before he died and also worked a lot with Esric? Mr. Hodnett never held himself up to have known any Creek Indians, but you kind of felt that might be the next claim he was going to make and he'd of made you believe it too? Mr. Hodnett told Dr. Glass to go back to his office and tend to sick folks and let him tend to the land line and the law?

That trial was more interesting by far than anything I'd seen in a coon's age, as they say? I didn't even go about the Big Star for close on two weeks except to run in and out for groceries I just had to have? First off they chose the jury, and all twelve of us were patients of Dr. Glass, wouldn't you know it, and one of us even colored because that's something they're real careful about these days? If I'd been old Prissy Britches Green Coat and Mr. Screven, I'd of just quit right there, but they acted like they knew something I didn't, you know, sort of smug and smirking? Well, it turned out they did, and it took me a while to figure it out, and if it hadn't of been for me they'd have won that law suit in spite of adverse possession and peaceful coexistence and established usage and all the evidence in the world and would have walked off with sixty acres of the old Glass homestead and it would of been subdivided by now and covered up with split-level, three-bedroom, ranch style brick? With two car garages, for pity sakes? It has been truly said by all the lawyers in the land that you never know what a jury is going to do?

All the evidence that was presented, and it took them two days to do it, or at least a day and a half added to the selection of the jury which was more fun that choosing sides for a baseball game, favored Dr. Glass? It was open and shut and plain as the nose on your face as he would of said if he had met me in the Big Star along about then? Old man John Wesley Hodnett did a great job and made the other side look like the fools they were in spite of him being eighty-odd? Or maybe even because of it, who can say for sure? He paraded folks through that witness box who had hunted on that land fifty, sixty years ago, folks who had farmed it on shares for the Glass family when it was still in cotton, women who'd picked berries and gathered poke on it when they were little girls, and even had the Negro man who'd strung the barb-wire when Dr. Glass fenced it in for cows? He had the tax assessor with his maps who swore that ever since he'd owned it Mr. Screven had been paying taxes on one hundred and forty acres and Dr. Glass on two hundred and sixty? I mean, Mr. John Wesley Hodnett was on the ball! Old Prissy Britches Green Coat would cross examine every time and try to show that a witness was lying or even imply that Dr. Glass was paying them off, and he just generally showed himself and acted nasty and kept Mr. Hodnett hollering, "I object," till he got to where he said it right weary and bored-like, and the judge sounded that way too when he sustained? The judge never one time in the whole trial said, "Objection overruled," that's how good a lawyer Mr. Hodnett was, and Dr. Glass was sure smart to have changed over to him?

He was plumb cute, too, Mr. Hodnett was, in addition to knowing his law and a heap about people in general? He wore one of those little miniature roses in his lapel like people grow nowadays in pots under those fluorescent lights and all? He used to have a big rose garden outdoors, but when he got too feeble to tend it to his satisfaction he went to Gro-Lux and raised little baby ones in the house and put a fresh one in his coat every morning, summer or winter didn't make any difference to him after he took up with the Gro-Lux, and it made him look real sporty and like a gentleman at the same time? He had his grandson in court with him on that case, which Little Buck was a junior in law school and Mr. Hodnett was using him as a helper sort of like a brick mason's apprentice or an intern at an operation?

Mr. Screven and Old Prissy Green Coat hadn't been able to muster any single witness who was worth a hoot about that line being where it had been setting for a hundred years, and finally they called their new-fangled surveyor with his yankee accent to the stand? Mr. Hodnett was a little deaf and he played like he was considerably deafer than he was? Sat with his hand cupped behind his ear and all and asked folks to repeat every now and then? I mean, really now, I think Mr. John Wesley Hodnett could hear what he wanted to hear? When Prissy Green called that surveyor up, before they had a chance to swear him in or anything, Mr. Hodnett leaned over with a coarse old deaf man's whisper and said, "Little Buck, I'm not going to waste much of the court's time on this witness. I'm just going to ask him enough questions to show the jury he doesn't know what he's talking about." Of course, we heard it. You could of heard it plumb to the back of the room, I expect? Priss Green hollered, "Objection," and that time, too, the judge said, "Objection sustained. Mr. Hodnett, will you please lower your voice when you wish to speak confidentially to your clerk?" But by then, of course, the damage was done because the jury had certainly registered the remark and anybody with peacock brains could listen to the yankee surveyor and know that Mr. John Wesley Hodnett was dead right? You see what I mean about him being cute as well as smart?

Oh, everything worked out fine for Dr. Glass's case on that witness stand? Esric Lee explained about survey lines and established usage and local history before and after the Creek Indians and before and after the War Between the States for that matter until even a child could understand it? And he was real cool under cross examination when Priss Green tried to discredit him and get him rattled and all like that, which is just part of courtroom procedure and a decent jury doesn't pay it any mind at all? Unless it works and the witness breaks up? It looked like for a while there that Priss Green was hired by Dr. Glass instead of Mr. Screven, because every time he tried to maneuver some witness it would blow up in his face?

Even the black man made old Priss look silly and caused his face to turn red, and if you think that green coat and yellow tie looked good underneath a red face and buck teeth that were sort of gray then you've got another think coming? I was sure that Bug-Eye had never been on a witness stand before, and I'm sure he must have been a little nervous about it although you couldn't tell by looking at him? Only way you could tell about his nerves was that he was answering questions in a Negro accent so thick you could spread it on a biscuit with a case knife, and all of us in town know that Bug-Eye can talk as proper and white as any of us? Except that he still says judge-ment and pres-i-dent, but even Andrew Young does that if he's not careful? Bug-Eye, of course, is not his real name? It is Booker T. Purdue, but when he was a youngun and anybody would aggravate him he'd draw his fist back and holler, "I goan bug yo eye out, fool!" and all the other kids and then everybody in town commenced to calling him Bug-Eye and kept it up? He has been monstrously successful and yet everybody likes him because he is just a nice person and knows everybody and helps anybody in the whole county who will stand still long enough to be helped, makes no difference black or white? He started off as a sharecropper, one of old Uncle Garland Purdue's younguns, and soon as he got to be a muscled-up young buck he worked out in slack season for day wages? That's how he came to be hired on the Glass place to help string the pasture fence right straight down the property line that was in dispute?

He got drafted when he was eighteen and went off to World War II and got decorated and all and when it was over he came home instead of migrating to some big city? Used his mustering-out pay for capital instead of show and went in business and has wound up so far owning two dry-cleaning establishments and four laundromats and a brick house with three bathrooms? And his wife drives a Buick and him a pick-up truck just like all the old-time white folks in town who've done good and yet kept their heads through all this progress? Everybody likes Bug-Eye, and goodness knows he is familiar with proper English and college and all that, for hasn't he sent his own children and Lord knows how many others on off to the university, including those two Dandridge boys who could only be called by even the most broad-minded "poor white"? And one of them has done well, too, although the other one is still in the penitentiary? Which all goes to show you that even Bug-Eye can't put something in a body's gene pool that wasn't there to start with, as Dr. Glass would say when he gets to talking about heredity and diabetes and such?

Bug-Eye got on that witness stand that day and if you shut your eyes you'd of thought Step'n Fetchit was back among us in spite of Civil Rights and everything? He was saying, "Naw suh," and, "Yassuh," as broad and thick as if he was fifteen years old and still picking cotton on halves? Priss Green didn't cotton to what was happening and began asking meaner and meaner questions so as you could tell from the jury box that he was going to show us he could by-God discredit at least one witness? First thing you know he'd dropped the Mr. Purdue and was saying "Booker T." and him not even having known Bug-Eye at all before that day, and we all of us use courtesy titles for the colored now unless we know them real well for years and years? And I don't blame them, I'd of marched in Selma, too, for pity sakes? I have seen Bug-Eye's wife in the Big Star from time to time buying salmon steaks or live lobster and not flouncing around putting on airs and showing out about it either? If you have good sense you're likely to have good taste, but there's only one of them you're born with? You have to work on the other. And Bug-Eye Purdue's family was a model to all of us if we'd just stop and think about it? Up from share-cropping is every bit as important a step as up from slavery? There are plenty of folks in our town who can vouch for that, and the biggest portion of them is white, not black, and all of them are obliged to have good sense even if they have not yet acquired good taste like Bug-Eye's wife?

I sat there and knew that Priss Green had to have good sense or he couldn't have finished law school and passed the bar and all that, but his attitude toward Bug-Eye was as much of an advertisement of his taste as that coat and tie? I got to thinking that he was probably born a sharecropper himself and was feeling sorry for him because I have this tendency to be tolerant of just about anybody but not necessarily of just about anything? Come to find out later, when I had time to check on it, Priss Green's daddy used to be a very wealthy attorney his own self over in Alabama, which goes to show you that lots of money can't buy good taste either, but that opens up a whole new can of worms, as Dr. Glass would say and we won't go into that right now?

Priss Green may be pretty good at leading a witness, but when he started doing it to Bug-Eye, he made what I would call a serious error in judgment? If a lawyer discredits a witness it looks good for his side, but if he slips up and lets the witness discredit him, he is held up in public as a fool and that reflects on his client, too, and that hasn't got one thing to do with a blind woman holding a sword and a set of scales but it sways juries like you wouldn't believe?

Old Priss Green leaned forward real confidential like and said, "Booker T., you weren't but fifteen years old when you were stringing that barbwire for Dr. Glass, and there are obliged to be a whole lot of things you did back then that you don't remember too clearly. Am I right?"

"Yas, suh. I reckon they's a heapa things we all disremembers as the years go by, but I sho recollect putting that fence down that propity line cause it was the first bob wire I'd ever stretched. That stuff like to et me up, but I was getting two dollars a day daylight to dark and that was big money in them days." There was a little titter ran through the courtroom, not enough for the judge to take notice of but enough to make folks think things were going to get entertaining, because say what you will, white folks do love Step'n Fetchit? Priss Green had little enough sense to think it was favoring him?

"Right, Booker T.! It was the first barbwire you'd ever stretched and that was probably the first line any white man had ever pointed out to you and said, 'This is a property line,' because ordinarily you wouldn't know what a property line was. Am I not correct? You'd just blindly put barbwire where some boss man who was paying you two dollars told you to put it, right?"

I saw Little Buck nudge Mr. Hodnett like he was egging him on to object, and I saw his granddaddy shake his head ever so slightly at him, and you could tell that old man John Wesley Hodnett was telling Little Buck to give Bug-Eye his head and Priss Green enough rope and have faith that they were both going to manifest what the good Lord had given them? I just love Mr. John Wesley Hodnett, although not as good as I do Dr. Glass, and I know that he has been using Bug-Eye's laundry ever since he opened the first one, which they are awfully good about getting the right amount of starch in shirts and sewing buttons on without being told?

Bug-Eye looked at old Priss with a big frown between his eyes, and so help me Hannah if he didn't reach up and scratch his head? Then he came out with, "What you say, white folks?"

Old Priss leaned plumb over the witness box almost. "Booker T., back when you were fifteen years old it is entirely possible that Dr. Glass came down there where you were stretching barbwire and said, 'Boy, nobody'll ever know it. You just run that ole fence over here. Nobody'll know the difference because the folks on this side of the line live in Atlanta and don't ever come on the back side of their land anyhow, and I'll make it worth your while.' Now, it's entirely possible that could have happened to an innocent fifteen-year-old colored boy working for a powerful and influential white landowner, isn't it?"

Little Buck gave Mr. Hodnett another dig with the elbow, but the old man didn't even look at him, just sat there holding his ear forward with his hand and trusting Bug-Eye with everything he had?

Bug-Eye leaned forward in his chair so it looked like from where we sat that he was nose to nose with old Priss.

"Effen you knows so much about how things was when I was fifteen years old, how come you don't set up here and tell it flat out instead of axing me all them querstions you making up in yo own head?"

Well, old Priss backed off pretty quick, I can tell you, and got this very dignified tone in his voice? "Booker," he said, "there is a great deal of confusion over the matter before this court and I am attempting to clarify it." And he made the mistake of pausing for that to sink in?

Quick? I mean that Bug-Eye was quick. He shucked Step'n Fetchit before you realized it and you'd of thought Dr. Ralph Bunch was among us?

"Counselor," he said, "the confusion is obvious and so is its source. Let me contribute to your efforts at clarification by pointing out that if you in any way seek to impugn the integrity of either Dr. Glass or myself, you are making a serious error in judgment."

Well, sir, you have heard of listening for the pin to drop, but I don't believe anybody in that courtroom took a breath for a full minute? I myself was wondering how many of the white people in that room could of used *impugn* properly, and Priss Green's face got so red it looked as if it was going to start blinking like Christmas lights there for a while? Finally he swallowed and sort of wiggled like he was trying to pull what dignity he could still muster around him and said, "Your honor, I believe I have no further questions of this witness. He can come down."

When Bug-Eye stood up to leave the witness box he looked over at the jury and never the least bit changed expression, but he winked at me? Yes, he did, too, he winked right at me just as sure as the sun came up this morning and still never changed his expression at all? There I was in the full bloom of my womanhood, you might say, sitting in a jury box in my pink voile blouse in the middle of Georgia right out in public and I had been winked at by a black Negro man? And you know what, I didn't feel the least bit insulted? It was a quick, clean, sort of off-hand wink like you get from your partner when you've been led to and she's sitting over there got a void and a trump she's going to lose next time trumps lead? It told me that he knew how I felt about Dr. Glass and that he felt the same way and he'd done all he could and now it was my turn?

I got to remembering the day the schools integrated? Everybody was sort of strung tight and looking for maybe something to happen on account of a lot of talk that had been going on in the lower element and all? Every time a bus pulled up to the school house, Dr. Glass stepped out from one side the front door of the school and Bug-Eye from the other and they met in the middle of the walk and shook hands with each other? Never said a word, they did, just shook hands? Then they walked to the bus, and when the driver opened the door they walked into school together leading the children? There was a whole crowd of folks watching that morning, including the high sheriff and his deputy and the city policeman, too? They were there to keep the riff-raft under control, you know? They watched two buses unload like that and then the high sheriff hollered to the others, "Let's go to Melear's and get a cup of coffee. Ain't no call for us to hang around here no longer." The riff-raft just don't stand a chance in our town?

I sat there in that jury box and didn't listen to half of Priss Green's summation because I got to thinking about my daddy and how he'd roll over in his grave if he could know that his only daughter had been winked at in her pink voile blouse in the courthouse by a black Negro man and that she liked it and even gave him a slight nod of her head? When you come to it, my daddy would be whirling like a spinning-jenny out there in the graveyard about a lot of things? This progress business has got to come on you gradual and you almost have to be there and live through it, if you're going to be able to stand it, let alone like it?

It'd take my daddy a day and a half laid up in the bed to get over just one trip to the Big Star, and if he got a good look at Sally's eyes and ears he'd probably holler for a dose of calomel and follow it with a broken dose of salts? My daddy was an old-fashioned upright pillar of the community and was fond of saying, "What's right is right and what's wrong's wrong," but I personally have had to modify that a little in light of all that has happened in my own life?

First news you know that trial is over and argued and we are filing into the jury room and they shut the door and the bailiff props his chair alongside it and won't let anybody in or out, and there's nobody in that jury room from then on till the verdict except those twelve men and women? It's the moment of what they call high drama, even if the bailiff is just Mr. Willie Green Avery, all of whose children I went to school with and I've known him all my life and he's just as friendly and plain as he can be when you run into him in town? When he props himself in that chair outside the jury room, though, and sits there with his arms folded waiting for the jury to knock from the inside and be let out, he even looks different and it's not just because he's got his teeth in, either? He's not smiling and friendly; he is strictly all business and represents the dignity of the court same as the judge does? He didn't even let on he recognized me by so much as the flicker of an eyelid when we went in that room at three o'clock in the afternoon, although I am sure he knew every one of the twelve of us except maybe the white-haired retired man from Peachtree City who wears the copper bracelet on his right wrist for his arthritis and goes to Dr. Glass when the copper lets him down?

I looked at my wristwatch and thought this ought to take thirty minutes, an hour at the most, and I'd be home in plenty of time to get Wallace his supper and let his sister go? You just can't find good help any more, what with the lunchrooms in the schools and Cluett-Peabody and all, but Wallace's sister had promised to stay with Sally while I was on jury duty? Well, my stars alive, at six o'clock Mr. Willie Green Avery looked in the door and asked us could we reach a verdict in thirty minutes, and by that time it was plain we couldn't and the judge called us back out and told us to reconvene at nine o'clock the next morning? Gave us all those solemn instructions about not talking to anybody about this case under penalty of what all he would do to us if we did? I am here to tell you that a judge is worse than a daddy and the meanest school teacher you ever had all rolled into one? He is stern and strict and leans overboard to be fair, but I have never yet seen one willing to be late to supper over a hung jury? Judges keep awful regular hours from what I can see and don't interrupt their schedules for anybody, and that probably comes from all that exposure to the lady with the blindfold on? If that lady ever got a good peek at some of her judges, I believe she might make them put out a little harder?

I was honest and legal, which the two are not always the same, as anybody with one eye in his head can tell you, and I did not discuss the case with a living soul? But the judge never said a mumbling word about discussing other jurors with somebody, and as soon as I got Wallace fed and watched him settle himself down in front of the TV set and all, I got on that telephone? I had to check on English Drennon? English is twenty-two years old and Dr. Glass had delivered him and raised him through his shots and strep throat and a few cuts here and there and one broken bone, although his mama said it wasn't broken it was just fractured? The Drennons are fine upstanding people who don't owe anybody anything and I have known the whole family all my life, and when they were striking the jury I saw Mr. Hodnett lean over and ask about English and you could tell he thought English was too young, although he had cut his pony tail off when he finished high school and had been wearing shoes whenever he went down town for the last year or so? I had seen Dr. Glass give Mr. Hodnett the big nod for English and I knew that meant he trusted him?

Well, sir, that English Drennon was the stumbling block and the holdout on our jury? It didn't take us five minutes to elect the

copper bracelet as our foreman, and we took a vote right away
after about ten members had discussed the evidence so as it
wouldn't look cut and dried? The vote came out eleven to one for
Dr. Glass with that English Drennon being the only one for Mr.
Screven? Everybody took turns explaining the facts of the case to
him real patient like and you could tell they all thought he was
confused about the evidence because of his age and all? Then we
voted again and he did the same thing? None of the Drennons, or
the Englishes either, for that matter, are retarded? They're mule-
headed and contrary at times but they've never had one that was
retarded and I knew it? I couldn't figure out why English
Drennon was voting against Dr. Glass, who had after all brought
him into this world and been good as gold to him ever since?

When Mr. Willie Green Avery knocked on the door with the
message from the judge, I sidled up to English and asked him
what was the matter with him. He's got blow dried hair and
almost all his zits have gone and he's turned out to be a right
handsome boy for a Drennon, though there's just not a thing he
can do about that low forehead, they are all afflicted with that?
He had two neck chains on, and all the young men unbutton their
shirts halfway to their belly button now if they've got the least bit
of hair on their chest? It must be to show the chains, for we've all
seen hair, for pity sakes? I mean, a lot of the grown men do it,
too, and some of them have a big old irregular blob of gold
hanging round their neck, too? Comes from having their high
school class ring melted down and hanging on a chain instead of
knocking around in the back of some dresser drawer where
anybody's class ring is supposed to be after you've got old enough
to have better sense? Dr. Glass told me in front of the Sara Lee
display in the Big Star one time that folks waste more money on
vitamins than anything else in the United States, but I disagree
with him? I think it's high school class rings?

English had done had his melted down, I'll have you know, and
him just twenty-two and he even had a little chip diamond set up
in one corner of it, the Drennons being all inclined to be just a

little bit flashy? On the other chain around his neck, in the edge of what little hair he had to show, was a real dainty woman's ring with a set in it, and that meant that English was in love and had promised to be true to some girl and that he was proud of it? While I was talking to him out the corner of my mouth so everybody else wouldn't hear, I kept trying to see what kind of stone it was? The gold looked real but the stone was pink and probably didn't amount to much?

That young whippersnapper said, "Miss Myrtice, I've knowed you all my life but you may as well know. I've made up my mind and I know this jury vote has got to be unanimous or they have a mistrial, and I aim to set here from now to Kingdom Come. You can't talk me out of it."

Bout that time old Peachtree City Copper Bracelet asked if we needed to take another vote or did we think we should declare a hopeless deadlock or did we think we should ask the judge to recess us for the night? And I spoke up real quick and told him I'd appreciate it if we asked for an immediate recess since I was tired my own self and also I needed to get home to my hard-working husband and fix him and my little girl some supper? I wasn't about to throw up my hands and give in to any Drennon with two neck chains that quick and easy, I can tell you?

Like I said, soon as I got Wallace settled and Sally in her room supposed to do her homework, I got on the phone to do a little investigating? I called up Pauline Willmott, because I knew she went to the same study group with English Drennon's mama? Soon as Pauline and I got through the politeness and the catching up you always have to do when you haven't talked to somebody in a good long while, I asked her what she could tell me about the Drennon boy? I never mentioned the case to her and it had not yet made the rounds that I was on jury duty, so Pauline didn't know it and I was not breaking any law even if the judge should happen to find out about my call? You know what she told me?

"Myrtice, I think he's finally quieted down a little bit. You know he works part time with that new surveyor that folks hire when they can't get Esric Lee and the rest of the time on the dock at Georgia Highway Express. I understand from his mama that he's fallen head over heels in love with that little Brandi Screven with the big eyes and cute figure, but she's just sixteen and he's twenty-two. English's mama says Mr. Screven is real strict, won't let Brandi have her ears pierced with but one hole and doesn't want her dating at all, let alone some wild boy that much older than she is."

Well, sir, that did it and everything fell into place and fit together like a jigsaw puzzle and I had trouble keeping my voice disinterested until I could wind down and get off the phone with Pauline? I talked a while and asked about her recipe for hush puppies and then hung up, but my brain was whirling the whole time enough to make me dizzy-headed? I told Dr. Glass once in the Big Star dairy corner, where they sell yoghurt and all such fancy stuff as that, that I was dizzy in my head, and he'd been up all night and was feeling sort of gruff? He said, "For God's sake, Myrtice, you can't be dizzy anywhere except in your head," and I've tried to remember that but a language habit is hard to break? When I hung up that phone from talking to Pauline I never slept a wink the whole night? The which is just a way of speaking and means that I kept waking up off and on with the same thing on my mind? I knew what I had to do and I knew that I was going to do it, but it was a hard decision to come up on a lady because there are just some things in life that you are supposed to ignore and pretend never happened?

Next morning I put on my red and white polka dot and marched in that jury room and listened to them review all the evidence one more time and never opened my mouth to say a word? Then I let them take a vote just to see if that English Drennon had come to his senses after a good night's sleep? But he hadn't, he still voted no? The colored lady on the jury raised her voice at him and he let her rave and rant and then just as cool as a cucumber said to her, "You know what the penalty is for intimidating a juror?" I mean somebody had coached that smart-aleck!

That's when I took over? I said I sure didn't want to intimidate anybody and that I wanted to say that for the record and all? But that I did want to reason very gently and sweetly with an old neighbor, and I went over to the corner of the room next to the toilet door and said, "Would you mind stepping over here just a minute, son?"

Well, he did, he could hardly refuse, don't you know, when it was put to him like that? I put my lips up real close to his ear and whispered low as I could?

"English Drennon, if you don't straighten up and fly right this very minute I am going to tell Mrs. Screven what I saw you doing to your little sister's Shetland pony down in our back woods year before last when you were a grown man, at least physically and in spots, and sure ought to know better, and do you know what the penalty is for that?"

Well, he turned white as a sheet and his eyes got plumb black and I thought for a minute he was going to faint away on me? But I got him set down and we took another vote and this time it was unanimous and the Glass homestead was saved? And Mr. Screven had learned what "more or less" means and I could hear my daddy again saying, "What is right is right and what's wrong's wrong." I was sorry Bug-Eye Purdue was not in the courtroom when old Copper Wrist announced the verdict, for I would have loved to of winked back at him? That judge can set up there all he wants to wondering if he's going to get done in time for a golf game and thinking that justice is blind? Well, I could tell him real quick that his goddess may be wearing a blindfold all right but that this is one Georgia girl who has learned how to goose her and make her use that sword to good advantage?

Although it was the hardest thing I ever did in my life? Like I already said, there are some things in life you are just supposed to ignore? Especially if you're a lady? And sex is certainly the thing I have ignored the most and enjoyed the least the longest day of my life? It didn't come easy to me to even admit to English Drennon that such a thing existed, let alone that I had been an eyewitness to him having carnal knowledge, as they say, with that pony? I knew exactly how the poor little thing must have felt, for pity sakes, even if I have never had a bridle on and my head tied to a tree?

That whole trial was good experience for me, though? It is what has given me the courage to face what I aim to do now, and that is going to be even harder on me than saving his homestead for Dr. Glass? It will give me the strength to talk about sex in public, which I know I am going to have to do no matter how upset it makes me? In fact, being upset on the witness stand in a ladylike way, of course, is not any handicap at all if the witness knows what she is doing? I'll remember to wear dark skirts and high-top blouses, but I do think for the last day I can wear my white organdy with the ruffle down the front?' By that time everybody in the courtroom, let alone the jury box, will know beyond the shadow of a doubt that I am a perfect lady?

I figure the whole trial won't take more than a week and I can stand anything for a week? God knows if I can live through what I have with Wallace for a year of days and face the same thing, same speed, up hill, down hill, round the curves all the way through the rest of our life together, then I can make it through a week? And when we get to the sex part I know to be shy and reluctant and dignified, and whatever I do not to be cute or let the opposition's lawyer get me mad or rattled and make me say something smart aleck that will get the jury tickled?

I remember back before integration when Bessie Lou took out a bastardy warrant to make Arthur Murray Scofield pay child support for their six-month-old baby? And there was no doubt at all it was Arthur Murray's baby because it had that distressed monkey look with the left eye off center like all the Scofields have, plumb back through Arthur Murray's granddaddy? Arthur Murray didn't want his salary garnisheed and he hired himself a lawyer on account of he was timid as all get out to start with and on top of that stammered like a yellowhammer when he got nervous? It was only going to be heard in Ordinary Court but when Arthur Murray showed up with a lawyer, the Ordinary asked Bessie Lou did she want a postponement till she could hire a lawyer, too? And Bessie Lou said, "I don't need no lawyer because I'm not going to tell nothing but the truth nohow, and besides, Right is on my side."

Well, it went all over town and everybody laughed at what a fool that lawyer of Arthur Murray Scofield's made of Bessie Lou? He never put Arthur Murray on the stand atall, just cross-examined Bessie Lou? She swore that she had cohabited with Arthur Murray for six months before she got pregnant and that she knew it had to be his baby and nobody else's? I personally am going to use *consortium* if I have to use such a word to describe it at all, and God knows I probably will? *Cohabit* is a legal word, too, but *consortium* covers more territory? Arthur Murray's lawyer asked her if on or about the night of so and so when she had an argument with his client at the Blue Goose Cafe was it not true that she had left the Blue Goose in the company of two colored soldiers from Fort Benning? And Bessie Lou said she certainly had and that the reason she had done so was because she was mad with Arthur Murray and wanted to show him he wasn't the only rooster in the chicken yard?

Then the lawyer asked her was she aware that those same two soldiers, the which one was from Alabama and the other from Philadelphia, had come back to the Blue Goose less than an hour later, laughing and bragging in public how easily they had both experienced sexual intercourse with her, using repeatedly the term "like taking candy from a baby?" And Bessie Lou was being prim and dignified and still had Right on her side and she said, "I heard about it. My sister wait table in the Blue Goose and she told me and she also told me Arthur Murray heard it, too, and left without paying for his catfish sandwich or even eating all of it, come to think about it." And the lawyer said, was the report of those two soldiers true? Bessie Lou said, "Well, yes sir, I cohabited with both of them but I made one get out of the car twell the other one got done and promise not to look."

Then the lawyer really bore in and asked how was she so sure her baby was Arthur Murray's? She said, "Cause he the only one I've ever let cohabit in me his own self." The lawyer said what did she mean by that and would she explain it to the Ordinary? And she did? "I made them two soldiers put on protection. You know, them rubber things. But I always welcomed Arthur Murray just like he was, including the next night after them two soldiers was long gone back to Ft. Benning and we made up." The lawyer got persistent and asked how could she be sure the two soldiers did indeed avail themselves of the protection she demanded? Bessie Lou got indignant and straightened up and said, "Cause I knows. I told 'em to and I knows they did. Land sakes, I didn't just get down there and look — that wouldn't a been decent!"

Then everybody laughed and Bessie Lou cried and the Ordinary found in favor of Arthur Murray, and the town had to grow up around them before everybody forgot it? Of course, four months later Bessie Lou married Arthur Murray Scofield, and when that baby started first grade he was in one of the bus loads of children that Bug-Eye Purdue and Dr. Glass led into the school house? He was the cutest little thing you ever saw, had on a white shirt and clean as a pin and carrying a red, white and blue striped book satchel and looking for all the world like a little bitty Arthur Murray? When he was in the sixth grade, Bessie Lou was elected president of the PTA and presided real well at meetings and all? Say what you will, there are mostly good people in this town?

There will be no fun and frolicking when I get on the witness stand, I can promise you? As I have previously implied, I never could stand sex anyhow and it is certainly no laughing matter? I will never forget how shocked and horrified I was on my wedding night? Oh, I knew what was supposed to happen and all because I certainly was not stupid, but I was just not prepared for how I was going to react to it? I couldn't help it, I busted out crying and boo-hooed for a solid hour till I finally got the hiccups? Poor old Wallace offered to take me back to Mama, but we had driven all the way to Panama City for our honeymoon and was signed up to stay a week and I wasn't about to go home and admit something was wrong? The last person in the world I wanted to see was my mama, but I thought if Wallace came at me one more time in that fix men get into so quick a-pumping and a-pounding and performing consortium all over the place, that I would just go jump in the ocean? We had a place right on the beach and the Gulf of Mexico kept lapping and whispering and slopping and sloshing all night long? So did Wallace. I had thought a man would consortium once and then roll over and go to sleep like they do in the movies and even here of late on TV, the which no wonder the country is coming up on moral bankruptcy what with all our children have got laid out there for them to look at? Not that Wallace, for pity sakes, he just kept coming back and coming back? I thought he'd never quit and I guess he wouldn't of if I hadn't got the hiccups, for even when he was comforting me about crying and all he kept feeling and fooling around and getting himself excited all over again?

The thing that came as a complete shock to me and which nobody had ever told me about and which I had never mentioned to a living soul till it was too late and Wallace and I had already suffered medical malpractice was the one thing I had never heard mentioned anywhere among ladies? It's a delicate subject and talking about it is like Bessie Lou said on the stand, "It just wouldn't be decent." I still can hardly bear to discuss it, but I know it's got to come out and I have been braced for it ever since I acknowledged the Shetland pony to the Drennon boy? What I'm getting around to admitting is that I never knew till I experienced it firsthand that all that old mess comes gooshing out of a man when he gets to the end of consortium like somebody racing a bicycle? I didn't, I didn't know it?

I begged Wallace to put on protection but after a couple of times of that he balked on me, said it was like washing your feet with your socks on and so forth; you've heard all those comparisons by now your own self, I am sure? They're all what they call male chauvinistic nowadays but was what was called "coarse" when I was growing up? Wallace had the idea that if I got enough of it I would learn to like consortium, and I had the idea that if I had to live the rest of my life having consortium all that much that I would go stark raving crazy and have a complete nervous breakdown? So I learned real early to fake it?

Being pregnant helped? Dr. Glass had a rule that said no douche after three months and I told Wallace that certainly applied to consortium also? I didn't get indelicate enough to be specific, but what could roll out of Wallace was worse than any douche in the world, even if you had misunderstood the doctor and used a cup full of water and a quart of vinegar like Pauline did one time and we called her Pickled Polly for three months? Wallace and I had little Sarah Martha, three miscarriages, Wallace Junior, who got run over and died, two more miscarriages, and then a hysterectomy, thank God? That Wallace still couldn't get consortium off his mind, and I feel like I have spent half my life dodging and doubling back like a rabbit on the run and making excuses?

The only time Wallace and I ever got down and tried to discuss it like they say you should with each other, I lined out a schedule that I thought was reasonable and he thought I was kidding and laughed himself into such a good humor that he grabbed me and we rassled around and wound up doing consortium in the breakfast room, for pity sakes? I was dead serious and thought after ten years he should of been pleased with Christmas, Easter, his birthday, and our anniversary, but he laughed so hard I didn't want to look like a plumb fool and went along with the joke? My stars alive, changing sheets is one thing but scrubbing the breakfast room is another, and I couldn't even fuss because I was the one who had insisted on wall-to-wall carpet in the first place?

My hysterectomy didn't help a thing? Dr. Glass didn't do that kind of surgery himself, but he made the mistake of telling Wallace that the Atlanta doctor had left both my ovaries in? That didn't leave me much excuse, and my stars alive I've wished a million times they'd cut those things out and hung them around my neck or thrown them in the Chattahoochee River or anything but leave them in there where Wallace thought it was business as usual? After the operation, of course, I quit mennerstrating, and then I didn't even have my one week's vacation every month? I never went more than four days in my life, but I always wore a Kotex an extra week and enjoyed the rest it gave me? Wallace, bless his heart, never tumbled to it and was always sweet and kind to me during what he called "my time?"

Only time I ever heard what I'm talking about coming out of a man even mentioned was at bridge club back when I was still in it? Like I said, that's one thing ladies just don't ever talk about? Pauline Willmott, the one we used to call Pickle Polly, said her husband was going to have an operation and naturally somebody said, What kind? Bubba Willmott is fifteen years older than Polly and no telling what they were going to do to him now that he was fifty-four? The which nobody was supposed to call him "Bubba" anymore? Since progress had come and we were all having to struggle with prosperity, Bubba had got him some cards engraved for his insurance business said "J. Brooks Willmott" and all the newcomers in town called him "Brooks"? He also had taken to blow drying his hair and polishing his fingernails? Wasn't too long after that he showed up with a gold bracelet, a diamond finger ring, and you guessed it — a neck chain with his melted-down class ring on it?

When we asked about Bubba's operation, Pauline said it wasn't too serious, they were just going to trim up his prostrate glands? Dr. Glass says, "Good godamighty, there ain't but one r in that word; if you put in two r's that's how angels fall and we all know angels ain't got 'em?" To tell you the truth, when he told me that I was ordering ribs at the deli in the Big Star and I believe to my soul he'd had himself a little toddy, although Dr. Glass ordinarily doesn't drink at all? And besides, it's not like him to say *ain't*? At any rate, it is hard for me to remember everything and I am forever forgetting and saying *prostrate* and it's not like it was a word you were going to use much anyway?

Polly went on to say they weren't going to make an incision on Bubba, that this was what they called reaming him out, the which sounds awfully coarse in itself to my way of thinking? Said they were going in from below through his you know, and of course all of us did know and just nodded our heads? Then Polly said did we know about informed consent? That was before I had ever been called to jury duty, so of course I didn't? Well, Bubba's doctor had to inform him of all the consequences that might come up as a result of his operation and also get his signed permission to go ahead and do it anyhow and that is informed consent? And his wife got involved in the procedure because the doctor told Bubba that he would be able to function but he would have no emission and to be sure and tell his wife that ahead of time, but it sort of sounded like one of those new cars with lead-free gas, to me, the way they were talking about it?

One of the girls, I think it was Patricia but I'm not sure, wanted to know what in the world the doctor was talking about, and Pickle Polly just as brazen as you please up and told her? Said, and I'll never forget it, "Oh, he'll still ejaculate and everything except it'll be backwards and go into his bladder instead of into me." The very idea of hearing something like that ringing right out in the air in your very own bridge club with girls you have known all your life, for pity sakes? You see what I mean about progress and prosperity? I can tell you the very idea of Brooks Willmott ejaculating at all, let alone backwards, and having it discussed during a four spade bid for game and rubber got me so flustered and upset that I reneged when trumps led and got caught when I laid it on Patricia's ace of diamonds? But if you think that was embarrassing, you should have heard what Pickle Polly said next? She giggled and said, "I told Bubba it was fine with me because from now on he'd be the one have to get out of bed and clean up instead of me." Can you believe that? Great stars alive, I don't have any idea what this world is coming to?

Later on I got to thinking about it though, and I decided that this was real progress? Like, you know, that this operation was the Big Star of sex and might even make consortium more tolerable for me, and it looked like the way I had it figured that there were at least another twenty, twenty-five years I had to put up with it, for pity sakes? Things dragged on and three or four weeks later I called Pickle Polly up and told her I was working the crossword puzzle and what was the technical word for that operation that Bubba had had? And she said which one? Well, I have never yet lowered myself to discussing parts and members on a male, so I said, "The one he had down there?"

Down there is a nice enough term; after all, my grandmother used it, and it covers everything anybody's got any business talking about out loud anyhow, male or female? Nobody says it any more and during the mini-skirt craze it sure quit applying anyhow? I used to watch those younger women bent over the freezer section in Big Star fishing out the Lean Cuisine they wanted and wondered if my grandma wouldn't switch over now and call it *up there*? Pickle Polly said, "How many letters?" and I just grabbed a number out of the air and said, "Nine," and she said, "Must be *vasectomy*. What paper's that puzzle in? Things are sure coming to a pretty pass. I've got to run, the kids are already in the car."

Well, I had what I wanted, or at least I thought I did, and I wasn't worried one minute about getting caught because Polly has never been known to pick up a crossword puzzle in her life? Next week or so I ran into Dr. Glass in the Big Star trying to decide if the mussels were fresh enough to suit him but they weren't, and he finally settled on a pound of the little bay scallops? I pretended I was interested in the flounder although Wallace won't eat anything but bream or crappie and I have never yet seen them in any store, but I used the flounder as an excuse to visit with Dr. Glass and pick his brain a little? Finally I got around to what I wanted just about the time the boy had wrapped his scallops in that heavy paper and put a little ice in with them so's they'd be sure to stay fresh till Dr. Glass got home with them? Scallops are quick to go bad and stink on you if you don't hurry? I said, "Dr. Glass, how much trouble is it for somebody to get a vasectomy?"

He said it wasn't hardly any trouble at all nowadays, that he did them in his office under local? And then he said who was it? And I told him, Wallace, my own husband?

And he yelled at me? Yessirree bobtail, Dr. Glass yelled at me right there in the Big Star with yankees and Japanese and Cuban immigrants and Lord knows what all pushing their carts around? There was even one man in a turban with a woman who had a red dot on her forehead and a diamond in her nose and all wrapped up in a window curtain?

"Good godamighty, Myrtice, your husband doesn't need a vasectomy! You've already had a hysterectomy, for God's sake!" is what he said? I was so embarrassed I could have shriveled up like a snail with salt on him? The fish market boy heard every word of it and he's colored, too, on account of the Big Star is big on Equal Opportunity and all like that? I lowered my voice and explained to Dr. Glass that he very well knew how I felt about certain aspects of married life including consortium, this being well after Bug-Eye Purdue and I had come through in court for him and he knew I used legal terms a lot? He asked me what I thought a vasectomy for Wallace would do for my sex life, and thank the Lord he was keeping his voice down now? I have found throughout life that if you whisper to somebody in public places that nine times out of ten they will whisper back, it's just human nature?

I lowered my eyes because you just can't hardly look straight at somebody else when you're discussing things of that nature and told him that it would give me a little peace and would not interfere with Wallace and that part of his life to amount to anything? And Dr. Glass got the wrong idea. Just because I used the technical word, and how was I to know that J. Brooks Willmott had also had a vasectomy years and years ago before he had his prostrate reamed? After all, Polly and I had only been together in the bridge club going on five years, for pity sakes?

Dr. Glass didn't explain any misunderstanding on his part to me? He just raised those big old bushy eyebrows of his at me that'd look for all the world like John L. Lewis except Gallimore trims them for him every time he goes for a hair cut and for that matter burrs his ears out, too? Then he said, "Well, whatta you know! That's awfully broad-minded of you, Myrtice. I've heard about open marriages but I never thought you'd agree to one. Does he already have a girl friend? Have Wallace make an appointment; I do them on Friday afternoons."

It flashed over me all of a sudden like that Dr. Glass thought for some reason I was farming Wallace out to concubines or such and I almost opened my mouth to correct him, but the Big Star was like Grand Central Station that day and you could tell Dr. Glass was in a hurry to get in the ten items or less express lane, the which is No. 10 and stays lit up twenty-four hours a day? Can you believe the progress in this town, we've got twelve check-out lanes in the Big Star no less? I had told Wallace way back yonder when we had that discussion about Christmas and Easter which led to him ravaging me in the breakfast room that if I ever caught him messing around with another woman then one year later he would have been dead exactly twelve months, and I meant it? The very idea, for pity sakes!

I have never been one to look a gift horse in the mouth, as they say, so I called Mabel, who is almost as old as Dr. Glass and has been with him forever, and made Wallace an appointment? Then I set in to explain to Wallace that he was scheduled to have a little minor surgery done on him down there? Of course, he snorted around like a rebellious mule even with me telling him that it was done under local and there wouldn't even be an incision and it was a very simple procedure and after all, Brooks Willmott had it done? I like to lost him there, for Wallace has never been the least bit pot-gutted about Bubba Willmott and has all our insurance with J. J. Bowers; says you can't trust a man who grew up in this town all his life and then took to wearing neck chains and polishing his finger nails? He may be right, but that was not the topic, so I let it lay? I finally had to promise that I would let him have consortium twice a week for the next ten years and then once a week from then on, that Wallace being known ever since he was a little boy and sold puncheons in Colored Town off the back of his daddy's truck as a sharp trader?

I tried to jew him down to only once a week after five years but he wouldn't budge, so we finally came to terms and off he went? I should have tumbled to something being wrong before I did, now I look back on it, but I didn't? He came home from the doctor's office a little spraddle-legged but otherwise in good shape? Said Dr. Glass told him he'd already discussed this with his wife and didn't reckon he needed me to sign a form. Said Dr. Glass was in a big hurry and had 'em stacked up like cord wood and was cutting guys faster than Jess Travis with a barnyard full of pigs to neuter and charging two hundred dollars a head for doing it? Said Dr. Glass told him to come back in six weeks to check and be sure the operation was a success and in the meantime not to have no sex without a condom? I mean that Dr. Glass can line it out plain without any medical terms at all when he's dealing with some- body like Wallace who is not easily impressed in the first place and could care less in the second? Wallace told him he didn't do condoms and that six weeks had done got to be a short span to him and he'd just keep on doing without till he came back?

Said Dr. Glass looked at him right straight and squeezed his shoulder and said, "Well, son, I hope things are going to be a lot happier for you now. You be careful, though, and I would certainly advise you to be discreet. Is the next one ready, Mabel?"

I didn't want to get too specific, since I had not previously even mentioned that part of it to Wallace, but I did ask him if Dr. Glass had said anything to him about going backwards or informed consent? Wallace said no, and he also hadn't told him that every time he got up out of a chair it was going to feel like he was leaving parts of himself in the seat? I will not mention which parts because sometimes Wallace does talk coarse even to me, and suffice it to say that it is all grouped together down there anyhow?

Well, I can tell you I like to of had a fit? Six weeks went by and there I was laying up in the bed keeping my part of the bargain and trying not to think that twice a week for ten years is one thousand and forty but at least it wasn't going to be messy consortium when all of a sudden Wallace let loose and commenced just to flooding me? I have never felt so betrayed and scandalized and mad all at the same time in my life? I let out a scream and hollered for a towel? Wallace jumped up and ran for the bathroom and he was still leaking, for some of it pumped out on the bathroom floor on account of I saw it with my very own eyes and will never forget the sight if I live to be a hundred? When he turned to come back, he stepped in it and his feet went out from under him quick as lightning, since that is the slickest stuff in the world, let alone on a tile floor? He went up in the air all slow and graceful, like he used to do when he won the pole vaulting championship for the state his senior year?

Except he didn't come down in any bed of shavings? His whole body was stretched out and falling free and his neck cracked on the edge of that little old wooden stool I've got in there so's I can reach the top shelf of the linen closet where I keep the extra toilet paper at? A lot of my friends still keep theirs under the lavatory, but I had a leak one time that got a whole six-pack of Charmin soppy; so I keep mine in the linen closet? Wallace crumpled up and just laid there? He was the stillest thing I've ever seen in my whole life? You could tell before you got to him that he was also the limberest, and his arms and legs just sort of melted around into the floor and wasn't moving?

I managed to call Dr. Glass and he called the EMS and I mean they all came in a hurry? You think the Big Star is an example of progress over the A&P, you should stop and consider for a minute how much progress the EMS is over the hearse which used to be the only excuse for an ambulance we had around here? I mean, EMS worked on Wallace to a faretheewell?

All of it was sort of a dream after that? They got him breathing again and strapped to a board and all, but he wasn't conscious yet? Dr. Glass gave me a squeeze and told me to call my sister and follow the ambulance because he was going to ride in it all the way to Atlanta and the Shepherd Spinal Center? Which we did and there I practically lived for the next six months?

Turned out Wallace had severed the spinal cord in his neck and that's when I first learned what a quadriplegic is? We got off the respirator after six weeks, but he still can't move anything at all from his neck down? I have learned more than I ever cared to know because they won't quit and give up on anybody at that Shepherd Spinal Center, I am here to tell you; it is more a sign of progress than any Big Star you ever went into? I learned to bathe and to catheterize and all about bed sores, and I have even learned about machinery and lifts and elastic hose and how to turn somebody twice as heavy as you in the bed? I can get Wallace in his wheel chair and out of it all by myself without any trouble now and without hurting my back?

He can't move anything at all from his neck down but he does real well guiding his wheel chair with his tongue? I saw on TV where they have trained monkeys to help quadriplegics, but Wallace just grins and says he's got the cutest little monkey in the world already, and besides, we can't afford one?

He's right, too, you know? About not being able to afford one, I mean to say? We've used up his insurance that he had through his job and it paid over two hundred thousand dollars to the Shepherd Spinal Center and then a fortune for the lift and the van and the motorized wheel chair?

I can't leave Wallace to get a job and if I did I'm not trained to make enough that would pay a nurse and have any left over to speak of? And besides, I don't want to? It's beginning to turn out that I not only love Wallace, which I have never doubted for a minute, for pity sakes, but that I am more in love with him than ever before? I am finding out there is a heap more to consortium than I thought the first time I heard the word, for it certainly is not all sex?

We have used up our savings and have sold all the cows and the fancy cars? The only thing we have left is Wallace's disability Social Security and the land we live on that his daddy left him? It is part of the old family homestead and I don't aim to see Wallace lose it if there's any way on God's green earth I can keep from it?

That's the only reason in the world that I am going to sue Dr. Glass? He's retiring next month anyways, so it won't hurt his practice, and I found out that his insurance has what they call a tail on it? It is not anything personal against Dr. Glass at all, the only thing personal being Wallace's homestead? I'm not even upset about Dr. Glass hollering at me in the Big Star over the mangoes and papayas when I told him about the big mistake he'd made on Wallace, operating on him and all and not explaining to me that a vasectomy would not dry him up and make him go backwards? He said I was the silliest damn goose he'd ever seen and some days he wished he hadn't taken that cord from around my neck when he delivered me, and then he stormed out of the Big Star without buying a blessed thing? I still love Dr. Glass and I wouldn't lift a finger to hurt him, but I sure love me and Wallace better than I do any insurance company in the world?

I've got my plans and I have about screwed up and got my courage to where I am ready to move? Dr. Glass has got two million in malpractice just sitting there never been tapped, plus personal liability insurance you wouldn't believe, and I aim to get enough out of that insurance for me and Wallace to live out the rest of our lives on without worrying? And I'm not going to mess up anybody's homestead? I'm going to drain those insurance companies down to where they're dry as a chip, though?

I have already talked to Priss Green and he is going to take the case, him being the only lawyer I've ever watched that I think is low-down enough to represent me properly in this case? I jewed him down to a tenth when he started off wanting a half? I aim to sit there by him and pick the jury my own self because after all, who is better qualified than I am for that? He has just addressed juries, he's never personally sat on one, for pity sakes? I aim to get Bug-Eye to help me in the colored community and I'll get all the colored on the jury I can? Plus all the women?

I know the testimony may get personal and raunchy on cross-examination and all, but I can guarantee you nobody will laugh at me in that courtroom? I aim to have Wallace there every day in his wheel chair and there is nobody in the world can laugh while looking at a high school state champion propped up and strapped in a wheel chair? That jury's gonna look at us and then look at all the assets the insurance companies own, and it's not even going to be a contest!

I'm going to win that case, I can tell you right now? Loss of livelihood, lack of informed consent, loss of consortium — you name it, we got it? Especially informed consent? If Dr. Glass had called me in to sign a paper like he was supposed to instead of just trafficking around with me in the Big Star and I had found out what all that a vasectomy really is and what all it really isn't, none of this would of ever happened? I can guarantee that because if I had of known that Wallace wasn't dried up, there would of been no consortium on that night? I'd of had a cake in the oven or the worst headache you ever heard of or some ironing to finish, or something, 'cause I know all the ways to double back when I'm on the run?

No sirree bobtail, I sure wouldn't have gone to bed without a towel and then there wouldn't have been any screaming and Wallace wouldn't have jumped up before he finished and none of this would of happened? There's no way for anybody to say there was informed consent?

I hope nobody gets the idea that I don't love Dr. Glass, but what's right is right and what's wrong's wrong? And what goes around comes around, and I'm going to win, you just wait and see?

FUBAR

IT NEVER CROSSED my mind that any of them was crazy, and now I look back on it most likely they all was. There's some things a few years'll give you if you keep your eyes open and your guard up. One of them's a little sense. Maybe not a whole lot, but then a little sense is better'n none atall. I finally got myself some and that's the only reason I'm living today. Course along with the sense come a whole new set of friends, and that helped, too.

I didn't aim to get in no trouble, but at that age I guess I sure wasn't aiming to run away from any either. At the time I had done convinced myself that all I wanted was a job, and I was hell-bent and determined I was going to get one at Freddy's. I had run with the Sunday School crowd ever since my daddy died when I was eight years old. I'd joined the Boy Scouts because Elbert lived next door and his mama gave us a ride to meetings, but I never got past Tenderfoot. I was one of them boys that grow off fast, and besides I was large of my age and I didn't like being bigger than all the scouts in my troop. On top of that, all of them still had their daddies, and back then that was still an ache in my gut worse than being hungry, tired, or sick or all three at once. Mama never would cry, so that sure didn't leave no room for a big boy like me to cut loose, but there were times I'd watch my friends with their daddies, or just listen to them drop a remark about something one of them had said, and I sure wanted to sit down and cry till I hiccupped.

My granddaddy taught me to work and he learned me to be tough and not ever cry about anything. Just like he learned my mama and all her brothers and sisters. School teachers all tell you that you ought to say *taught* instead of *learned*, but my granddaddy taught me how to work and he learned me not to cry, and if anyone can't tell the difference, all I can say is one of them lets you talk to folks and guide them and the other one just needs a set jaw with an eye that can shrivel your feelings like salt in a snail's shell. By the time I was ten he had me on a tractor; by the time I was twelve I could fix anything that broke on it and I could work in the fields way past dark. I'd do it, too. I'd do it and be real proud of it, just to watch my granddaddy spit tobacco juice and hear him tell somebody at the store, "That boy works hard as any nigger you ever saw and better'n most white men you'n find nowadays. Ain't like when I was a boy," he'd go on. "All of us was raised to work and didn't know nothing else. He's got a lot of git-up and go about him." I wanted him to love me so bad I'd have done anything he wanted. That's where I learned how to work and got it so in my bones that to this day I feel guilty if I ain't working. I wanted him to love me and I wanted him to step in and be a daddy in my life. Looking back I realize he didn't do neither of them.

When I was thirteen years old I looked like a grown man and was strong as a bull. The coaches started talking football to me, but back then we didn't have a junior varsity team and wasn't no way I could play till I got to the ninth grade. I got my growth and my build from my daddy's side, but I still felt like a little kid inside. A six-foot two-inch kid. I asked my granddaddy about my daddy one day; told him I still missed him so bad I couldn't hardly stand it. My granddaddy hadn't ever mentioned my daddy to me, and yet I knew they'd worked together a long time. I could remember my daddy on the tractor and my granddaddy with a hoe, both in the same field. And I could remember my granddaddy stepping over to the store for a Co-Cola or setting for a half hour under a shade tree to fan with his straw hat while my daddy kept that tractor chugging and clanging, never letting up till dinnertime.

When I said I missed my daddy, he rared back and spit a long stream and told me that my daddy never would have amounted to nothing if it hadn't a been for him. My daddy, he said, was wild as a buck and didn't study nothing but laughing and having a good time, and he never would have settled down and held a regular job. My granddaddy set him up in the produce business and taught him all he ever learned about farming. Why, the only reason he was able to afford that nice brick house for me and my mama, which we didn't really need nohow, was because of what my granddaddy had done for him; he never would have amounted to a hill of beans otherwise. Then he told me in a real flat voice my daddy was dead and gone and I had to put the past behind me and the cantaloupes was overdue for turning.

Well, sir, I felt like the hungry man they talked about in church who wanted fish and got a serpent and then asked for bread and got nothing but a cold, hard rock. I asked about my daddy and got my granddaddy. Big I, little you. That was when I commenced thinking my granddaddy didn't really care about anybody but himself. He never even laughed about anything unless it was a put-down on somebody he didn't like, and there sure were a heap more folks that he didn't like than he did. All the things he told wound up making him look smart and important and the other fellow dumb and trifling.

I asked my mama if I had to work for Granddaddy, and she gave me a look and then set her jaw and turned off. In a minute she said one word. "No." We never mentioned it again. My mama is not somebody you do a lot of talking to, and I sure didn't dare tell her about Daddy. She never talked about him, but she's never dated another man and that in spite of her being the best looking woman in the whole county.

Anyhow, that's how I come to be looking for a job. And the reason I wanted to work at the Freddy's Fubar Filling Station was because everybody who hung out there laughed all the time. They laughed at things other folks were scared of. Seemed like all the funny folks in town swarmed to Freddy's. It was on one of the corners across from the courthouse where the two highways crossed and was easy to get to, but I always felt like the same folks would have hung out there if it had been down behind the burying ground. I know they would if Freddy had run it because he was the one that drawed them in and kept them coming. You never knew what Freddy was going to say next.

First time I personally run into anything out of the ordinary there was the first time I ever went in there. It wasn't a place that school kids felt welcome in. We all went another block on down to the drug store or else some of the tough guys would head over town a couple of blocks to Burson's Cafe where you could play pool and cuss a little and get a thumb dog from Buck. You couldn't cuss much because Buck wouldn't stand for anybody saying the Lord's name and the F word or he'd threaten you with a cue stick, but you could use all the others and he'd just grin. That and his weenies was part of growing up in our town. Buck's weenies were just regular old weenies; it was watching him fix'em that made them special. He'd grab a bun and then lick his thumb like some folks do to turn a page in the phone book. Then he'd spread the bun open with that same thumb and reach in the water and pull a weenie out with his hand and lay it in there. It was fun to watch a guy the first time he ordered a hot dog at Buck's. It wasn't no place for a candy ass, I'll tell you that.

The afternoon I went into Freddy's for a Coke was right after I started watching my granddaddy and deciding he didn't really ever think about nobody but himself. There was about a half dozen in the station, a couple of them playing checkers and Boss cleaning out his fingernails with his Barlow, and nobody paid me any attention. I got my Coke out of the box and put my nickel on the register, and about that time Lamar Hester rolled up in his sawmilling truck. He came in hollering for Freddy and said he needed a drink and needed one bad. Freddy said yeah, he had a drink and he'd let him have one, but just one. And he reached up under the register and pulled out a bottle of liquor and handed it to Lamar. I'll never forget it. Lamar stood spraddle-legged right in the middle of the filling station between the stand for maps and the butane heater. There was two fly swatters hanging on the wall next to the bathroom door underneath a calendar with a picture of Miss Turpentine Queen on it. Just the ends of the fly swatters were showing, for they hadn't been used in four months. Lamar took the cap off the bottle, throwed his head back, and swung that bottle straight up. When he did, Freddy stuck the muzzle of his pistol right behind Lamar's ear and said, "If your Adam's apple moves more'n once, I'll blow your goddam brains out the other side your head."

Well, sir, I tried to squeeze in between the fan belts and the glass case with the Moon Pies and goobers in it, but nothing happened. Lamar took one swallow and laughed and handed the bottle back, and Boss kept working on a split nail with that old pocket knife and it seemed like business as usual at Freddy's Fubar Filling Station. One of the checker players jumped a king and said, "Freddy, you got to watch that damn fellow. It's just three o'clock in the afternoon and he might be one of them alkyhawlics. Hand that bottle around, why don't you? I didn't know you had an extry one hid out or I'da done been in it."

Nobody said a word when I come in, and far as I know nobody said a word when I went out, but from that day on I was fascinated with Freddy's.

His name wasn't even Freddy. It was Carter Lee Cantrell III, but most folks in town had plumb forgot what his name really was and couldn't of told you any more'n they could sing out the real names for Boss Cleveland or Mouse Stinchcomb or Polly Parrott or Custard Mize, let alone Miss Bunch Brown. Come to find out he'd got his nickname from the Li'l Abner comic strip where everybody went around for weeks asking, "Are you ready for Freddy?" and Freddy finally turned out to be the undertaker. Carter Lee had picked up the name because he could outdrink all his buddies, and when they'd get to talking about how liquor was going to kill him, he'd brag that when all of them was dead, he'd embalm 'em in half his Old Crow and drink the rest. And then he'd laugh and yell out, "Are you ready for Freddy?" And the name caught on.

When he took over the filling station, he personally put the sign up, and when I found out what Fubar had meant to Freddy and everybody else who went off to World War II, I nearly died and thought for sure the missionary ladies would run him out of town for it. But nobody ever objected that I heard of, and I finally decided that either the missionaries didn't know what it meant or that it wouldn't have been genteel to notice it. Sort of like you're not supposed to notice or snicker if somebody poots when there's company around, although your mama will frail hell out of you if you slip up and do it when there's just homefolks there. Mama don't talk much but she's hell on pooting.

I got up my nerve to go back to the Fubar a coupla days later. The same two guys was playing checkers and far as I knew they played there every day but Sunday. They didn't neither one ever go to church but they'd been raised not to play checkers on the Lord's day. There was a different crowd warming the butane heater and they was laughing at old Harley Prince. There was a bottle going around in a sneaky way with folks turning it up but looking sideways out the window while they swallowed. It was against the law to drink in public back in them days and we had a marshall in town who'd make a case against you in a minute if he caught you at it. Harley Prince wasn't in the Fubar but he had just left and they was all laughing at what he'd said. Harley was a newcomer to our town, hadn't been there more'n ten or twelve years, and he'd been to college and smoked Parliament cigarettes and all that, but still he hung out at the Fubar now and then. He talked fine proper English all the time and he'd get off these real good zingers without ever cracking a smile. He didn't rightly have no business hanging out in the Fubar, what with his college education and all, but he hadn't been raised here and didn't know any better.

Seems he was at the heater and had just took a drink when Hardup Betsill come in. Hardup always deserved a heap of credit, I thought, for growing up in the middle of ten sisters who babied him to death and still getting in the produce business and winding up rich. The only thing was he never could keep from bragging. Lots of times he was lying, too.

Once they said he was with a crowd of fellows in Atlanta and they all told the waitress that Hardup was going to pay the bill, and he was good-natured and said he would but that she'd have to get him a blank check. And when she asked him what bank he wanted it on, Hardup said, "It don't make no difference, I got money in all of them." Folks in town just took things like that as his ways and didn't pay it no attention. Except to laugh at him.

That afternoon he'd wandered into Fubar's and bought himself a pack of crackers and a Pepsi because his third wife wouldn't let him drink no liquor and she was about thirty pounds heavier'n him and twice as mean, so he minded real good. He turned around to Harley Prince and said, "Harley, I've told everybody else but I ain't seen you. Did you know I'd bought my wife a house in Florida?"

And Harley dead-panned it and said in that kind of lofty way he had, "No, I didn't, Hardup, but I'll tell you right now if she's going to run it herself you'll lose money."

And it went plumb over Hardup's head. He said, "Oh, it ain't for rent, it's just for pleasure." Hardup is pretty slow about everything but produce, and since Harley Prince never cracked a smile but just said, "Indeed?" everybody else in the Fubar felt like they weren't real men if they give it away by laughing, so they all held it till Hardup and Harley Prince had done walked out together.

That was the day I asked Freddy for a job and that was the day he give me one. I felt like I was going to belong somewheres and on account of that I was going to amount to something.

It didn't take me long to figure out that except for Hardup everybody that hung out at Freddy's Fubar had one thing in common and that was liquor. Freddy had liquor hid out everywhere and the only place that made me nervous was the tire casings. If you snatched a tire off the pile without feeling around in it first, you were liable to sling a bottle out and break it, and that created more commotion than a weasel in the hen house for sure and certain.

Most of the regulars brought their own, but Freddy was always good for a drink if any of them had run out. Freddy hisself killed two quarts every day. He drank vodka before dinner time and bourbon in the afternoon, and I never saw him when he was thick-tongued or staggering. He usually had a smart answer for everything and laughed at things you'd never thought was funny till Freddy got hold of them.

Him and Lamar Hester used to crank up and laugh at each other every day about six o'clock. Lamar'd come in from the sawmill and set there till he got to feeling good, and then him and Freddy would start jowering with each other about who was going to live the longest. Freddy and his folks went to the old doctor in town, who had moved in as a young man but hadn't ever really been looked on as anything but a newcomer cause he wasn't born here and even had a wife who come from Michigan. Lamar's family had all took up with the young doctor. He'd been raised in our county and come home to practice medicine, and he might still have a lot to learn, which he did, but at least he was one of us. Old Doc talked proper all the time and wouldn't get out of bed at night unless you was born a Calhoun or a Carmichael. Young Doc was the one everybody took their field hands to and Lamar liked him because he'd see his sawmill hands when they was sick or cut. Old Doc said "whiskey" and Young Doc said "likker." Each one of 'em said that was what was going to kill Freddy and Lamar. Freddy and Lamar would get to laughing about it and turn their bottles up. They even had a bet about who was going to live the longest. Only thing kept 'em from putting the money up was they couldn't agree on somebody they could trust to hold the stakes. They talked tough but you got the feeling they was friends.

"Here you come as wall-eyed as a hung-up dog and it barely six o'clock in the evening." Freddy said one day. "That means you ain't got your own bottle again and that you're ready for Freddy."

"Here's my bottle, you spindle-legged tumble turd," Lamar fired back. "I even brought you a drink, and don't say I never gave you nothing. Punch Stinchcomb made this batch his own self. Run it through a radiator down on Ginger Cake Creek and caught it in his mama's slop jar. I think he might have even rinched it out first. It's been aging ever since yesterday and it's guaranteed to clear your head and shrink your liver. You look like you're nine months pregnant and you're the one what's ready for Freddy. Drink up."

"Shut up, boy. That whiskey's going to kill you. Your eyes are redder'n a fox's ass in pokeberry season."

"You're flat out wrong, Freddy. Whiskey's going to get you. Likker's what's going to kill me, and I got a medical opinion to back me up. But I still bet you five hundred dollars I outlive you by at least ten days. Have a swallow!"

"Lamar, I wouldn't drink that shit if you had a gun drawed on me with the hammer cocked. I've always heard that the worst liquor ever came through this county was back in thirty-two when Judge Ballard paid off an election bet with a gallon that'd been made out of ice cream cones. Even Ferrol McFarland and Lawrence Hightower couldn't drink it. Mr. Lawrence told me he couldn't get it past his nose even when he held it out at arm's length and come in fast as a wood duck. That stuff you've got is stinking up the whole station. You'll have to drink it in the bathroom or under the grease rack."

"Trouble with you, Freddy, is you done drunk whiskey instead of likker until you ain't nothing but a sissy. You don't know bad likker. In New Guinea oncet I had buddied up with a coupla yankees. Wasn't nothing else in the outfit to buddy with or I never would of sunk that low. They was always making fun of me being from Georgia and the way I talked and all. Nobody but the officers had any alcohol on the whole island. Them two yankees and me got hold of a whole mess of dehydrated potatoes and some sugar from one of the mess sergeants and set us up a still out in the jungle. They'd never heard of such, but there sure wasn't anything else to do on that goddam island. I mixed up the mash and rigged a condenser out of parts from the motor pool and we let it sit for about a week before we decided it was time to run it. It was a little green but the weather was awful hot and we had to run it. Now that was bad likker.

"One of them boys was from the Bronx and other from Brooklyn and they had trouble drinking it, but I shamed 'em into it. I drunk the most of it trying to set them an example, and when I come to you know where I was? I was tied up like a hog, slung from a pole with my head hanging down backwards and a bunch of barefooted savages was trotting through that jungle with me. The soles of their feet was tougher'n Biscuit Tarpley's. Come to find out them fuzzies come by the still when I passed out. Bronx and Brooklyn sold me to them. The CO seen Bronx and Brooklyn come walking across camp rubberlegged and laughing and stopped them. He had got used to seeing three of us wherever one of us went.

" 'Where's Georgia?' he asked. And they giggled and he says, 'You're drunk! Where's Georgia?' And they commenced dying alaughing and told him I'd passed out and they'd sold me to some black folks and when I woke up I'd be a slave and that'd teach me a lesson about being from Georgia. The which is a bunch of bull shit, for none of the Hesters far as I know ever had no slaves back in the old days, and I sure as hell wouldn't be bothered with owning one of the sorry bastards now; it's all I can do to pay 'em sawmill wages and kick they asses home ever night. You couldn't give me a slave. But yankees think we all used to be up to our elbows and butt-holes in them and they ain't nothing going to change a yankee's mind about the South. Ever.

"Thank God the Captain stepped in. He hollered, 'Hell, these people don't own slaves. They're going to eat him.' And Brooklyn laughed louder and told old Bronx I'd be upset but that I'd probably think it was better'n none atall, and the Captain plumb exploded and said they'd have to find me before I was carried into a village or it'd be too late, that they was gonna cook me and eat me. And he got up a detail and found the path I was on and rescued me. He had to buy me back; those spooks didn't want to turn me loose. They was bandy-legged and fuzzy-headed and all of 'em had big thick scars they'd cut into they faces and sharp pointy teeth. One of 'em had a chicken bone through his nose, and none of 'em spoke no English to amount to nothing. The Captain wound up trading three machetes and two sacks of sugar for me and throwed in two boxes of matches for boot. I had the worst headache I ever had in my life."

Freddy laughed, "It's a damn good thing for you that captain was in charge, Lamar. If it had been me they'd never have got but one machete and no sugar at all. Hell, no wonder the government's nearly bankrupt; squandering money and overpaying for sorry trash like that."

"You kiss Old Rusty, Freddy. What hacked me was that Brooklyn and Bronx had sold me in the first place for only two coconuts and a string of beads. And come to find out those natives do eat folks. They call it 'long pig,' and that's what everybody in the outfit called me after that night, 'cept they finally just made it plain 'Pig Hester' and it followed me plumb through the service. Here, take a drink outa my bottle."

By then Freddy'd done got to where he could drink anything.

"Don't care if I do. How'd you get even with Brooklyn and Bronx?"

"I never did. When we left New Guinea, Brooklyn got hit in the leg going in on a beach head. Bronx and me dragged him through the water and commenced trying to run with him and a sniper got Bronx square between the eyes and then sprayed Brooklyn's guts all over my face and he died in my arms hollering Jesus and cussing Japs. Ain't nobody called me 'Pig' since and better not, by God, nobody ever do it again. Hand me your bottle. Mine's empty. You're right about my liquor stinking, but it don't smell as bad as Brooklyn's guts did."

With that he threw his bottle up against the wall and broke it into a thousand pieces, and Freddy laughed fit to kill and hollered, "That ain't no fireplace, but kill this'n and throw it, too. You got a home in the Fubar."

Now, you think after that I'd ever be satisfied working anywhere else? I could have played football for three years and plowed cantaloupes for twenty and missed all that story.

One of my favorite folks was ole man John Jenkins. He come in ever morning at eight o'clock just before I left for the school house, got a Co-Cola and a sack of roasted goobers without speaking to nobody, and locked hisself in the toilet. He was always still in there when I left for school and I asked Freddy once what time did he come out, and the Fubars started watching and he always stayed in the toilet exactly an hour. Freddy took to banging on the door ever now and then when he'd think about it and hollering, "Whatcha doing in there, Mr. John? Everthing coming out all right?" But old man John always stayed his full hour and when he did come out, he still didn't speak to nobody and just walked on out the Fubar. I never saw him in the house or out lest he had his hat on. He died in his sleep one night. Lamar Hester asked Freddy did he reckon the Co-Colas killed him and said he'd of been safer drinking liquor. Freddy laughed, but every morning after that between eight and nine he locked the restroom door. If a stranger came in and wanted to use it, Freddy would bang on the door and holler, "Mr. John, everthing coming out all right?" Then he'd tell the man he'd have to wait till nine o'clock cause Mr. John was in the john. Harley Prince said he was glad Mr. John's last name hadn't been Trapper.

Freddy always opened up the Fubar hisself and heap of times I knew he'd slept there all night. It wasn't that he got too drunk to go home. I never did figure out why he'd sleep in that old station now and then. I guess he stayed drunk all the time but he never seemed drunk to me, just didn't give a damn and made jokes about most everything. Real early one morning this car load of folks from out of town pulled up and Freddy came prancing out the station all dressed out in one them wide hats and a shawl with a hole in it that somebody had brought him back from Mexico. He was running forwards two steps and backwards one and bowing from the waist. He had a ukulele in his hand and when the driver rolled down his window, he bowed real deep and hollered, "Good morning! Are you ready for Freddy?" and the driver acted real dignified and said, "Fill it up, please."

And Freddy said, "Fill it up? Fill it up? I can play you a tune, but I can't fill'er up for another half hour." And the man smiled real nice and wanted to know how come, and Freddy hollered out, "Cause, by God, it's too early in the morning! I ain't even puked yet!" Then he laughed like crazy and that's the first time I ever saw a fifty-year-old man scratch off. Most of our trade was local.

That was also the morning Harley Prince insulted the Masons. Masons was the only thing in our town stronger'n the Baptists, and everybody that amounted to anything seemed like was in the Lodge, and they was also the only people, the way I could see it, who took themselves as serious as the Baptists. Bobby Lee Bowers had worked up to Shrine and come by the Fubar selling tickets to the barbecue they had every year up at the Lodge Hall. Everybody in the Fubar had bought at least one. Harley Prince walked in all straight-back and dignified, and Bobby Lee walked up and said, "Mr. Prince, I'd like to sell you a ticket," and Harley said, "A ticket to what, my good man?" And Bobby Lee said, "To the

Masonic barbecue." And Harley barks out, "Sorry. I do not support Communist Front organizations." And everybody sucked in their breath except Freddy. He let out a laugh and whooped, "You're really ready for Freddy." Then he grabbed his pistol and shot straight up and everybody cleared out for a while.

Hawk Forts was the mayor and he wasn't a regular except on Monday and Friday mornings. He had the concession on the condrum machine in the men's toilet, and he took out the quarters on Monday and put in the rubbers on Friday. The Forts family had a heap of money and at one time had owned nearly the whole town, but everything was tied up in the estate and Hawk sold them rubbers to get his spending money. He got elected mayor every year and that paid twenty dollars a month. Harley Prince said when he observed the qualifications for public office in our town that he did believe he would offer for City Council his own self, even if he hadn't been born and raised there. Freddy kept at him and promised he'd support him, and Harley actually announced. He might have overcome Freddy's endorsement and insulting the Masons and got elected, too, because his opponent didn't amount to nothing and was sorry as gully dirt, if he'd only kept his mouth shut.

About a week before election, Mel Johnson tracked him down in the Fubar and gave him a check and that did it. Mel had the insurance agency, and the Baptist preacher's wife had run into Harley's car when his wife was taking their little girl to school and tore up a fender. Mrs. Prince was pregnant again and Mel Johnson had the preacher's car insured. When the check came in, he hunted Harley up and give it to him because Mel was always real prompt and dotted his i's and crossed his t's. And Harley looked at the check and then swung around to everybody in the Fubar and announced real formal, "I accept this check for damages to my automobile, but I proclaim before God and these witnesses here assembled that if my unborn child grows up to be a Baptist, I still have a claim against Johnson Insurance Agency." Freddy got so tickled he shot twice that morning, but sure enough

Harley got beat. He come by the Fubar on election night and took so drunk they had to take him home. He still talked real formal, drunk or not.

I'd been working for Freddy about six, seven months I reckon; at any rate I'd done turned fifteen and I was muscled out more'n ever and was six-three and shaved every day. Whenever one the Fubars happened to notice me, they'd say I looked like my Daddy and that always made me feel good and I wouldn't have left Freddy by now for nothing. On a Friday evening just before supper time, there was a crowd of Fubars there. It was summer time and they was setting on benches out front and it wasn't good dusk-dark yet. Bob Marston had just come up and somebody said to him, ain't it been a pretty day. Bob was bad to look on the dark side of things ever since he'd been sheriff all them years and had to put up with criminals and also their kinfolks on visiting days, and he hardly ever smiled anymore. That evening he had just dropped by for a minute. You could tell because he didn't have his bridge across his upper front and his tushes was all that kept his upper lip from sucking in all the way, and he was in his undershirt with his galluses hanging down. And he growled back, "Yeah, it has been so far, but it ain't too late yet for some sonbitch to come along and mess it up."

About that time here come Harley Prince and somebody asked how he was and he said he was very upset and Freddy says, "How come?" And Harley looked real mournful and says, "I discovered that my wife doesn't trust me." Freddy comes back with, "Whatcha mean?" And Harley says, "She's gone to visit her sister in Birmingham and I just found out that she took the diaphragm with her." Well, sir, Freddy got out the pistol and shot and everbody laughed, including me, although it was going on two years before I caught on to what was funny. Bob Marston laughed for once till he nearly choked and said, "I just be goddam." After that everybody passed their bottles around and broke up and started home.

When Lamar Hester drove up that evening wasn't nobody left but Freddy and me and Hardup and Burdell the black boy that Freddy'd hired to wash cars since I'd built up his mechanic business so much I didn't have time to wash and shine. Burdell was about forty, forty-five years old and would probably have worked for nothing because he couldn't hold no regular job, and I'd caught him a hundred times sneaking drinks from Freddy's bottles. I hadn't never told on him and he was my friend as much as he could be anybody's friend. He'd had so many fits his brains was addled like a setting of eggs in a thunderstorm. He had to take pills every day to keep from having spells, and he still stayed with his mama.

I'd found out a long time ago that black folks don't "live" anywhere. They "stay." You ask one of 'em where he lives, and he may have been in the same house for twenty, twenty-five years, and he'll say, "I stay on Redwine Road." Burdell's mama worked in the grammar school lunch room, and every now and then she'd drop by the Fubar to bring her boy his pills when she found out he'd forgot them.

That particular evening Lamar Hester got on my case. "What kind likker you drink, boy? Or has Freddy got you fubarred on whiskey?" I sort of sidled off and grinned and never said nothing. But he wouldn't leave it alone. "Freddy, big as that boy is it's time he had a drink." Now I hadn't ever had the slightest desire in the world to even taste whiskey, but somehow he had me on the spot and feeling like I wasn't tough.

"Come on, boy, you don't even have to drink my white likker; old Freddy'll give you some of his bottled in bond, I bet."

"Lamar," I said, "I don't want no drink. If I did, I'd take one."

"What's matter? You fraid you'll be one them alkyhawlicks from the Fubar? You scared you'll turn out to be like Freddy?"

That struck me wrong. "Freddy ain't no alcoholic. He can quit any time he wants to. And what's wrong with being like Freddy? I wouldn't mind that atall."

Lamar laughed so hard he sprayed spit five feet. "He'n quit any time he wants to! I told that to Young Doc oncet and he said, 'You dumb bastard. That's what every alkyhawlic in the country says. Go ahead and drink yourself to death; nobody else can stop you.' And that's been eight years ago and I been doing my dead-level best to follow his advice, but them dumb damn doctors don't know everything; I ain't dead yet. Freddy don't want to quit! But you're wrong! Ain't no way you'd want to turn out like that bird-legged, pussel-gutted turd head. You probably couldn't hold your likker nohow."

I'd done got hot. "I'n drink good as any of you if I take a notion. And I'n put it down fast as any of you, too."

"Boy, you done lied now. When I's your age I killed a quart in ten minutes on a bet. You ain't in the class with no real drinking man."

"That ain't nothing. Anybody could do that."

"Awright, you muscle-bound young smart aleck. I got a hundred dollars says you can't swallow no quart of likker in ten minutes."

Freddy had a quart of rum in the old tire casing by the water cooler. I don't know what come over me but I grabbed it out and broke the seal and turned it up and never let it down till it was gone. It didn't take two minutes. Lamar Hester let out a yell.

"Foul! I call foul! That had to be colored water. You couldn't do that."

Freddy says, "You're wrong. That was a brand-new bottle. And you gotta pay me for that in addition to his hundred." Lamar hollered. "I been took. Can't no kid ain't never had his first drink do that in a thousand years."

I reached in the hole in the plaster down behind the candy machine and pulled out a new quart of Freddy's vodka. Mr. Boston it was.

"I still got five minutes. I'll show you," I told him.

To this day I don't remember getting more'n half way through that second bottle, but Freddy told me later that I drained it and then made it to the grease pit before I fell. He said in about ten minutes it come back. Said it shot straight outa me like a busted hydrant. Went ten feet out and he thought it'd never stop. Young Doc said later that was the only reason I didn't die, but it was three, four years before I told him about it.

I slept till Sunday. Freddy and Lamar had dragged me to Freddy's cot in the store room and Freddy called my mama and told her Mr. Laverne Williams and his boy had come through and invited me to Steenhatchie, Florida, to fish for the weekend. Told her we'd tried to call her and Freddy had give me ten dollars and permission to go. Freddy said he'd rather have faced two mad dogs and a turpentined bobcat than my mama if he took me home drunk. He was more'n likely right.

When I woke up on Sunday I felt worse'n hell. The bad part was not remembering. Freddy was feeding me Red Rock ginger ale and tomato soup, and I noticed his hand shaking and asked him what was the matter.

"You got to me, kid. I ain't ever before in my whole life had anybody say they wanted to be like me. And I decided maybe I am an alcoholic and that I'm by God going to quit. I haven't had a drink since Friday night when you fell out and scared the living shit out of me. I can quit cause now I want to quit."

It was Tuesday morning before they had to take him off. I'd always heard that you saw snakes when you got the DT's, but Freddy didn't. He had grasshoppers. He'd be talking good sense to you and then all of a sudden he'd jump and yell and start brushing on his shoulder or snatching the air in front of his eyes or even picking 'em off your sleeve. At first everybody thought Freddy was just going on with his foolishness, but then the sweat commenced to pouring off him in gallons. Lamar Hester and Hawk Forts was alaughing and pretending to stomp the grasshoppers on the floor and Lamar was really having a good time.

"Freddy, you're a real sissy. Comes from drinking whiskey instead of likker. I got the shakes and horrors that time they locked me up for a week where I couldn't git at no likker, and I had snakes in my cell crawling all over me. In and out the bars. And even out the nose of another prisoner. What kinda man sees hoppergrasses? You want I should get the fly swatter for you"

I could see Freddy's eyes. The blue was all gone and all you could see was the black. He was scared to death and the sweat had soaked every thread on him and he was beginning to blow when he breathed. I sneaked around to the phone and called Bob Marston. Freddy didn't have no kin left in town except for an old maid cousin, and she worked in Atlanta at the tag department and was so big in the Baptist Church I sure didn't want to call her. Bob growled and grumbled but he took care of it.

They had to cuff Freddy to take him off, but I told him I'd run the Fubar till he came back and he hollered to me that he still wanted to quit and wasn't no grasshoppers gonna make him break his promise to me.

They took him to the VA Hospital. Bob came back by the Fubar and told me they put him on the floor where they had the alcoholics and mental cases, and when he left they had Freddy in a strait jacket and you could hear him hollering two floors down even on the elevator.

"They got him in a semi-private room with a goddam nigger. That's the U.S. gov'mint for you. Us veterans go off and fight for this country and then they don't respect none of our rights atall. I don't know what this country's coming to. Looks like it's going to be the schools next, in spite of hell."

Well, the black man did bother Freddy but not the way Bob thought it would. Which that word *nigger* is one I have done got completely out of my vocabulary. Ain't nothing in the world would make me madder'n being one except for somebody to call me one. You got to consider other people's feelings in this world. Now I'm trying to remember to say "mobile home" instead of "trailer;" folks have done got touchous about that. Freddy's room was right next to the elevator, and every time it would stop at that floor the elevator bell would go "ding." Hardup said it sure did sound for all the world like a car pulling into the Fubar. And every time the bell would go "ding," Freddy would pull and jerk at the strait jacket and try to sit up in bed. He'd look over at his roommate in the other bed and yell, "Get up off your goddam black ass and check the oil and tires and wipe that windshield!" And the poor fella didn't know what to think and would lay there and pull the sheet over his head and get as far over on his bed as he could.

This went on for three days no matter how much medicine they give Freddy. The nurses were about to go crazy and I guess the poor black man did, from hearing it so much. When Freddy finally come to himself and quieted down and they took him out of restraints, all of a sudden the black man went wild. They had to put him in the strait jacket and every time the elevator would go "ding" he'd rare up and yell over at Freddy, "Get up off your goddam white ass and check the oil and tires and wipe that motherfucking windshield!" And Freddy would pull the sheet over his head and edge away as far as he could.

Freddy sent me word that he hadn't forgot his deal with me and for me to clean out the station as only I would know how to do. I knew what he meant, and I got shed of every bottle he had hid out, including the one behind the trap door in the ladies' rest room and the one buried in a box under the drum of used motor oil.

Like I didn't have trouble enough, Burdell the black boy got hold of one of the bottles and also forgot to take his medicine at the same time. Him and I was there by ourselves, and I had put him to work on a lube job while I patched a tire so Mrs. Turnipseed could pick it up on her way back from Ruby's Grocery. I heard this godawful noise like a wild animal crying on a werewolf show, and Burdell was sort of in a half crouch with both arms swinging back and forth like Mr. Muggs. He kept on with that high-pitched wail and his eyes was looking plumb through me and it scared me so bad I couldn't help but start to run. And about that time I heard this crash and looked back. He had fell over and cut half his face in two on a tire rim and was jerking and flopping like a chicken when you wring its neck. I was afraid he'd trip the hydraulic catch and the car'd squash his brains out, so I run back and snatched him out through the blood and grease, and he was still jerking and flopping and chewing his tongue. You could tell he'd wet his overalls and it smelled like he'd done the other, too. I knew better'n to call Old Doc, even if Freddy did use him and it was Freddy's station and all. I got ahold of Young Doc and he come and give Burdell a shot in the vein and stopped his fitting and then called the colored hearse and sent him off to Grady Hospital. That was my first and only epileptic fit.

I'd of quit then, but I couldn't let Freddy down. The Fubars turned out not to be so damn funny when you had to do all the work at the station and were having to step over them to get it done. Freddy left out the hospital before they wanted him to. The black man had got to him with that "goddam white ass" business, not to mention the "motherfucking windshield" and he flat out left. He walked out that hospital in nothing but a split-tail hospital gown and showed up in the Fubar right after sun-up one morning barefooted as a yard dog with no drawers on and nothing but little strings holding that gown together in the back. He never would tell how he managed to get out of that hospital and plumb across Atlanta and back home in that outfit. He swore he couldn't remember, but it's something I have always wondered about. Freddy could talk anybody into anything when he set his mind to it.

He didn't drink no whiskey. First news you know he had a new Co-Cola sign. It left off the Fubar and just said Freddy's Filling Station. It had been up over a week before anybody noticed it. Harley Prince said, "We have this day sacrificed honesty and diluted euphoria, I see," and that was the end of it. That Harley Prince was educated. Not that he ever done anything with it but he sure as hell had it. He always walked straight and toted his head too. He has been a credit to our town.

Lamar Hester didn't let nothing change him. "What's the matter with you, Freddy? Them doctors get to you? They die, too, you know. It's just that when we do it, it's the likker what kills us. They don't actually live any longer, it just seems that way. You don't really want to quit, you're just trying to prove you can."

Within two weeks Lamar Hester was dead. He'd set up a sawmill way the hell out in Shakerag, and he commenced throwing up blood 'bout middle of a Monday morning. They had to bring him out in a logging truck and he died in Young Doc's office before he could get the ambulance. Young Doc told Lamar's brother that he had varicose veins coming out his liver and wrapped around his isogaphus and he never stood a chance. Freddy closed the filling station and put a wreath on the door for Lamar's funeral.

Next day Lamar's oldest sister, the one who never married and lived over in Jonesboro, come by the station. She was pale but she wasn't but a little red-eyed from crying, and when I told her that Freddy had gone to the post office, she give me an envelope for him.

"Please give this to Mr. Cantrell. Lamar gave it to me five years ago and made me promise on the family Bible I'd deliver it when he died."

The envelope had printed on it in pencil, "You win. Have one for me." When Freddy opened it, there was five one-hundred-dollar bills so crisp and new-looking you couldn't hardly get them apart. I heard Freddy say, "Well, I'll be a son of a bitch. Why hadn't I thought of doing that?" Then a minute later he said, "He really was ready for Freddy."

For two, three days Freddy was right quiet and didn't laugh much. I figured he was grieving the best he could for Lamar and I felt like he really needed me, so I worked hard as I could and never said nothing. The Fubars were pretty quiet, too.

Then one afternoon Freddy took drunk. Where he got it I don't know, for I am sure and certain he never left the station. I reckon I had missed some when I was cleaning up. I have said that Freddy could take a drink and never show it, but this time he got falling down, limber-legged, tongue-tied drunk. I guess it was from being dried out so long. Anyhow, he finally passed out and I put him to bed on the cot in the stock room.

When I got to work the next morning, he was up and sober and had swept out the tire bay, and I thought everything was all right again. Then 'bout seven o'clock I come through to get a screw driver and caught him turning his bottle up. It wasn't more'n a third empty, so I knew he'd just started on it that morning. I never said nothing about it and he acted like I hadn't seen him nor him me.

Harley Prince come by for a minute and one of the checker players said, "Welcome back from your fishing trip, Harley. Did you catch anything?" And Harley said, "I'm not sure. I'm on my way to the doctor to find out." And Freddy laughed like always.

I got busy pumping gas and lining out work for Burdell and it was about eight-thirty before I realized Freddy wasn't around. I looked in the station and the rest room door was locked. I even knocked on the door, to keep up tradition and all, and said, "Mr. John, Mr. John, everything coming out all right?" Then I saw Freddy's keys laying on top the cash register, and I knew he was somewhere around, for he had locked the toilet door as usual. I wondered how come he had laid his keys down, for he usually kept 'em on his belt with a chain, but 'bout that time the bell went "ding" and I went running out to check the oil and tires and wipe the windshield.

Later on the checker players had settled in and one of them yelled at me, "Where's Freddy? It's nine-thirty and the door's still locked and I need to step out."

I grabbed up the keys and unlocked the door and there was Freddy. I took one look and commenced dying laughing. He had his head twisted way over to one side and was bugging his eyes almost outa his head and was running his tongue out at me like some kid playing Ugly Face. He was the tallest and skinniest and stretched outest I'd ever seen anybody, and all of a sudden he sorta swung around real gentle and passive like and I saw that he was hanging from the pipes by an electric cord. I realized that he'd stepped off the toilet seat and that he'd meant to do it and I hollered so loud they never did find all the checker buttons.

They sent for Bob Marston and Young Doc, and a bunch of 'em cut Freddy down and took him away. I was sitting on the cement propped against a gas tank crying my guts out. I couldn't help it and couldn't stop it and I didn't even think about who might see me. Young Doc come over to me and squatted down a while and didn't try to say anything. Just patted me. I finally managed to tell him how horrible it was that I had laughed. Then he told me that he'd been called to a heap of hangings and always had the same impulse, said the face of a hanging victim was ridiculous and one we usually associated with comedy, that nobody thought of sticking your tongue out in a tragedy. Then he left, and directly I picked myself up and went home.

Well, I'm playing football now. Coach is proud, says he'll get two good years out of me. I'm staying full-time with my granddaddy. We've got the best crop of turnip salad he's ever seen and we start cutting it for market on Monday. After that the collards will come off.

My granddaddy is still mean and tight and he still don't ever think about anybody but hisself. It don't bother me anymore that he won't cry. I'm cried out my own self. For the rest of my life, I suspect. We don't laugh much, neither.

He hasn't changed. I'm staying with him because nobody else will and because whether he'll admit it or not, he needs me.

He may not have changed, but I have. I have come to see that in his own way he loves me. He loves me because he does need me. And I need him, too. You know why? I need him because I love him. There's a difference there. I know that, even if I don't understand it yet. Someday I will.

Porphyria's Lover

I HAVE HAD plenty of time to think. The rain set in early tonight. We've had so much wind off and on that there are probably some trees down between here and the lake. Other than the wind and the rain, there hasn't been a sound and I've had nothing to do but think.

I haven't moved a muscle for hours; at first for fear his head wouldn't stay balanced on my shoulder, and then it seemed like I went into a trance or something and couldn't force myself to lift so much as a finger. I've been sitting dead still in the dark all night long and there's been nothing to do but think. And think and think. I'll probably have the damnedest crick in the world, to say nothing of being stiff and sore, but the thinking is over. It's getting gray outside and the rain has about let up and I know what I have to do. I've considered everything. This is it. Eliot was right when he said life goes out, not with a bang, but a whimper. To hell with him. What did he know?

There are not many men around who played football in high school, got an AB from Suwanee, and taught English at Stratford

Academy before they married rich. It wasn't just rich, either; I had plenty of chances before if that had been all I was looking for. She had to have more than money and looks if I was going to marry one. God knows I'd cracked more than my share of little wriggling cheerleaders and homecoming queens and beauty contest winners. In fact, the guys always kidded me about being a stud and I guess, to tell the truth, I have been.

I work out enough to keep good delineation and my waist is still thirty-four. I've been told so often that I'm good-looking that I long ago decided it's true, and it's been years since I made a pass and got turned down. Of course, that's part of my image as a stud; I learned in high school and college that if you pretend indifference or unawareness long enough the chick will wind up approaching you. People are just naturally more appreciative of something they have to beg for. Then it's quick and simple, ashes hauled, over and done with. Biff bam, thank you ma'am, and let's cut another watermelon in another corner of the field. That way they never get to you, never get to know more than that they've been well laid by an educated, good-looking athlete. They keep wondering what you're really like and what makes you tick. It's a real gas to be polite and just barely friendly at the country club to a slit you've screwed through the mattress three nights before. It drives them crazy. I've never been what anybody could call pussy-whipped even one time in my life. By God, I am a stud.

The first night I met Tiffany I knew she was the one I was going to marry. That is, if she checked out to have as much money as she had class. I was bored with bedding chicks and tired of Stratford Academy. It was time to make a career change and also to settle down. I was coming up on thirty, and if you're not married by then people begin to think you're gay. I've been accused all along of never looking out for anybody but No. 1, which doesn't make a helluva lot of sense to me. After all, in the ultimate analysis, who else are you supposed to look after? I've just got the sense to do it a little quicker and a whole lot slicker than most people. Like I said, Tiffany had class.

When I found out about her old man and that she was an only child, I mapped out my campaign and we were married six months later. It was the easiest thing I ever did and also the smartest. I had it made for life. High rolling on Easy Street. Nobody ever had more fun than I. It's hard to believe you can ride that high and fall this far, and that's a lot of what I've been thinking about all night.

Mr. Adkins was easy. I'd maneuvered around enough professors and headmasters to know the value of courtesy and pretended deference, how to kiss a little ass and phrase questions just right to make an older guy feel important. The trick is when you're around one who's really as important as Harlowe Adkins, the big corporation president, that you remember everyone else is doing exactly the same thing to him and you've got to be a little understated and innocent about it. I played it cool. I put the rush on Tiffany. I didn't look at another woman the whole time, and if I made a few trips out of town it was always very discreet and under an assumed name. Whenever I wound up in any place where they asked your name. Most places like that you didn't need anything but your first name anyhow. I always used "Roscoe." That's the private name I gave my dick when it started growing and got so important, and it always amused me to hear some total stranger try to get cute and intimate with a name like that.

Tiffany was head over heels in love with me within three weeks, but that was a foregone conclusion. You couldn't expect her to resist a good-looking guy five years older than she who was built like a Greek god and could handle headwaiters and discuss music, art and poetry. She was lithe and blonde with tiny ankles and high cheek bones and she moved everywhere like an aristocrat. We were the most gorgeous couple in the state and heads really turned when we went to the beach. I was proud of her.

Like I've said, Mr. Adkins was easy. All he wanted was the assurance that Tiffany wasn't going to be swept off her feet by some lazy fortune hunter who, as he put it to me once when we were drinking together, wasn't worth his weight in goose shit. I've always been a high energy person and worked hard; there's nobody I ever worked for who wouldn't give me a super rec. On top of that I went to church at least twice a month and nobody in town had ever heard of Roscoe and his exploits. Mr. Adkins within two months got me out of Stratford and put me in his bank. I worked up so fast you wouldn't believe it. It wasn't long before Mr. Adkins bragged on me and promised me the presidency in a year or two. That's when he told me to start calling him Harlowe. You'd better believe I liked that. By then Tiffany and I were talking marriage and I was scared to death she was going to want me to call him "Daddy." I've never called anybody that. I never will.

Right after that I made it a point very unobtrusively to be changing clothes in the bathhouse with Harlowe and let him get a look at old Roscoe. I found out a long time ago that men are just automatically impressed and a little in awe of somebody who's got one a lot bigger than theirs. They may make jokes about being hung and stepping on your meat but, by God, there's some envy there, and where there's envy there's got to be a little feeling of inferiority. I believe in playing every card you've got. It's a long way to the top. Harlowe had the Olympic pool in his back yard but I had a sight more to put in it than he did. I swear it seemed like he had more respect for me after that.

I played the lovesick swain right up to the hilt with Tiffany. In fact, I didn't make but two trips out of town the whole six months we were courting and those only because the pressure built too great. Tonight I'm thinking that I loved her. At least I came closer to it with her than I ever have with anybody else. She sure as hell adored me. In fact, she worshiped me. She used to fuss and say there was a part of me I kept to myself and that I never let anybody really get to know me, while she gave everything she had. I guess she was right. A whole lot of that talk is a bunch of shit, put out by folks who aren't concerned with getting ahead in life.

Women are quick to cry and get swollen eyes and red noses and whine that you don't love them any more, like that had any relevance to anything. A lot of men say they don't understand women and I always keep my mouth shut; it's not up to me to help the dumb bastards. But, by God, I understand women. They were created to serve and they all know it down deep in their hearts. It's atavistic. Some of them may raise hell and kick against the pricks, you should pardon the pun, but they'll have nothing but contempt for you if you weaken and let them boss you. I've never had the problem.

Tiffany was easy. At least for a while. Our honeymoon was a blast. She turned out to love sex and old Roscoe was a real St. John the Conqueror for those two weeks. We probably set a record. At least Tiffany thinks we did. That's why she was so shocked later. It took me awhile to teach her other things. She never could understand why I wanted my shirts and ties hung separately in the closet and color-coded. She made fun of me for having the hip pockets in my slacks sewed up but then it never dawned on her that buns are as important to a guy's appearance as they are to a doll's. What I had the most trouble getting her to do properly was fold my socks and line them up in rows instead of rolling one inside the other and throwing them in the drawer like balls. When she'd rebel, I handled her like I used to do Mama. I'd just quit speaking and ignore her and pretend to be moody and withdrawn. She couldn't stand it. The whole twelve years of our marriage I never apologized once. Come to think of it, I never did to Mama, either. Of course, with Tiffany I had the extra advantage of withholding Roscoe until she straightened up.

Breakfast was another thing I had to teach her about. Why women think they have to change a man's habits, I'll never know. They are constantly checking though to see if you're going to let down and allow them to rule instead of serve. Tiffany used to roll her eyes and sigh a lot but she finally realized I wanted my breakfast the same way every morning. She got to where she'd just shrug her shoulders and fix it to suit me. After all, I'd done a lot of research and so had the nutritionist at the gym, and I knew what had vitamins and minerals in it and where the empty calories were. I was not about to defile my body with eggs or with pork filled with nitrite. I had a big glass of orange juice, a bowl of Special-K with skim milk, and Sunkist raisins to sprinkle over the top. I poured fresh honey over all this and it was a good start for the day. I haven't used refined sugar since I was twenty years old.

Once Harlowe took me and Tiffany to Sunday brunch in San Francisco when we were there on a banking convention and he happened to be passing through at the same time. It was open air on a rooftop and the menu was loaded with gourmet items, and you were supposed to sit around for a couple of hours reading the Sunday paper and rubbing elbows with the ultra rich. They didn't have Special-K and I made the waitress go out to a grocery store and find some. It took an hour to get it and they billed Harlowe five dollars for one bowl of dry cereal. The waitress hated me and you could tell Harlowe and Tiffany were embarrassed. They were so well-bred, though, that they ignored the incident and made small talk with me about the bank. I loved it.

Tiffany seemed to think that just because she'd grown up going to fancy places and foreign lands that she had an edge on me about etiquette and so forth. She had more sense than to say it but that unspoken attitude was there just as real as the knowledge that her family background was better than mine. I guess it was in our fourth year of marriage that we went to Barbados on a convention. Things had already been pretty rocky between us a few times. This was to be a sort of second honeymoon and bring us back together and all that crap. I played along with it and romanced the hell out of her. There wasn't anything else to do in Barbados.

We caught the eye of this older couple from New York and they latched on to us; bragged on how attentive I was to my wife and how refreshing that was in this day and age. You know the sentimental trash people can hand out when they think they're reading you straight and all the time they're just interpreting actions according to their own values. This guy had three teenage sons at home. He kept saying he hoped they would grow up to be like me. We ate our meals with them and went to the evening parties with them and Tiffany and his wife shopped together while we were at meetings.

He was from upper state New York and named Robert Rensslaer. Tiffany said he was old money. After one day it was, "Just call me Bob." I was beginning to wonder if he had a special personal interest in me, but I gave him a couple of opportunities to step out if that was what was bothering him and he didn't notice; so I decided he was straight. Bob was big on fitness and was really into jogging. Of course, I'd been running four miles every morning before breakfast for seven years and I'd made Tiffany start it for the last two. She hated it but always had enough class to pretend she liked something if she was going to do it anyway. The streets in Barbados were rough as hell, impossible to run on. I checked at the desk and they told me to go to the race track but to watch out for the horses because they worked them sometimes real early in the morning.

I got Bob and Tiffany and we took a taxi and set out. Bob's wife was glad enough to sleep late at the hotel. When we started running it was full daylight but not yet sunrise, and the race track was perfect. After about twenty minutes I had already lapped Tiffany twice and Bob once and was really settling into my stride. Good sweat, good pace, good rhythm. Somebody was breaking three young horses to harness but they were off to one side, not bothering us at all. I heard somebody yell, "Look out for the horses!" and then the fast and faster feet of runaways. I pulled over to the side of the track but never slowed up. All of a sudden Tiffany screamed like a banshee and I looked back. Bob Rensslaer was crumpled up in the middle of the track and the horses went hell for leather past me. I had to turn around and jog back to him; there was nothing else to do. The dumb bastard was out like a light with blood oozing from both ears and a dent in the back of his head you could put your fist in. Or a horse's foot.

Tiffany came tearing up, trembling all over, shaking like a leaf. Said she'd listened to the man yelling and got off the track but Bob never budged. She'd watched the horses tear by her and trample him down. I yelled for an ambulance but the race track boy said there wasn't one on the island, that we'd have to get a taxi to take him to the hospital. Bob was still unconscious and as limp as a rag when I helped load him into the taxi. I gave the driver a five, told him to head for the hospital and slammed the door. Tiffany wanted to know if I wasn't going to go to the hospital with him and I said hell, no, there was nothing I could do for him. I was no doctor and the man was obviously feeling no pain. I sent the taxi on.

That woman actually tried to create a scene right there in front of those Barbados natives. My own wife. She started arguing with me.

"The least you could do is ride to the hospital with him in this strange country," she said. "He doesn't have his wallet with him; they won't be able even to identify him in those jogging shorts."

I was furious. I grabbed her arm and twisted her off to one side where the black men couldn't hear and told her to get on back to the hotel and tell Bob's wife to go to the hospital, that she by God could identify him. Then like any sensible person would do, I started back jogging.

Tiffany was fit to be tied. She started running alongside me. She was literally screaming.

"You can't mean you're going to finish jogging! What sort of self-centered, obsessive bastard are you?"

She was obviously losing control and there's no way in the world to deal with a woman like that. I just lengthened my stride and ran off and left her. I ran another full forty minutes to make up for the time I'd lost. When I got back to the hotel, the help was all agog about the accident and told me Tiffany had carried Mrs. Rensslaer to the hospital. I did my situps, showered, and ate breakfast. I had figured they might not have Special-K in Barbados and had packed my own, which was a godsend. When I got back to the room, Tiffany was flinging clothes into suitcases.

Bob Rensslaer had died about fifteen minutes after the women got to the hospital. Mrs. Rensslaer was in complete shock. Tiffany was going to fly to New York with her. The hotel manager would arrange all details with the Barbados officials and have the body shipped. Tiffany was white as a sheet. She wouldn't even look at me. Her voice was flat.

I got a cold chill. I realized that this was a true crossroads. Tiffany and Harlowe were real close, although he was very careful to keep his nose out of our business. There was no telling what she'd tell him if I let her go home without me. Harlowe had been good to me but I didn't have complete control of either of the banks I was managing for him and we'd pretty well lived to the edge of my salaries. If Tiffany walked I'd be in the street the next morning with nothing but the clothes on my back. I had too much time invested and my prospects were too good to relax and tell her to kiss my ass, which was the way I really felt.

I played it just right. I ate a lot of crow. I was injured. I was misunderstood. How in the world could anybody think I was uncaring? I never brought out the point that Bob Rensslaer was a dumb New York son of a bitch for not hearing a drove of wild horses and getting out of their way. I was nice. I was sweet. In the end it was Roscoe carried the day for me. He was superb. Tiffany wound up sweating like a mule and crying like a baby but she went home with me. There's never been any doubt since who was head of my house, although Tiffany never was exactly the same again. Roscoe's a real whoremaster and he's never let me down.

When we first got married I really and truly intended to be faithful to Tiffany, but I soon found out that Kipling was right: "The more you have had of the others, the less will you settle to one." I didn't cut anything unless it was really prime, though, and I was careful as hell not to get caught. If there were any suspicions, they were never voiced. I'd found out from listening that wives really get suspicious when the husband slacks off on sex; so I never did. Like I said, Roscoe has never failed me.

I've sat here tonight thinking about things that I'd pushed back and forgotten. Like when I first discovered how important and impressive Roscoe is. I was twelve. My mother used to make me go to church, which gave me the name all over town of being a model child. I had to go to RA camp that summer and the preacher who was head of youth activities for the whole state singled me out to room with him. I was all gangly and awkward and flattered as hell. He had been to our church on speaking tours a couple of times and every Baptist in the state looked up to him and thought he was handed down. I was still young enough to halfway believe all that religious crap, and when he crawled in bed with me I remember that I was embarrassed and a little ashamed because my pajamas were faded and old and he was so polished and sophisticated.

When he put his hand in my crotch, it never crossed my mind to object. It was like being touched by God. That's how important he was to Baptists.

Roscoe jumped up like he was on a string. I would have let that man do anything he wanted to. He never said a word. He took my hand and put it over on his thing and it was to this day the tiniest one I ever saw on a grown man. I still remember how shocked I was. I was embarrassed for him but at the same time all of a sudden so proud of Roscoe I couldn't see straight. He played with him for what seemed like hours and finally jacked me off and I went to sleep. The way the bed was shaking, he tended to himself, too. The next morning I was afraid to even look at him. I was ashamed of liking what had happened and somehow felt guilty and that it was my fault. He was matter-of-fact and unconcerned and didn't even mention it.

I learned a lot from that preacher. He'd meet with groups of boys all day and make talks with that wonderful booming voice of his about the Lord and the love of Jesus Christ, and he could sing hymns to stir your blood. He'd laugh and talk and tease the little kids, and everybody worshiped him. He was a prophet of God but at the same time one of the fellows. Every night when the lights were out he changed. He grabbed Roscoe and made me hold his but he never said a word. It was almost like it wasn't happening if you didn't talk about it. You want to know about living a double life and getting away with it? Man, he was a master at it! I mean, he was cool. Like I said, I learned a lot from him.

I was only twelve and next to the last night I was there I couldn't stand that silence any longer. I spoke out in the dark. "Do you think what we're doing is wrong?" He didn't say a word. I felt his little old thing go soft in my hand and after a minute he turned Roscoe loose and got up and went back to his own bed. I waited a while and tended to Roscoe and then went on to sleep. I've never the first time since then wondered whether or not anything I do is wrong. I learned an awful lot that week.

With the start I got at RA camp, I've had a double life nobody would believe and nobody ever knew about it. Not Tiffany. Not Lance. Nobody. I learned when I was a senior in high school not to mess with any man you know or who knows you. I learned it the hard way, but even that one time I did nobody ever suspected. I got away with it. Clean.

Barge Tumey was a hunk. On top of that he had a good personality, made straight As, and was as quick-witted and funny at a party as anybody you could ever hope to see. He was center and I was quarterback, and we double-dated a lot and hung around together. One afternoon Coach held us late after practice and everybody had left the locker room but us when we finally went to shower. We were in the middle of a winning streak and Coach thought we had a shot at the play-offs. We were feeling good. Buck naked and in top form. Barge bent over in front of me like he was going to snap the ball and I stepped in real close to him, said, "Hut," and let my hands go on through his legs and hold his real balls. That's been ages ago and I still get excited when I remember it.

He didn't jump away like I thought he would, or laugh. Or clench his fist and threaten to deck me. Instead he wiggled on back into me and got hard as a rock. We made it to the showers and I've always thanked God that Coach or nobody else happened in. Roscoe was fit to be tied, and Barge and I relieved each other right there. When it was over, Barge looked at me white as a sheet with wide eyes and said, "My God, I can't believe this happened!" I laughed and said, "Don't ever mention it and it didn't." Then I snapped him on the ass with a towel and reminded him that we both had dates that night.

We were both going with cheerleaders, but we'd had to quit double-dating. Mine thought she was in love with me and I was tapping her regularly, but Barge had really fallen for his and wasn't into anything but heavy petting. He kidded me about robbing the cradle because mine was just a freshman but I'd told him women were like cows; if they're old enough to bleed, they're old enough to butcher. I took mine to the Dairy Queen, then parked in the cemetery and laid her and was home on the books by ten o'clock. Mama worked eleven to seven at the hospital and she hadn't been gone ten minutes before here came Barge. That's been years ago, but Roscoe still raises his head and gets up every time I remember it. Even tonight. Even now. When it's too late. When it's all over.

I let Barge in and he stood there trembling with his hands down tight by his side. He said, "Old buddy, I need to talk to you." And I stepped out of my shorts and said, "I don't think that's what you need at all." Then I undressed him while he just stood there like a helpless maiden and took him in my bedroom and did everything to him before daybreak that I'd ever heard of at that time in my life. He moaned a lot but never resisted once. Every time he tried to say anything I'd say, "Hush," and turn Roscoe loose again. God, what a night!

When he was dressed to leave he said, "I guess this means we're queer, doesn't it?" I laughed and clapped him on the back, and I've never yet seen a more beautiful torso in my life. "I'm not queer and never will be!" I told him. "Just relax and enjoy life. You can come study with me any time you want to when Mama's at work. That's the only time I want you to open your mouth. But I want you to open it wide then." I patted him on the ass and pushed him out the door.

Poor bastard. He couldn't handle the double life. He'd go wild and laugh and cut up with me and Roscoe, but he got morose and moody everywhere else. People started commenting on it. Football season was over but Coach was one of those who made a fetish of trying to look after his boys. He called me aside and told me he was worried about Barge, his grades were falling off, and did I think he was fucking around with marijuana? I didn't laugh, I just looked puzzled and said, no, I didn't think it was marijuana.

Then he said, "My God, he's not dripping acid is he?" and I told him no again with a straight face. Then I looked real sincere and troubled and told Coach I'd be glad to help Barge study and get his grades up any night he wanted to come to my house, and Coach pumped my hand and told me what a fine fellow I was. There is nothing that follows a guy through life more effectively than a solid recommendation from his high school football coach.

I told Barge about it and he didn't even laugh. He'd try to drop me, and then when he couldn't stand it any longer he'd come back to study. He couldn't get enough of Roscoe. The trouble with Barge was he wanted to analyze and talk everything to death instead of just enjoying life and going on about his business. I laughed and preached to him about if it feels good, do it. Barge got obsessed with the idea that he was homosexual. My God, a 210-pound hunk who had chicks falling all over him worrying about something like that. I went through the cheerleading team and cracked every twist who wasn't going steady and half of those who were, to prove to him that a guy's not queer just because he likes to study with a buddy.

It didn't do a bit of good. He came in two weeks before graduation walking like a Zombie and talking like one, too. Sort of way off and far away. "Cile was going to let me have it tonight.

She took off every stitch she had. And I couldn't make it. All I could think about was you."

I laughed. "That's a high compliment, old buddy, because your little Cile is choice. If you don't get it up next time, let me know and I'll be glad to go in for you."

"Don't laugh, dammit," he said. "I've decided I'm in love with you. More than I'd ever thought I could be in love with anybody. It scares the hell out of me."

I laughed again. "Relax, Barge. This isn't the end of the world. Be like the woman who wrote the verse:

'And if I loved you Wednesday,
Well, what is that to you?
I do not love you Thursday —
So much is true.

And why you come complaining
Is more than I can see.
I loved you Wednesday, — yes — but what
Is that to me?'

Everything's cool, man. Keep it that way."

That's when he started crying. I mean, the tears were raining down. "You don't give a damn about me. You don't truly care about a living soul in this world except yourself. Well, I realize that I'm queer as a three-dollar bill, no matter what you say, and I'm not spending the rest of my life in this kind of misery. I'm either going to a Christian counselor or I'm going to run my car into a bridge."

Well, now. That gave me a chill, sure enough. I didn't want him talking to a counselor. Once somebody blabs their guts to somebody else, the easier it is to do it again. If you don't say it, it didn't happen, and if you don't hear it, it never was even thought of.

"You don't want to do either, Barge," I said. "This is what you really want." I moved behind him, reached around into his groin, and pulled him back to me. I knew exactly how and where to touch him. That's what he was in love with. Not me. When we were through, he started to leave.

"I'm still going to a counselor," he said. "I'm so mixed up I can't stand it."

I laughed. "Hell, Barge, it won't do any good. No matter how it comes out you're going to spend the rest of your life around the fellows pretending that you think jokes about queers are funny and hoping nobody finds out about you. Have you ever heard how many psychiatrists it takes to change a light bulb? The answer is, 'Only one, but the light bulb has got to want to change.' Forget the counselor."

He didn't laugh.

"It won't do any good, old buddy," I told him. "And if you hit the bridge doing less than eighty, that won't do any good, either."

He didn't. The State Patrol was chasing him and clocked him at ninety when he hit. The motor was in his chest and he was in the back seat. They didn't open the casket. The guys on the football team were honorary pall bearers and everybody else was crying so hard nobody noticed that I didn't. God, that was a close one.

Later that summer I rushed Cile for about three weeks and I didn't tap her until the second date, out of respect for old Barge. When I went off to college, I never answered her letters. The one thing I learned from all that was that if you're going to have a real double life, don't ever mess around with a guy that you know. Or who knows you. You can't really trust anybody in this old world.

I always was more mature emotionally than other guys my age. In college I was president of the fraternity my junior year and most people don't make that until they're seniors. I quit coming home except on Christmas. That town didn't have much to offer me anyhow and I was glad to be rid of it. Mama got married again. If indeed she'd ever been married in the first place. I've always wondered about that, but what the hell difference does it make? At any rate, I didn't have to listen to all that whining anymore about when was I coming home. I established a hostile relationship as quick as I could with her husband so at least he wouldn't want me around, and that got her off my back. She was getting to be a real pain in the ass and it was a relief to be shed of her. There's nothing in the world you outgrow more completely in college than a mother. Here again, though, if you don't talk about it, it didn't happen. Leave people their dreams whenever you can. As long as they don't step on your toes.

It never crossed anybody's mind at college that I was getting it on with men. Except that one time. I was always so careful not to go to the gay bars except a long way from home. Who in the world would have thought I'd ever run into somebody I knew from Suwanee in a bath house in San Francisco? I was punking a whole line of guys, one after another, in and out, and I spotted him about third from the end. Talk about sang-froid and savoir-faire. I never batted an eye. I just popped him extra good, finished the string, and hauled ass out of there. Back at school he tried to approach me. I denied everything. He said I was famous in San Francisco for my staying powers and everybody thought my name was Roscoe. I said I must have a double. Then he made a pass at me. I threw him out of my room and beat the living shit out of him in the hall in front of witnesses.

It was the right choice. The discipline committee had a hearing and three other students turned up to testify that he'd made passes at them. He got kicked out of school, broken ribs and all, and I didn't even get demerits for fighting in the dorm. My counselor did tell me that he thought I'd overreacted, that all I needed to have done was refuse. I told him, "I'm sorry, sir, but if there's one thing I can't stand it's a goddam faggot."

Like I said, Kipling was right: "The more you have had of the others, the less will you settle to one." It applies to both genders. There's some sort of pressure that builds up in you and you just have to release it. I've always been very circumspect about it. Out-of-town business trips are the best cover ever devised, especially if you come home horny and bang your wife the first night back. You would not believe how wild this country was getting there for a while. There were some guys who bragged about making it a hundred times in one weekend, but I maxed out at twenty. I never did drugs and I never let anybody in my ass. Nobody ever deserved that much control over me.

I've seen them shooting up and sharing needles with people they wouldn't nod to on the street at home. Even early I had sense enough to know that was a sure way to spread disease. I didn't worry too much about clap and syphilis; after all, they can be cured. I got hepatitis once but blamed it on raw oysters in New Orleans. I was having a high old time and enjoying life because Roscoe didn't have an enemy in the world and never met a stranger. We did a guy in Atlanta once, Roscoe and I, who was high on coke and said he wasn't satisfied. I'm the one who greased the live hamster and stuck it up him. I didn't tape its jaws, though, and you never heard such screaming. I eased on away from there, but I assume the hamster died first. I read a month later in an Atlanta paper that the police were searching for a known homosexual named Roscoe. It never entered anybody's head to look here. Certainly not for me. If you don't tell it, it never happened. I say, a known homosexual. The very idea.

The world was sweet. My apple. Tiffany and I had a good life together. When she'd get pissed, she'd threaten to stir up my sock drawer or mess up my closet, but she never did. Harlowe kept increasing my responsibilities and my salary. We built a new house and a swimming pool. I was limiting my trips out of town to about once a month, usually when Tiffany was on her period. New Orleans. Atlanta. New York. San Francisco. Seattle. You name it. Roscoe grumbled a little because we didn't go more often but he just had to put up with it. He's a vain little bastard and it's true enough that men admire and appreciate a noble dick more than women do, but business is business. He was getting more than his share of both and was just spoiled rotten. I will say this for Roscoe: He may have strained and fumed along the way, but he has never sulked on me. Not until tonight.

We had the best of all possible worlds. I had the perfect double life. Then some asshole, you should pardon the pun again, brought in that virus from the green monkeys in Africa. Of all places, for God's sake! AIDS. Auto immune deficiency syndrome. HIV. It wasn't fair. It still isn't. The sun dimmed, the laughter stilled. Keats said it best:

> I saw pale kings and princes too,
> Pale warriors, death pale were they all.
> They cried, "La belle dame sans merci
> Hath thee in thrall."
>
> I saw their starv'd lips in the gloam
> With horrid warning gapèd wide;
> And I awoke and found me here
> On the cold hill side.

You had better believe that I bailed out. Quick. When I read that the bath houses in San Francisco had closed, I just laughed; I hadn't been near one in six months. I have always been a person of discipline and self-control. Hell, I could give up anything. And I did. How was I to know it was too late?

I had been a good boy and done without for over six months. Tiffany gave Lance to me. She literally dumped him in my lap. We'd built the house. Harlowe shook his head at it costing over three hundred big ones but you could tell he was sort of proud. Indoor-outdoor swimming pool, marble floors, three-story foyer. It's a real show place. We could afford it, too. Tiffany hunted all over Louisville for a decorator to suit her and wound up flying one out of Chicago. He cost her an arm and a leg but we could afford that, too. He's been more than worth it.

Lancelot Waddell III. Old money by accident, good family by fate, interior designer by choice. What a guy. He and Tiffany fell for each other like a ton of bricks. Never disagreed about the first thing. Heads together all the time like two sides of a gold coin.

They shone with blonde hair and class. Giggling together like two school girls. I knew the minute I laid eyes on him he was gay. Cool and sophisticated with just a touch of priss, a hint of twitch. He had a good handshake and a level gaze, but his eyes shifted down from my face to my crotch. Ever so briefly but ever so definitely. I felt Roscoe stirring around, but I turned away and fixed a drink.

I played that one so cool that Lance didn't tumble to what happened until later. I pretended to be the dumbest, straightest hunk you ever saw. I let Lance come to me. I let him be the aggressor and I never acknowledged the first suggestive glance or tentative touch. He and Tiffany were wild about each other and I worried a while that he might be AC-DC and cuckold me. No sweat. Turned out later he'd found out when he was fourteen that he couldn't get it on with women, although he had hundreds of them wanting him through the years. I've known dozens like him. A face so beautiful it'd stop a woman's heart, a body out of the Acropolis, but a loin that would leap to life only for another man. I knew we were made for each other. It nearly drove Roscoe crazy, but I waited.

He and Tiffany got so close that she started finding him other decorating clients. She had such good connections that pretty soon his firm opened a branch in Louisville and Lancelot Waddell III bought ten acres not four miles from our new house and built himself a two-room innovative hideaway that is so avant-garde it was featured in Architectural Digest even before it was finished. The guy had taste.

He was staying with us while he built his house. By the time it was done he was calling us his family and said Tiffany was the sister he'd never had. When it happened between us, Tiffany had taken Harlowe to Nashville to a family reunion for two days and they'd excused me. Lance was reading by the pool and I stripped and swam ten laps. Then I walked toward him, and guess where he kept staring. Even after all that exercise and cold water I could feel Roscoe stretching. I told Lance I was tired, to fix us a drink and bring it up to mine and Tiffany's room. When he got there I had the sheet down just enough to show hair and a flat belly but not Roscoe. That did it. I felt like a bride.

Lance had a good degree of control. At least at first. Although why everybody thinks they have to talk things to death I'll never understand. Guess what he wanted to talk about after he'd initiated things and it was obvious to a blind man what was going to happen. AIDS. He told me that he had some condoms and that he really thought we ought to use them. Said he'd had quite some variety of lovers in the past and he sure didn't want to run the risk of passing something he conceivably might have on to somebody he cared as much about as he did me. I nearly laughed in his face. I told him I'd never been with a man before, he'd have to teach me what to do, but that he sure didn't have to worry about disease from me and I wasn't scared of him.

What a night. Roscoe went wild. By sunup I knew Lance was my slave for life. Now that was a double life that was so contorted it'd take a team of Philadelphia lawyers to figure out. Lance didn't want Tiffany to find out because he felt that he'd betrayed her by seducing her husband and he loved both of us more than anybody before in his whole life. I sure as hell didn't want anybody, anywhere, to find out anything. Anytime. I never let him know that I wasn't a virgin before he made me. The town never tumbled to anything. Nobody talked about any of it so none of it ever happened. Only Roscoe knew the whole truth. I had a key to Lance's house and dropped in often when Tiffany thought I was jogging. We never got caught. Until now.

I can't remember when Tiffany started hounding me about wanting a baby. I kept evading the subject. I wouldn't have minded one to carry on my name and all that crap, but they're so demanding when they're little. The truth was I didn't want a wife with stretch marks, sagging boobs, a flabby belly, and a loose snatch, but I had more sense than to mention that. Finally Tiffany just announced that she was going to stop the pill and I shrugged and let her get away with it.

What a nightmare. She was pregnant in two months and it damned near ruined her. She swelled all over. Even the bridge of her nose was swollen before it was over. How anything that good-looking and classy could wind up like a waddling troglodyte is a travesty against nature. She threatened to miscarry at three and a half months and I was relieved as hell when the doctor said no sex. No less a trooper than Roscoe was about ready to cull that. I had Lance for fallback, thank God, so I was able to play tender husband to the hilt. Even Harlowe bragged on me about being attentive and insisted on picking up the tab when I traded for a new Porsche.

Lance absolutely lost his head. He brought Tiffany some little gift at least two or three times a week. He kept her in flowers. He walked in one day with fresh roses and I said, "Hell, fellow, if I didn't know better I'd think this was your baby."

He got tears in his eyes and said, "In a way you'll never understand, it is." And Tiffany reached up and kissed him. Talk about your double life! It was enough to make your head spin.

The baby was a girl. Tiffany named her Danielle after me and everybody worshiped her. Lance even added a codicil to his will. I'll say this; she was a beauty. A little more in the doctor's office than most babies, but we all thought that was just Tiffany being over-zealous. Tiffany got her figure and her looks and her class back and things were going along smooth as silk.

When Danielle was sixteen months old, all hell broke loose and the world came down around my ears. Sick. Wasting. Cough. Weight loss. Specialists. Hospitals. Consultants. Laboratory tests. Nobody had time for me. Lance wouldn't leave Tiffany's side. Pneumonia. Pneumocystis carinii. Nobody would look anybody in the eye. Danielle's blood test for HIV was positive. And so, of course, was Tiffany's.

I laughed and called it ridiculous and refused to have a blood test. Tiffany must have got it from kissing Lance, I said. Lance tested negative. How in the hell could that be? I ask you, what's fair in this world? Harlowe got a steely glint in his eye and a flat tone in his voice and told me that he would get a court order if necessary. He buddies around with three Superior Court justices and I knew he wasn't bluffing. I shrugged my shoulders and laughed and let them draw the blood. There it was. Positive. Positive for AIDS. Some meddling son of a bitch checked tests they hadn't told me about. It was positive for syphilis, too.

I denied everything. I hollered dirty rest rooms, public toilets, everything I could think of. They all ignored me. When Danielle died, Tiffany and I sat together at the funeral. Neither one of us cried. Harlowe and Lance took care of that for us. When we came home from the church, I followed Tiffany to the bedroom ready to comfort her. She had a completely impersonal tone in her voice. Her eyes were dull.

"Get out," she said. "Don't you dare touch anything or anybody in this house ever again."

When I went in the hall, Harlowe had a gun. "Out!" he said. "You're in the street, you phony bastard. Get in that goddam car you've polluted and leave this town. If I ever see you again, I'll blow your nasty filthy guts and blood to kingdom come."

He meant it. I drove around for a while trying to think. Lance was my last refuge. Lance had enough to keep us both in style. I might have to come out of the closet and move to Chicago, but Lance would take me in. I'd found the knots in my armpits and groin three weeks ago. I'm no fool. I knew what was in store for me.

That's why I came out here last night. And what did I meet? What did I get? He wanted to talk! He wanted to talk about some slut he'd met in the hospital. She has three kids. Her husband was an IV junkie who gave her AIDS and then skipped town. The woman had passed the AIDS on to her baby who was two years old now, and dying in the room next to Danielle's. That's how Lance had met the bitch. Her two older kids are four and six and their blood has tested negative. She told Lance that she had watched her parents back away from those two children and refuse to touch them. They wouldn't let the kids come close to them. Wouldn't even speak except clear across the room and that not very friendly.

The bitch cried on Lance's shoulder, all jacked out of shape about who was going to look after her two older kids when she and the baby were dead and gone. Lance has always been a sentimentalist and he bought all that maudlin shit. Told me he had let the woman appoint him as their guardian and had already set up a trust fund for those brats. Said he'd never seen anybody in his life as grateful as the mother and he was going to bring her out here as soon as her baby died to stay for her last weeks or months. Lance even said he was thinking about marrying the woman, for God's sake!

Then he wanted to talk about us. Talk, talk, talk. He wanted me to confess to playing the field before I'd ever met him. He wanted me to admit I'd infected Tiffany and therefore Danielle. I held my ground. I admitted nothing. He was cold. I reached for him and pushed against him. He was as limber as a corpse. I put his hand on Roscoe. I had to win Lance back. Roscoe was pushing and surging. Nothing on Lance had stirred. Then I said it. I'd never said it to anybody before.

"I love you, Lance," I said. I really meant it.

"Did you love Danielle, too? Did you love Tiffany?" His eyes were tired and old. "You haven't the faintest concept of what love really is. The trouble with you is you've never learned that there's a difference between love and sex."

He shouldn't have said that. All of a sudden Roscoe died. Limp as a dishrag. I was cold. Empty. There was nowhere left to go. Nothing left to do. This moment was the last I'd ever have with Lance.

I found a thing to do.

All my fingers, ten of them, I wound his lovely pulsing throat around, and strangled him. No pain felt he. I am quite sure he felt no pain. Nor did I.

I propped his head up on my shoulder and I have cradled him through the night into this gray dawn. I have just dialed 911.

Before they get here I may put a bullet through my mouth. Or I may let nature take its course and die in six months, threatening to spit on any jailer who offends me. I haven't decided yet. I still have a few minutes.

Only this I know. It was for a while a beautiful world. Now it's an ugly world. It's just not fair. I never talked about it and still it happened.

> "And so we sit together now
> And all night long we have not stirred.
> And yet God has not said a word."